This is a collection of short stories I wrote over a long period. It gave me great deal of satisfaction and enjoyment, and I hope it will do so equally to you dear reader. The stories cover a number of genres from spooky, to fantasy and science fiction. I had fun writing them and there is nothing more satisfying than shaping a decent plot from a compelling beginning, to a well-rounded conclusion. A well written short story is the ultimate test of a writer's abilities.

Also by the same author:

SF
Worlds Beyond Ours
The Wizard of Kalar
Galactic Sniffers
InterGalactic Rogues (2015)

Historical
Murder in Hattusas
Madduwatta's Rebellion
Mittani Kidnapping

Free at Last

And Other Short Stories

Sasha Garrydeb

London
2014

Published in Britain in 2014
by ABC Publishers
24 Treadgold Street London W11 4BP

e-mail: abcpublishers@ntlworld.com

Printed in GB by ABC Publishers

A CIP catalogue record for this book
is available from the British Library.

ISBN 978-09548144-3-4

Printed by
ABC Publishers,
Notting Dale,
London W11 4BP.

Contents

𝕱𝖗𝖊𝖊 𝖆𝖙 𝕷𝖆𝖘𝖙

A rider!' shouted the sentry from the gate tower to the *Tesserarius* below.

The *Tesserarius* yelled back the all-important question, '*Ours?*'

The sentry stared hard into the predawn distance of the white winter landscape. '*Yes*,' he bellowed back.

In no time the rider was galloping up the snow covered approach road to the fort and through the gate, cantering his sweating horse along the *via principalis*. It was the road leading to the *principia* of a Roman camp, the command centre. The rider slid off the horse outside the *principia* and jumped to attention before the Optio, second in command of the cohort, barring his way to the Commander.

'Well?' the Optio stared angrily.

Ashen faced, the *cursor* crashed his right fist across his left breast in the Roman military salute. 'Sir! Urgent message for the Centurion.'

'*Y—e—s*, spit it out—damn you,' burst out the Optio.

'I come from the Turma guarding the Hanging Stones. The Druids have gathered for the winter solstice. We're holding them back but there's too many. I was sent for reinforcements, *sir*.'

The Optio swiftly pushed open the door leading inside. 'Well get in there. Report to the Centurion,' he ordered.

The *cursor* marched in and repeated the message, handing the Commander a wooden tablet. Then he stood to attention—waiting.

'Licinius, read this.' The Centurion handed the opened tablet to his second in command.

'It's from Mannius at the stones.' The Optio stared at the wax indentations. 'He says your Gwern is leading the Druid attack. Can't be right. The ungrateful swine. You should've executed him instead of making him your *Cacula*. I told you nothing good would come of it.'

'I sent him on an errand to Durnovaria[1],' the Centurion retorted. 'What's he doing up there?' 'Where's the Decurion?' he demanded.

The Optio answered. 'I saw him at the stables. He was just getting ready to go on patrol. Do you want him?'

'Yes. Quickly.'

The Optio dashed out.

The Commander of the hill-fort garrison at Hod Hill in the south of Britannia was grim faced. His Celtic slave, who he'd sent with a demand for provisions and replacements to Durnovaria[1], was leading a revolt up at Stonehenge. It was only four years since the Iceni revolt—and it was still painfully fresh in his Roman mind. This outrage had to be nipped in the bud. Hod Hill was a small garrison where he commanded a single cohort of the IInd Augusta, only eighty legionaries, with the rest of the Legion at Isca. There was a *Turma* of thirty-two cavalry in his command—but that was all. He'd have to manage.

Outside, early drums and pipes proclaimed that Saturnalia was nigh upon them. The next day would be the festival of the winter solstice, marking the "*natalis solis invicti,*" birthday of the unconquered sun. The sun had managed to survive—and after this feast day—would begin to climb higher in the sky. Days would begin to lengthen, and the sun would strengthen from then on. But, the merrymaking and presents would have to wait. Putting a stop to the Druids took precedence. The Governor of Britannia had proclaimed from Londinium: "High priority—end the Druid menace to good Roman order—at all cost." That's just what Aelius Marcus was going to do—Saturnalia or no Saturnalia. His *cursus honorus* depended on it.

The Decurion burst in. 'What's all the fuss?' he demanded.

This was Officer to Officer. The Centurion was in command but the Decurion was his equal.

The Centurion was just as forceful. 'Flavius. Druids up at the stones. They're trying to hold their primitive version of Saturnalia. We've got to put a stop to it. Take your *Turma* and wipe them out.'

A smile broke the Decurion's rugged features, 'Right away.' The Decurion's comportment brimmed with pleasure at the task he'd been given. 'The Hanging Stones you say, eh. How many druids are there?'

The Centurion looked at the messenger. 'About three hundred—eh?'

The *cursor* nodded.

'What with my *Turma* and the *Turma* up there—we should make short work of them. That'll be the best sacrifice to Saturn *we* can make. See you later.' Flavius marched out, followed by the messenger, heading for the stable that was under the fort wall.

'Give him a fresh horse,' he told a stable lad, nodding at the *cursor*.

Shortly after, the *Turma* led by Decurion Flavius, galloped down the white road leading from the fort, swung left heading northeast towards the spreading dawn—making short work of the 27 *mille* to Stonehenge.

After some hard riding, the *Turma* saw the dawn proclaim the winter solstice. Flavius spied the great stone circle in the distance, standing proud on the white horizon. It had been a tough ride and his *Turma* joined forces with the resident *Turma,* which had been mauled but not beaten.

The way the sun hit the huge stone structure set in the snow, managed even to impress the hard bitten Equestrian Flavius. The combined Roman cavalry readied for another attack from the west. There could be no hiding in this white landscape. The wind blew hard and bitter with no shelter to hand. The standing stones protruded like a glorious statement from a long distant past.

To Flavius, from his horse, it seemed there were many more Celts than earlier suggested. Spears projected from amongst the tall stones, and a dazzling array came off the metal of the long Celtic swords hit by sharp sunlight.

The newly arrived Decurion shouted, 'Mannius—give the order.'

Mannius, the resident Decurion was in charge. He responded so all could hear, '*Right lads, lets finish this. Make 'em pay! Bucinator, sound the charge. Forward!*'

Every year the Druids appropriated the monumental structure and determined to hold their ritual—thumbing their noses at their occupiers. Last year they were thwarted—this year they succeeded. The sun had risen and the ritual was over. Now they had to get away with their lives.

The *bucina* rang out clear in the crisp frozen air, and the cavalry charged—hooves thundering across the frozen landscape. The *equites* drew their long Roman horse swords and as the two sides clashed, bloody mayhem ensued. Heads rolled in the snow, blood gushed from severed limbs. Metal collided against metal. Horses went down mortally wounded, spears sticking from their hides. Death rode unbridled among the winter scenery—red trying to outdo the white.

Slowly but with disciplined determination, the Roman side pushed the Celts from amongst the stones. Druids fought harder than most, dying with resolute hatred on their faces— fierce scowls etched permanently against Rome. After hard lengthy fighting the Celts began to retreat down the Avenue— then turned and ran for the trees on either side, hoping to outrun the horses chasing them.

Flavius let Mannius have the pleasure of harrying the remnants. He was wounded and dismounted outside the stone circle. A Celt spear had gashed his side and he felt dizzy from loss of blood. The *Equine Medicus* attached to his *Turma* was called and tended to the Decurion. After he'd been bandaged, Flavius went inwards between the stones—to the large altar stone. There, at its base, spread-eagled, facing heavenwards, lay a large naked Celt with a dagger jutting from his chest. He wasn't tied or restrained. Flavius stood, puzzled as to why the

Celt had allowed himself to be killed. The dagger in his chest wasn't Roman.

Mannius came back, panting hard. He dismounted and gave his reins to another *equites*. 'We got most of them. A few got away but we know which tribe they're from. We'll get them! So what's with you?'

'Look there—the slave Gwern.' Flavius pointed at the base of the altar stone. 'Let himself be sacrificed. Wonder why?'

'So *there he* is. I've been looking all over for him. I was hoping to run him through myself. That,' he pointed angrily, 'used to be a Chief of a minor tribe. Then he sided with Boudicca. Your Centurion bought him at auction a couple of years ago. You know the story better than I do. Good riddance to bad rubbish, I say. Bloody savage!' Mannius spat in the direction of the altar stone.

Flavius grimaced. 'Yes. But look at his face. He's smiling. They sacrificed him—and he smiled in death. Don't like that.'

'What's that on his head?'

They walked closer and inspected the crown of mistletoe.

Now Flavius scowled. 'Druid nonsense. It's their sacred evergreen symbolising fertility and continued life.'

'Why crown him with it?'

'Don't know. Come away Mannius. Look—why not come back to the fort and celebrate Saturnalia with us. Leave the place of death for this day. You can come back tomorrow. The corpses will still be here.' Flavius took Mannius by the arm, leant on him for support, and led him to their horses.

The two Turma set off back to Hod Hill at a brisk canter, leaving the dead Celt chieftain with a smile on his face—free at last.

Tesserarius = Non Commissioned Officer
Durnovaria[1] = Dorchester

Sasha Garrydeb

Impetuous People

My legs were pumping up and down the platform like demented pistons on a racing engine. I reached my right hand out—barely managing to grasp the accelerating vertical upright rail on the carriage. Gripping hard, I heaved, simultaneously lifting my right foot. It landed on the wooden step at the same time as my left hand reached the opposite handrail of the carriage door. I steadied, holding on tight with my right hand, I yanked the door open with my left, squeezed in, and then closed the door behind me.

Once inside the vestibule, I heard myself breathing dangerously hard. *That was a stupid thing to do,* I berated myself. I'm not as young as I used to be. I slid open the door to the corridor, and bounced down it from side to side, still breathing laboriously, looking for an empty compartment. We were crossing a series of switch-tracks making the carriage lurch around. Reaching the end of the carriage I found one person in the last compartment. I opened the sliding door unsteadily—and stepped inside.

'May I join you?' I was trying to control my breathing and be friendly.

'Certainly! Glad of the company.'

Seated near the window in the right corner, facing the engine was an elderly gentleman, smartly dressed in subdued navy blue—still wearing cashmere raglan. Grey balding hair, black bloodshot eyes. His friendly face looked into mine.

'Thanks,' I said, hoisting my navy-blue knapsack from my shoulders onto the overhead rack. I seated myself opposite the old gent.

A few moments passed. I listened to the da-da-da-dumta-da-da-da-dumta of the wheels as they sped over the expansion gaps between the rails.

'You were lucky!' He said, looking hard into my eyes—as if making a blunt point. There seemed to be fire in his.

'Oh! You mean...but—how the devil could you see me?' He was facing the wrong way to have seen me—and sitting on the far side of the carriage away from the platform.

'You really should know better,' he continued, ignoring my question. 'The next time, you'll rupture something—or—much worse.' He stroked his grey goatee sprouting on his chin.

'I'm as fit as a fiddle,' I lied. 'I do this every week.' More lies.

For just a nanosecond, a frown fluttered across his face. Then like a mask, the same straight concerned demeanour reasserted itself.

I thought, *what a peculiar fellow. Who does he think he is—my father? —— Now, why did I think that?* Trouble is; he sounded like my long dead father. That same note of concern—the brief frown, as if he *knew* I was lying. Suddenly, I felt distinctly uncomfortable.

This complete stranger, with one concerned remark, had pressed my buttons as if he were familiar with my deepest emotions. It gave me the creeps. Worse! I felt panic rise in me—throwing my mind back to the time when I was being bullied at prep school. The feeling of wanting to hide, find somewhere safe from the bullies. Another button.

Come on man; pull yourself together. You're thirty-nine years old. Those days are in the past. Ad merchants had no right succumbing to panic. All this was going through my mind, whilst seemingly calmly sitting in the compartment, looking out of the window. I caught a faint reflection staring back at me. I could see small beads of sweat beginning to appear on my forehead. My shock of blond hair was badly ruffled from the chase. I forced myself to breathe regularly, deeply, and quietly. I ran my fingers through my hair, smoothing it. I cleared my mind of the intrusions—forced the panic back into the recesses of my brain.

The old gent was holding something out in his hand. I looked at his face, confidently smiling at me. I looked at what he was holding. It was a handkerchief. His trousers were sharply creased—something I just noticed. Dumbly, I took the handkerchief and wiped my forehead. In the same numb manner, I tried handing the handkerchief back to him.

'Keep it. You may need it again.' He still had that concerned look on his face.

I mumbled, 'Thanks,' under my breath, then turned to stare at the green fields flashing by. I stared hard—I could almost smell the grass.

After a while, the hypnotic rhythm—da-da-da-dumta-da-da-da-dumta—of the carriage made me feel drowsy. My eyelids drooped and I tried suppressing a yawn.

The next thing I knew, I was being shaken. I opened my eyes and saw the old gentleman, his hands on my shoulders.

'*What are you doing?*' I exclaimed in alarm.

'You were having a nightmare—screaming—flaying your arms. I woke you—to calm you—in case you hurt yourself.'

'Oh! Right! Well, I'm all right now. Thanks.'

'You're sure?'

'*Certain.*'

'By the way. My name's Culifer.' It was the old gent.

He sat—waiting for me to reciprocate.

I counted to twenty, hoping I could avoid telling him my name. I know it was childish of me—even churlish, trying to ignore him.

My manners finally got the better of me. 'Mine's William. People call me Will.'

I noticed he wore a dark blue shirt, which was unusual—somehow sinister. It didn't fit. It ought to have been light coloured. Everything was dark, except the waistcoat; that was red. Seriously peculiar!

Above his black blood-shot eyes sat a pair of dark bushy eyebrows. Above that was a domed forehead. I had this sudden urge; this desire to claw inside his domed cranium, to cleave it apart, see what's inside. It was a strong impulse. If I'd a cleaver at that moment—I think I might have used it.

The da-da-da-dumta-da-da-da-dumta was getting to me. I found it difficult to block out. Da-da-da-dumta-da-da-da-dumta-da-da-da-dumta-da-da-da-dumta. I shook my head; put my fingers in my ears. Ridiculous. *I'm getting annoyed at the noise the carriage is making. How stupid can you get?* My brain was running away...out of control. It was grotesque. I sat, trying to hold myself together. If I stayed perfectly still, I might avoid falling apart. It was as if each cell in my mind wanted to drift away, to go their own separate ways.

Out of nowhere, a flash of white light momentarily blinded me.

Where the hell did that come from?

'Did you see that?' I asked Culifer.

'See what?' he countered.

'The light.' He must have seen it.

'What kind of light?' he queried.

'A white flash—you couldn't have missed it, surely?' I insisted.

I was getting frightened again. The panic was rising. On top of it all, my headache was returning. That morning, I'd woken up with a stinker of a headache. I put it down to a hangover—took some aspirins. It went for a while—now it came back with a vengeance. My back and neck muscles were tight.

'Are you all right?' Culifer was looking concerned again.

Damn his black heart. Why couldn't he leave me alone? I winced—then grimaced. The pain in my head was driving me nuts. A tic started in the corner of my right eye.

I noticed a couple of bulges appearing on Culifer's domed forehead, on either side, near his temples. I rubbed my eyes—Culifer stared back at me.

'You don't look too good,' he said, scrutinising my face.

Could those small bulges on the top of his forehead, possibly be horns? And the ears, are they not a little goat-like?

Is the beard hiding a muzzle? More to the point, is my imagination on the gallop—or am I seeing him, for the first time, as he really is? How could I have missed such an obvious connection? My mind reeled at the implications.

Culifer looked at me in a strange way—concerned—as if he was deciding, whether I had uncovered his disguise. I quickly glanced away, back out of the window, pretending to be fascinated by the countryside. Small beads of perspiration rolled down my face. I had great difficulty concealing my anxiety. I wiped the sweat with the handkerchief.

Again, I felt Culifer's beady eyes trying to penetrate my thoughts, boring into the side of my neck. What, with the -da-da-da-dumta-da-da-da-dumta, and this weird old man, I felt claustrophobia reaching out to me. Maybe it was time for me to think about leaving the train. If I were careful, I'd get away with a few bruises. The pressure was mounting. If I didn't do something, my mind would explode. Another blinding flash of light.

That does it. I reached for the Emergency Cord. Next thing I knew—my feet were being knocked from under me. I twisted and landed heavily on my arse. Then I felt the Vulcan neck-pinch. My last thought was, *too much bloody Star Tre....*

I opened my eyes. There was a warm hand on my forehead. She pulled it away—a young woman's hand.

'Lie still. You'll be all right.' Da-da-da-dumta-da-da-da-dumta nearly drowned her soft voice.

I was still in the carriage—lying on the seats. The Conductor was standing in the doorway, blocking it with his large frame. Other people were in the corridor, peering in through the window.

The old gent was sitting, looking concerned, talking to an elderly matron, occasionally nodding in my direction. I tried to rise. The young woman held me with the flat of her hand on my chest. She was good looking—auburn hair, green eyes, soft mouth.

'Lie still. We're searching the train for a Doctor. Here, drink this.' She held a white plastic cup to my lips. I took a small sip—gingerly. Warm tea!

I tried to hear what the old gent was saying to the matron. She seemed frayed all over—blurred at the edges. A caricature of an old matron. We'd probably use her in an old Hovis ad—sitting outside a cottage, spinning something. You know the sort of thing—long shot—black grocery bicycle comes to gate; young boy gets off—close shot—on Hovis bread. Camera follows boy grabbing the Hovis, taking it to the old woman. Bottom line—generation after generation eats the stuff.

Ah! I know who she is. An accomplice. My hearing seemed dimmed, somehow muffled. There was a strange musty smell. *I can see they're talking about me; planning something.* Again, I tried sitting up. A firm hand held me down. *Look at him. Butter wouldn't melt in his mouth. They don't know him for what he is.* Da-da-da-dumta-da-da-da-dumta. *I've got to get off this fucking train.*

Suddenly I remembered why I'd gone out drinking the night before. It all flooded back. Bust up with my wife. She's definitely gonna leave me. That last fling with the barmaid was the last straw. The barmaid phoning me at home like that— Gemma listening in—me making arrangements to meet her. Flaming row—kids screaming upstairs. Slamming the front door—going to stay with Ted for the night—drinking myself silly. Somehow, I managed to get through the day—at work. Then chasing this bloody train at Waterloo—trying to get back to Basingstoke—to Gemma.

*Fucking life! Better red than dead. Stupid thought. It's all falling apart. Why me? Shit job—shit life.———Who **is** that old man?* I lay there and stared at the two old fogies talking about me. Conspiring—scheming to...to...to *what*?

'He's only trying to help you.' It was the young woman.

She'd noticed me staring at the fogies.

'He's the one that called me in—and the Conductor. By the way, I'm a trained nurse. Call me Ellen. You've been unconscious for near thirty minutes. I've loosened your collar.'

'Uh! Yeah! Thanks.'

'So, what's *your* name?' she eyed me as all nurses do—kindly, with detachment.

'Wha? Uh! Me?'

'You're not really with us, are you?' she frowned down at me.

'Ehhm! I've got a lot on my mind. What did you say?'

'I asked you your name.' She was patient.

'Will; *yours*?'

'I just told you. It's Ellen. You're definitely not with us—are you?'

I resolved a plan of action, watching the two fogies plotting against me like that. The young woman was trying to get me to sip more warm tea. I wondered what was in it. I knocked it out of her hand, sending the plastic cup flying, the contents spilling all over my trousers.

Startled, she jumps back. I leap up, pushing her out of the way, and give the fat Conductor a head-butt. He staggers backwards out of the doorway. I push past him, heading right. People scatter, as from a madman. A young couple canoodling in the vestibule flatten themselves against the corridor wall. I rush past their astonished gaping faces, through the connecting diaphragm, into the next carriage.

On along the corridor. Quickly, people move to get out of my way—seeing the grim look on my face. Those that don't, get knocked over, and are brutally pushed aside. Behind me, a distant commotion. The pursuit is on. The old goat probably leading the charge—after my hide. *I must get off this **bloody train**.* In the next passage, I stop; try the doors, each in turn. All locked—at least *I* can't get them to open.

I run on, into the next corridor. Nobody in the passageway. My feet travel helter-skelter towards the next corridor. There, I desperately try the doors. To no avail. Locked. I'm frantic. Why are all the fucking doors locked? *How the hell are people supposed to get out?* I notice a fire extinguisher in the corner. I jerk that off the stand and give the nearest window a bash. It bounces off. I rotate my body, using a sweeping arm movement, taking the extinguisher through a wide curve and lunge it at the window as hard as I can. The glass in the door shatters. The extinguisher goes flying out. The wind comes gushing in. I lean out and open the door—then stop.

I turn to see Culifer coming towards me—down the passageway. Behind him, his cronies. For a split second, I think, *what the hell am I doing?* Only for a split second, though. Then I jump.

'*No-o-o-o!*' A woman's voice shrieks from the corridor. Another train comes thundering past in the opposite direction.

Culifer arrives, panting, out of breath. Behind him—commuters, the usual junket of people to be seen on trains, bystanders, all crowding to see what's going on.

Culifer exclaims, 'Don't know what got into him. Did you see that? Opened the carriage door and jumped—just as another train was coming in the other direction.'

"Ooohhs!" "Ahhhs!" And a chorus of "poor fellow," comes from the crowd.

"Must have been ill," someone comments.

"Mentally disturbed—most likely," someone else tries to explain.

The old gentleman inches away from the crowd. 'Impetuous people,' he mumbles under his breath. A devilish flicker of amusement crosses his face.

Forlorn Love

Vera Holubka was sent to Gulag 5151 in the far north of Siberia, sentenced to no less than ten years. She'd been condemned by the dogma driven Soviet State for currency dealing on the streets of Kyiv. For being a conscientious mother forced into private enterprise, for trying to make a living to support her family.

They'd all lived happily in a cramped apartment, Babushka, her two young sons, Hryhor and Volodia, and her husband Taras. She married young; but was utterly content with her dark handsome, young husband. Recently, he'd been thrown out of his factory job for striking a Party official, who'd been pompous, arrogant, and demanded bribes. So, Vera was forced to become the breadwinner.

Now, *that* life was just a distant memory to her—.

It had taken two whole weeks to reach Dolya, a hundred and eighty kilometres from the Laptev Sea in the Arctic North, just below the seventieth parallel. A harsh desolate, hostile place; biting winds freezing the marrow in the bones. It was already November; snow lay deep on the ground. The place was aptly called Dolya, for it was the prisoner's rotten fate landing them in this glacial wilderness.

Gulag 5151 was designated exclusively for women prisoners. The camp had no gates, no fences. It didn't need them. There was nowhere to go, nowhere to escape to. The fifty barracks sat on a vast undulating treeless plain, covered in thick snow, resting on top of the permafrost. Only an occasional miserly dwarf shrub protruded from the icy whiteness of the tundra.

The new arrivals trundled into the area in front of the main barrack, frozen, starving, and utterly dejected. They had walked over twenty kilometres in the icy winds, dragging their feet through the deep snow, egged on by shouts, curses and threats from the Mongolian guards who had collected them at the railway stop. A number of the prisoners fell on the way, unable to continue, and were callously left behind.

The moment the huge Mongolian Camp Sergeant laid his dark slit eyes on Vera's curvaceous figure, she knew she was in trouble. He had a leering look that made most women want to run in the opposite direction. Vera's twenty-two year old mind had found it hard to cope with the calamity thus far, leading to this camp—and now this!

That evening, the Sergeant had her brought to his room. He stared into her stunning hazel green eyes for a second; and though she fought ferociously, he was far too strong for her; he took her by force. Thereafter, each following evening she had been brought to his room; then taken back to the barrack where she sobbed herself to sleep. It had been going on like that for over a month.

Vera's loathing turned to disgust, then into deep hatred, finally flipping over into a perverse obsessive love. What she couldn't prevent, she now embraced. That was her Slavic nature. She emptied her thoughts of family, husband, and children. Over the past month, gradually, she managed to convince herself *she* chose this Mongolian monster to be her lover.

It was her mind protecting her sanity. She retreated from the reality of numbing cold, constant gnawing hunger. It was her way of escaping her grim surroundings, the continual brutality of the other prisoners. Now, she even looked forward to these visits to the Sergeant of the guards, to the filthy small room at night, to the stench of his foul vodka reeking breath.

One evening, she lay in her bunk in the cold barrack, running her fingers through her short matted auburn hair, mulling over what her Sergeant told her earlier that evening. After she gave herself to his grunting and groaning, he carelessly told her it was to be the last night; he wouldn't need her anymore; he'd found a far prettier newcomer to replace her.

Her mind simply refused to accept this. She lay under her infested blankets until the whole barrack settled, until the prisoners were asleep. Then she climbed out of her bunk, onto the cold floor with her bare feet, not bothering to cover herself with her shawl of rags. Slowly in a daze, she shuffled her way to a corner of the barrack, knelt on the freezing floor; and prayed with all her might to the holy virgin. She prayed the Sergeant would have a change of mind; prayed for the virgin to make her prettier, make her Sergeant love her again, as she loved him. She repeated the prayer, over and over, again and again.

At the five o'clock roll call, in the perpetual darkness of an Arctic dawn, guards found her frozen rigid body, still kneeling in the corner. A serene expression on her face.

Maternal Love

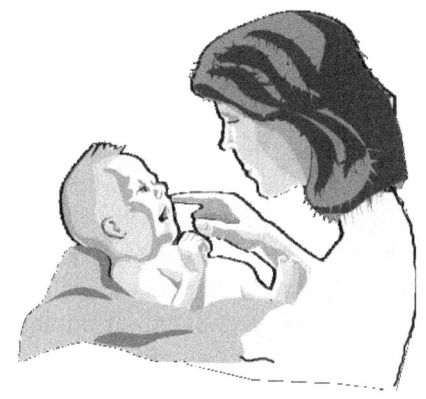

Vasia cocked his ears. 'Quiet—did you hear that? There—listen—*hooves.*'

'Don't be silly,' Vera chided...'Ahh!' she'd felt a contraction. 'How can you hear anything in this snowstorm?'

'I'm sure I heard hooves,' he insisted. 'Are you all right?' He was concerned for his pregnant wife; while at the same time, he sat down to his traditional New Year's Eve plate of pancakes with honey. Tomorrow would be the year of our Lord twelve hundred and forty in the little village of Chernobyl.

Abruptly—all hell broke loose. A tremendous pounding, and the front door—gave way. In the doorway stood a sardonic grinning Mongol, scimitar in hand. Vasia picked up the chair he was sitting on and in one motion threw it at the Mongol. The Mongol behind loosed off his arrow; it hit the chair, which crashed into the raised scimitar. Vera was standing, screaming.

Vasia picked up her chair and hurled it through the small window behind him. The snow swirled in through the broken glass, engulfing the room. The scimitar wielding Mongol advanced on Vasia; snow everywhere. Vasia picked up his pregnant wife and thrust her with all his considerable strength through the smashed window. He never felt the scimitar descend on his neck, severing his head from his body in one stroke. Both Mongols looked out through the smashed window into the snowstorm; shrugged their shoulders, and retreated through the shattered doorway.

Vera landed heavily, lying in the snow, until she caught her breath. Vasia was dead—she knew without doubt; his last act was to save his wife, and unborn child. Tears trickled down her face; she got to her feet and ran. Vera was alive, just—although swiftly freezing in the vicious blizzard. It was the damned blizzard that had muffled the Horde's arrival. They attacked under cover of the snowstorm, preventing the villagers from using their boltholes under the houses. One moment it was all quiet; the next, scimitar wielding Mongols broke down doors; killing all in sight. Now, the village was ablaze—everyone dead, or dying. Women, children, the old—and Vasia—her husband. The Mongols left no one alive. He'd pushed her out of the window, sending her out into the snow, contractions and all; somehow praying the snow would cover her escape.

No idea where she was now. She ran, walked, and stumbled along for as long as she could. A long time, so it seemed—and always away from the village—into the wind, using it for direction. Plodding through the snow, which came down like dry powder, unable to see anything in the total whiteout. Numb, she was climbing a slope of some kind, then stumbled and fell down the other side, rolling to the bottom. That sent her rigid with a prolonged contraction. She lay exhausted.

Instinct impelled her to begin digging into the flank of the hillock, frantically trying to burrow out a snow cave. The effort was enormous, the cold intense, the baby almost due. Shoving snow behind her, lots of it, burrowing further into the hillock, she patted the roof firm. Another contraction fixed her rigid—this one lasted longer. Looking around at her handiwork...*would it do?* To widen the cave she scooped out more snow, packing it back with her feet. Tenaciously, she'd dug out a small snow cave so she could deliver her baby. She had to be able to sit up in it, so she dug down a further arm's length, making a crater. It would have to do. *Need an air hole.* She poked her arm, and then her finger, through the top; felt air coming in, heard the wind howl outside.

In between contractions, she started tearing her petticoat. She needed three strips, then rags to clean the baby. The contractions were increasing in intensity—and length. The baby was coming—nature would take its course. There was no stopping it. Forcing herself to pant slowly and shallowly through her mouth, she attempted to slow the delivery.

Outside, the snowstorm raged, fiercer if anything. Inside the snow cave, it almost felt cosy, compared to her earlier exposure. The contractions were longer with shorter intervals. Sweat poured off her—and in these conditions, that could kill. She wiped her face. Another spasm overtook her, more prolonged and harder this time. She spread her legs in the snow, feeling her cervix dilate, pushing down hard, breathing regularly, and shallowly all the time. She was sure she was bursting, splitting in two. With each contraction, the baby moved a few millimetres.

She felt the baby's head shove through. Relaxing, panting, then pushing hard, the muscles of the pelvic floor parted and more of the baby came out. Breathe... breathe... breathe... pushshsh.... The baby's shoulders... more pushing.... the baby's trunk. Then in a rush...a slither...the baby entered into a cold white world. Liquid trickled out of her with the after-birth; she felt relieved, drained of effort and emotion. Her uterus contracted, closing off the placental blood supply. With all her effort, she leaned forward and placed the boy on her petticoat. She quickly but gently tied the umbilical cord in three places with strips of petticoat, roughly three fingers from the baby's navel, then two fingers from that tie, finally another two fingers from the last tie, then bit through the cord between the second and third ties.

Vera held him head down; fluid dribbled from his mouth and nose. She wiped the fluid, patted his back. The little one gave a choking cough, then another, then cried with all the energy his tiny lungs could muster. Screaming, she placed him back on the torn petticoat. Gently she pulled at the cord still inside her, quickly delivering the placenta and membrane, pushing the mess to the side of the cavern. She picked up little Vasia; a greasy white film covered fine downy hair on the bluish skin, making him slippery and difficult to handle. His forehead had streaks of blood on it.

She washed him with snow, rubbed him clean, and put him to her warm breast to suckle, cooing to him tenderly. Looking at her son feeding, she allowed herself to reflect on the past hours—her sweet brave husband. She cuddled her son, looked at him with glazed eyes; exhausted, she fell asleep.

Awaking with a start—she faintly heard men shouting. Horse's hooves beat against the snowy ground. She stirred and felt the baby stir. The air smelt stale and she realised the air hole had been covered with fresh snow. She had poked the hole just before she fell asleep. Now, she reached up and pushed her hand out of the snow cave, into the open air. She widened it making a hole through which she could see the blue sky. The snowstorm had run its course.

Again, she heard men's voices. Although the speech was distant, indistinct...she could just make out its lilt...Ukrainian...thank the lord. Hooves came closer; she let out a scream of relief—to let the men know she was there.

'Over here,' someone shouted.

'Where?' a deep bass voice wanted to know.

'Near that hillock—it's coming from below the snow.'

Vera screamed again—her son joined in. Above her head, there appeared a helmeted rider. The horse's head looked down on her.

'Well, I'll be blessed,' said the deep voice. 'Over here,' he yelled to the others.

He got off his horse and climbed into the hole with Vera. 'Here, let me take the little one,' he held out his hands for the bundle. 'You look almost done in.'

She gave him her screaming son. The big man put him under his fur cape, into the warmth. Vera got up; breathed deeply, and almost fainted.

'Go steady, there,' he put out his other hand to support her. With difficulty, he climbed out, then turned and pulled Vera out. Other riders, four in all, cantered up. One of them dismounted, took off his fur cloak and put it round her shoulders.

He asked, 'How did you get away from Batu's men?'

'That can wait; can't you see she's half dead,' said the bass.

She was hoisted onto the horse, behind her rescuer, and the baby handed to her. As they rode to safety, she thought, *you can't replace your father; but I'm going to tell you all about him when you're old enough.*

Illicit Love

Cautiously, Fabia sneaked out through the back way; wrapping a black *palla* cloak round her head, covering her face. If she was caught—the disgrace, not to mention the dire consequences. The *palla* made her look matronly, aiding her disguise. She stopped for a moment; listened; heard no one except the kitchen slaves squabbling, chopping, and clattering pans. With trepidation at her foolishness, she made her way down the alleyway into the narrow street paralleling Publicius Hill, the long ascending avenue on which her father's villa stood. The spacious villa jutted out from the northern slope of the Aventine Hill, overlooking the Circus Maximus, half way up from the temple of Diana.

At the fourth hour (10am), the street was busy, people making their way from the poorer southern slope, down to the Forum; some to listen to barristers defending their clients from the *rostra*, others to promenade around, meet friends; do some shopping. What denounced Fabia to the surreptitious stares of others was the absence of a personal slave accompanying her. Her attire, the blue dress, bearing, insisted she should have one. She had hoped that the multitude would conceal her intended rendezvous with Demetrius, which is why she chose this busy time for her libidinous intentions. Committed to her course of actions, she moved swiftly amongst the crowd, only to be jostled and elbowed by the ill smelling *plebes*. Pushed from behind, she stumbled into a merchant carrying rugs.

'Where's your head—with Maecenas?' scolded the merchant in base Latin with an oriental accent.

Fabia glared at him; *another foreigner,* then proceeded to shove her way farther along, a look of determination set on her face. She'd arranged to meet Demetrius at the northern end of the Boarium, in the firm belief that nobody *she* knew would frequent the meat market—making her discovery unlikely. At the bottom of the narrow street she turned left, threading her way through narrow alleyways to her tryst.

The smell from the meat market was strong, a light breeze blowing from that direction. The eager spring morning sun made little headway into the confined crevices between the tall housing, yet the heat was already stifling. Little beads of perspiration budded beneath the *palla* cloak as she strode out into the Boarium. Fabia hurried across the market place, avoiding bellowing beasts and noisy owners, making her way to the northern end where the live poultry hung on long poles by their feet.

Under the portico of the poultry market waited Demetrius, wearing a light grey toga, standing back under the columns in the shade, trying to be discreet. The twenty-four year old Greek youth had a pale complexion almost matching Fabia's—suggesting an indoor occupation. They met, touched hands furtively, mindful of onlookers and convention.

'Mistress Fabia...' whispered Demetrius, 'I'd almost given up hope...of you coming.'

'I'm sorry—Demetrius; it's difficult to get away.' She joined him in the shade, under the columns. 'My father has spies watching my movements. I sneaked away as soon as I could.'

'I'm glad you're here...' he wanted to say more but broke off, looking earnestly yet reverently into her face, searching for a deeper meaning. *Why is she interested in me?*

She looked away, 'We must make a move. You still want to...you know?' she asked.

The bustle from the market made it difficult to hear; they stood closer. Quietly he answered, 'I trust you. If you want to do the auguries on the Arx, I'll come and witness it.'

They held hands. 'I've been studying. I'm very *good* at it. My father belongs to the College of Augurs, you know.'

He didn't answer; simply stood and waited. He knew she was being blasphemous; but what could he do? He was in awe of her; the vigour, the sheer exuberance of her lovemaking had captivated and overwhelmed him. She was so young, but with the intense desire of one twice her age. He was totally besotted by her.

Quickly, they walked towards the Capitol; she in front, he, a few steps behind, as custom demanded; weaving through the narrow alleyways. At the beginning, there were few people,

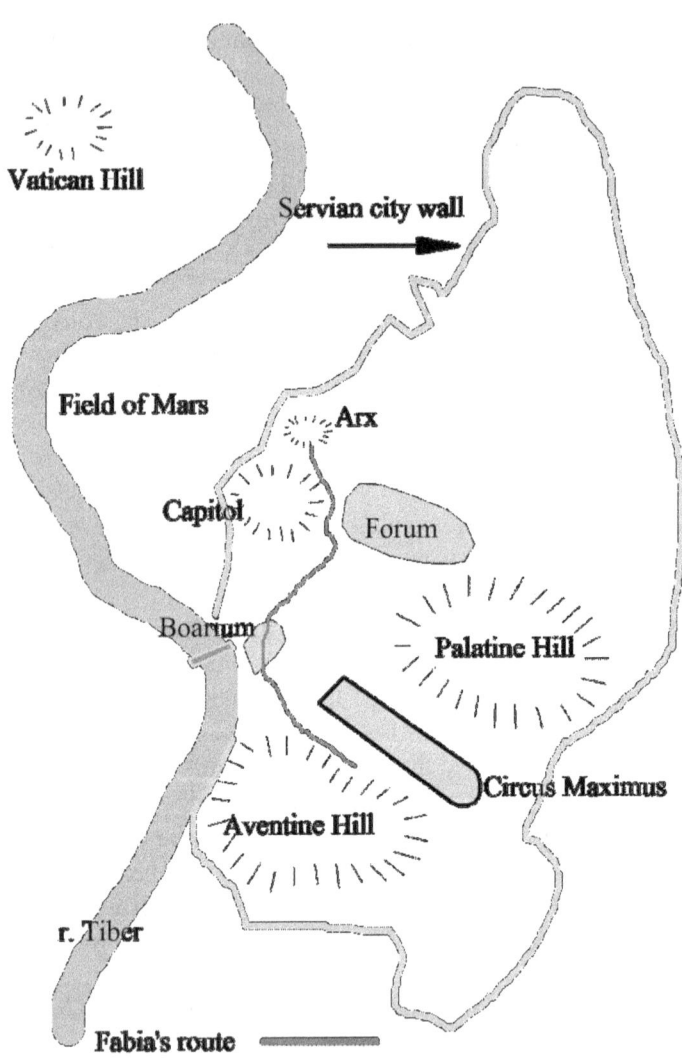

Rome 30 BC in the time of Augustus

then the throng increased as they neared the Forum. Before them, they saw the looming isolated mass left by erosion; the hill with the two peaks, the Capitol and the Arx; home to Jupiter Optimus Maximus, Juno and Minerva. They strolled up Jugarius Street, turned left at the temple of Concordia Augusta and then up the Capitoline Hill towards the steps leading to the top of the Arx. They climbed the steps to the Arx, which the temple of Juno Moneta shared with the Auguraculum, Fabia's goal.

From the Auguraculum, the permanent augury platform, Fabia intended to designate by word, the boundaries limiting where she would look for the auguries to the East; she badly wanted an eagle to soar in the circumscribed area, to vindicate her rebellion. Deep in this reverie, followed by her shaven headed lover, the two heard the heavy sandals of a procession descending from the Arx.

They pressed against the left wall to allow the haughty procession to pass by. First, they saw two burly gladiator bodyguards come into view. They preceded a litter carried by strongly built Dalmatian slaves with shaven heads, in ostentatious livery. Fabia froze. She recognised the livery. The litter stopped as it came parallel to the young lovers.

The curtain opened and out peered her father's face.

'So, you young vixen! You think to make a fool of me like your slut of a mother.'

Her face drained of blood. The Senator pointed at Demetrius and snapped his fingers. Two more bodyguards came from the rear of the litter and seized him roughly. Demetrius' features were emblazoned with terror. His ruin was written on his face.

'As for *you,* slave; you know well the penalty for cavorting with your superiors. He beckoned to the bodyguards.

'Take him back to the villa and lock him in the cubby-hole next to the wine cellar.'

'How...did you *know*...we were here?' her whiny voice was desperate.

'My informers overheard you making your plans,' he snarled. 'You seem to have forgotten who I am. I may have *been* your father, but I'm also a Senator of Rome, a Fabii. I can easily outmanoeuvre a mere child in intrigue.' He motioned to more bodyguards, 'Take her back to her chamber. Lock it. Put a grate over her window and secure it. Place guards outside her door and under her window. I want no more mistakes.'

On her return journey to the villa, she agonised over what she had done. Loath to admit it, at the outset, it had been an illicit sleaziness tugging at her rebellious fifteen-year-old heart, driving her in defiance of her father. Fabia's adolescent conflict had obliged her to begin an affair that placed her at odds with the mores of the disciplinarian society she felt afflicted by. When she was seven, her cuckolded father had cast her mother out onto the streets for her trollopy misconduct; now, Fabia had felt impelled to sink even lower.

She had seduced; been seduced; it made little difference, by a slave scribe. A Senator's daughter bedding a slave.... The shame on the family name was immeasurable. The old revered patrician name of the *gens* Fabia went back to Etruscan times and was one of the *gentes majores*....one of the Optimate families ruling Rome in 30 BC, under Augustus.

The Senator saw it as his duty to his ancestors to cleanse that name; the Greek slave was of no consequence. A quiet garrotting would take care of his impudence. His daughter; the law allowed only one punishment. She would be buried alive in a tomb; a fine meal would be provided and the tomb sealed; that way, none of his daughter's blood would be shed by the Senator.

Sasha Garrydeb

The Curse

A squirrel sprinted furtively across the gravestones, stopping now and then to scratch at a hole, trying to retrieve part of its food cache. It was dark, humid, with the wind drifting in from the nearby lake. A shallow fog hung over the silent graveyard. The full Moon slid from behind the clouds throwing an eerie white light over the late autumn landscape. Somewhere in the distance, an owl hooted, breaking the silence, sending the squirrel scampering for safety.

A short while later, footsteps trudged wearily along the gravel path between the tombstones. Two figures dressed in dark clothing whispered urgently to each other, the smaller, prodding the larger for emphasis with the bend of the crowbar he carried. Clearly there was an argument going on regarding the nature of their scurrilous presence late at night in a place they had no legitimate cause being in.

A broad Cornish accent whispered harshly, 'I tell yeh I saw it on 'er when the coffin was ammered down.'

A cultured voice rasped back, 'I told you to remove it *before* they put the lid on.'

'How could I with the family watchin an all? I weren't supposed to be near the casket—I'm only the gravedigger,' appealed his companion, trying to avoid the inevitable prod from the crowbar.

'You should have found a way. Now we have to break into her tomb. It's not good enough, you know.'

'Don't know what yer complainin fer. It could've been worse—we could've had te dig her up.'

They turned a corner onto a side path by a large ornate baroque tomb, with a marble angel crowning the ensemble. At that moment, the moonlight slowly disappeared, as cloud cover reasserted itself—the cemetery being thrown into obscurity. The small man reached his hand out to steady himself on a ledge of the tomb, when a loud piercing *m-i-a-o-w* emanated from the ledge, followed by claws digging into his hand. He yelled in pain, dropped the crowbar, and tried to swipe the black cat from him. No sooner had he touched the cat, then it screeched with fright, jumped away, bounding off into the Stygian darkness across the graves.

'Damned brute!' exclaimed the cultured voice, looking for the abandoned crowbar in the blackness. 'Tom, help me look for the….,' the small man left the sentence hanging, rubbing his hand.

'S'ok! I've got it. Here, take it.' The big man pushed it at his smaller companion.

'Well go on—you lead the way,' the cultured voice ordered, whilst he continued to rub his scratched hand.

A little further on, the hulk halted. 'I think this 'ere's it—can't see much in this bloomin' dark.'

'Stand back—let me get at the sepulchre door.' The smaller man felt for where the lock should be—and found a chain. 'Trusting souls aren't they.' He inserted the crowbar to break the chain—with no result. He tried a couple of times more—still the chain held.

'C'mon 'ere—give me that,' big hands grabbed the crowbar, inserted it in the chain and gave it a sharp twist. The chain snapped with ease. He then wedged the iron near the lock and tugged—it also gave way—the door creaked in the gloom.

'Keep it down—you're making enough noise to wake the dead,' urged the cultured voice.

'Huh,' snorted the big man dismissively.

The small man pushed his way forward, 'Stand aside.' He edged forward into the tomb. He sniffed the air, 'It doesn't smell right—aarrgh!' He lashed out at the enveloping cobwebs. 'You stupid big oaf,' he spluttered. 'This is the wrong tomb!'

'Ow do yeh mean?'

'There shouldn't be any cobwebs—not yet.'

'It's so bloomin' dark,' the hulk tried to excuse himself. 'We shoulda waited till the moon come out.'

The little man backed out of the tomb, clawing at his face, attempting to free himself of the clinging strands. 'So—where's *her* tomb?' he demanded.

'I think...must be the one next 'ere,' the response came in a whisper.

'Well, don't just stand there. Go and open it.'

This time the big hands tried to jemmy the door open quietly. Yet, again the smaller one pushed his way past—and gingerly inched his way inside. Once there, he lit a candle and held it aloft. Looking round, he placed the candle on a nearby stone ledge, freeing his hands for work.

'That's more like it,' he sighed, gazing at the newly installed coffin resting on a shelf against the far wall. 'Bring the crowbar—wait!' he countermanded. 'What's that green mist—there?' A puzzled expression on his face.

The big man scratched his head. 'What mist? Can't see nothin' there.' He handed him the crowbar and the small man hesitated—then warily jemmied the lid open.

'Pass me the candle,' he ordered. —— 'My god, look at her face!' he exclaimed. 'Looks like she died of fright.'

'Yeah. They said at the funeral, the mortician had trouble changin her look. Had to leave it as it were. That's why they closed the casket so bloomin' quick.'

The small man stared at the dead woman—as if transfixed. 'What else did you hear?' he inquired as he switched his gaze to the reason for their sacrilegious visit to the tomb in the middle of the night.

'I over'eard 'er brother telling one of 'er aunts, the emerald was given to some Celtic Princess by a Viking Chieftain way back in the thirteenth century—a sign of 'is love.'

'And pray tell, how did *he* know that?' There was a sarcastic tone in the question.

'Ow should I know? I'm just tellin yeh what I 'eard. D'yeh want me to go on?'

'Yes, yes. Get on with it.'

'The brother said, the Viking got it from the Lower Dnieper River in far off Rus. Then he said, an invading Norman Baron killed 'er Viking lover and stole the stone, afore driving his sword through 'er as well. And she'd put a curse on whoever owned it—and the curse, so the brother said, had taken many a life. Some of the owners had priests and even Bishops exorcise the stone, but none succeeded in lifting the curse, it's still there. Don't know where he got the story from—honest. Anyway, that's why the brother wanted the stone buried with 'er—so as to bury the curse forever.'

'Fiddle faddle. Tosh and poppycock,' spat out the small man.

'Yeah, that's what I think too, but you being a man of the cloth, I'd've thought yeh might put some more faith in the story.'

'Why should I? Being a priest doesn't mean I believe all sorts of nonsense,' the small man hissed as he reached for the emerald pendant resting on her still bosom. One sharp tug—and the chain snapped free from round the dead woman's neck. 'Now put the lid back on, and let's get out of here,' the small man urged, making for the door.

The big man did the priest's bidding and then followed him into the night. They closed the door of the tomb as best they could, then retraced their steps the way they'd come. As if to help them, the moon threw an accusing light on their activities.

'Don't ferget what yeh promised,' reminded the gravedigger.

Absently the priest whispered, 'Yes, yes. You'll get your hundred pounds, as soon as we get back to the rectory. By the bye. Did the brother say *how she* came by the stone?'

'Can't've been a month back when the dead woman stole the stone from 'er great aunt. That's what 'er brother said. That aunt was an obsessive gambler and won it from a Lord o the realm, at poker, in Bristol. The Lord died at the poker table, seized with pain—that's what I over'eard the brother say.'

The more the priest heard of the curse—and the stone, the tighter he clutched the pendant. The fog thickened around their ankles as they hurried back with the loot. What neither noticed in the dark was, a patch of vapour behind them, it had a green tinge to it—and seemed to be keeping close near the priest. Eager to scrutinise his treasure with more light on the item, the priest fairly ran to the rectory when they left the cemetery. The green foggy patch followed him.

Inside, the priest shuddered at what he'd done. Greed had overwhelmed him when he first caught sight of the green emerald. He had to have it. The idea—burying such a lovely thing.

'Eh, hemm!' came from the gravedigger.

'Yes, yes. Just wait there,' he told the big man. He went into his study and collected the promised hundred pounds. He stopped for a fleeting moment, wondering if he might send the gravedigger packing empty handed, then thought better of it. *Better pay him off, keep his silence.* It was the size of the gravedigger that made him think twice of double-crossing his co-conspirator.

He brought the money back and put it in the outstretched hand. 'Mind you, not a word to anybody,' he reminded the big man.

'What d'yeh take me fer—a snitch? I got me reputation to think of'.' The big man seemed offended at the reminder.

'Well—thanks for your help. Now, I'll bid you good night.' The priest moved to the door, inviting the gravedigger to leave.

'Err—yeh. Good night to yeh Rev. See yeh tomorrow.' With that parting shot, the big man eased his big frame though the door and vanished down the garden path.

The priest felt elated. He patted the emerald in his right pocket and went back to his study, sat at his desk and retrieved the pendant from his pocket. Switching on the table lamp, he gazed at the stone. Opening the top left drawer of the desk, he felt around for a magnifying glass. He was anxious to examine the stone closely. He wanted to drink in the essence of his sacrilege. At heart, this greedy priest was an evil man. He had taken his vows with his fingers crossed—looking for an easy life. The stone represented his way out—somewhere in the Bahamas—away from these country clods and their funny accents.

As the priest gazed into the heart of the emerald—the green haze that had followed him from the tomb slithered with wispy tendrils into the room and stole silently across the floor towards him. Over the hundreds of years since the curse had been pronounced, evil had etched itself into the glittering green by the potency of the malevolent influence from a crushed love. Now, this malicious energy was intent on claiming yet another victim.

'What's this?' He put his spectacles on and brought the magnifying glass to bear closer on the stone.

It seemed to him he discerned some features embedded deep in the emerald. As he looked intently, so the features cleared, and he perceived a Viking helmet.

'*N-o-o—this can't be!*' He shook his head. 'I must be tired,' he moaned aloud.

He sat back, away from the desk, with an air of desperation. '*N-o-o!*' he moaned again.

He could feel he was losing the stone. Something else held it, some demon. It was being torn away from him, and with it, his dream of an easy life.

The green haze lifted from the floor and gathered at the emerald—appearing to grow outwards. A malevolent Viking warrior's face loomed large. Green pitiless eyes blazed fiercely in front of him—fixing him rigid with their hypnotic glare. Instinctively, he shoved further back as the malicious face grew ever larger.

Fear had his cardiac muscles pounding beyond endurance. Something had to give—and it was the priest's heart. He slumped forward onto the floor, his face frozen with terror—and for one split second, the priest recognised the fear he'd seen on the woman's face in the coffin.

The Viking apparition hung—for a lingering instant—then gave a soundless hollow laugh before disappearing back into the stone, waiting for its next avaricious victim.

What the priest discovered, was that real evil, was easier to encounter than to escape.

A Day in the Life of Kra

Lud, the old crippled knowledge-keeper stood before the cave wall, red ochre on his fingertip, ready to dab more animals on the wall.

'Eraghhh,' he yelled at his son Kra, who was about to leave on the dawn hunt.

An eager clutch of the clan young surrounded Lud, waiting to be taught about animals.

'Eraghhh,' Kra yelled the parting back at him from the cave mouth, using his strong jaw perched on heavy features.

Neanderthals employed a primordial language, used fire extensively, made clothing, jewellery and tools, and took care of their sick and aged—but were especially skilled hunter-gatherers.

Dawn had infringed on the night sky; the chase was being readied. A hunting party had gathered, shivering in the cold of the cave entrance. They milled around beating their hands against their bodies, stamping their feet, waiting for the order to move off. Each daybreak warriors left the cave seeking fresh spoor signs, eagerly following their instinctive hunt routine.

Shadows danced high on the cave wall; cast there by the indispensable fire burning bright in the middle of the cavern, eerily imitating the purposeful movements of the people going about their pressing dawn concerns. From the women's area, at the far side of the roaring flames, a harsh shriek disrupted the quiet, followed by a thudding crash on the earthen floor, then an angry scream. One of the women had caught another pinching a scrap of food leftover from the previous night's meal.

Kur threw back his heavy fur cloak, causing his wolf teeth necklace to rattle. He grabbed and raised his enormous bone club to back up his threat. '***Bahnnna***,' the Chief's voice rose in anger—aimed in the direction of the squabbling women.

Silence descended like a thunderclap in the cave. Kur, the leader of the Wolf Clan insisted on silence at dawn—a calm before his band left for the hunt. Inwardly, he was striving to imitate the cunning of the wolf—he wanted his warriors to pause and sense the dangers about to face them out in the frigid hostile world. By reasserting his authority in the cave, he was helping the warriors centre themselves on their purpose, on the coming hunt, and on the landscape beyond the safety of their cave.

Gan, the shamán, a large wolf-skin concealing his craggy features, danced in a circle nearby. His shadow spread gigantically on the cave wall. He was intoning spells for the warriors' safe return, for the courage of the coming chase, for the bountifulness of the hunt.

This was what their lives entailed on the fringes of existence. The struggle for survival was a grim daily reflex activity spurred on by the empty gnawing in the pit of their stomachs. It was a stubborn tenacity that drove on their brief lives; lives that lasted only into their late 20's, if they were lucky. It was the same determination that drove all animals to challenge mortality for their survival.

Kur took his position at the head of the fur clad warriors near the cave entrance. He raised his right hand above his head, making a high circle, the sign of the Sun—he was asking the Giver of Life for a consecration—bypassing the shamán—reasserting his leadership over the clan. All the warriors copied his action and made the sign of the circle. He waited a heartbeat or two, and then led the column out of the cave.

Outside, in the snowy whiteness, near arctic conditions prevailed in the world of the Middle Palaeolithic. His warriors were all physically robust; their hundred and sixty centimetre skeletal frames had a muscular massiveness that indicated tremendous strength and endurance. All wore heavy fur clothing, carried wooden shafts, knapped spearheads at one end made that end lethal. Their hands and feet were wrapped snugly in tight thick skins.

Kur's broad, projecting, angled nose had evolved to conserve moisture under cold and arid conditions. All the clan were similarly blessed. He sniffed the air for any tell-tail spoor signs. Hair covered low receding foreheads; thick bony brow ridges over the eyes shielded them from the icy glare of the brilliant white snow. Their bulky trunks and relatively short limbs and digits were designed to conserve metabolic heat.

More snow had fallen overnight, which made the going more difficult. Heavy clouds in the sky foretold, more snow would fall before the day was ended.

The cave nestled snugly inside a sheer high cliff wall, tusks and fur skins from many slaughtered Mastodons sheltered the entrance, leaving a narrow covered passageway to the left. The people of the Wolf Clan had come across the cave many seasons ago. Sabre Teeth cats had inhabited it back then, and a fierce struggle had taken place for its possession. When the pair of long toothed cats were finally evicted with fire, the shamán purified the cave for many a sunrise before pronouncing it cleansed. It was his way of forging his power over the clan.

Snow sat heavy above the entrance—they were careful not to make too much fuss when leaving, lest the earth-borne vibrations cause a snowfall. Once out of the cave, the column began the difficult descent to the permafrost on the valley floor. Eyes were peeled for animal signs. It would be fortuitous if the warriors managed to corner a luckless beast prowling near home—preferably a giant reindeer—lots of meat. It had happened in the past, but so rarely as to be lost to recent memory.

Kur took the brunt of the march with a dogged perseverance and incredible stamina; he waded forcefully through the snow, pushing it aside with short sturdy legs, massive shafts bearing large joints. His followers reaped the benefit of his hard work. In this way, all seven warriors soon reached the sparse lower tree line where the top layer of snow thinned out. The chief picked up the pace and broke into a steady trot. Underneath the heavy fur, pronounced bony crests and sturdy ridges rippled under the strain where brawny muscles were attached onto the neck, back, shoulders, arms, hands, and feet.

They heard wolves in the far distance, howling, somewhere on the other side of the valley, where an enormous glacier rose into the sky, disappearing northwards into the vast icy whiteness. A yell of acknowledgement echoed from the warriors—a cry of respect for their spirit cousins. On the horizon, carrion ravens circled like specks in the wintry sky where the wolves had their kill. Pointless and sacrilegious interfering in their kill. The pack would have quickly stripped the carcass, leaving only bones. Yet the clan wasn't fussy. If carrion was available, they would grab it, or take it from whatever killed it. They could not afford to pass up any chance of food. They would even drag back to their cave an enemy killed in battle, and devour him with relish. They would crack open the bones; suck out the marrow-rich fat, and lick their lips afterwards. In this harsh landscape, it was eat, or be eaten.

The group pressed on with the hunt. They skirted a deep fissure crossing the valley floor, stopping to catch their breath on the far side. Kra broke off, leading two warriors to look into the fissure—they made frustrated noises looking down. Kra made angry faces, stomped his feet in rage. The fissure usually contained a few dead animals, but the clan could never reach them. There was no way down the icy crevasse—they could only stare longingly at the broken carcasses. Kur yell-grunted at Kra to join him. It was a command Kra instinctively obeyed; reluctantly he re-joined the group.

Kra, sometimes uncontrollable, headstrong, was still the best warrior, apart from Kur. His tenacity on behalf of the clan, always looking for ways to improve their lot, had compelled Kur to make him his deputy. Kra would settle and calm with time. As responsibility was placed on his shoulders, Kra would lose some of his hot temper, would relax his intensity to a capable dependability. He would have to; he was destined to be the next chief.

A few days ago, the clan had dug a deep pit a little distance from the fissure, in the permafrost, large enough to hold a mastodon, or a woolly rhino. They were hoping to catch the animals before they reached the fissure. Checking the pit the past two days, they had found it empty. This time they approached the hollow cautiously, hopefully—only again to be disappointed. The thin top covering with its layer of snow was intact. Heavy tracks nearby, pointed to a recent visit. The footprints suggested a young mastodon. The prints went close to the hole—but it must have sensed something, and turned back. The cow protecting it had probably called. They always travelled as a family group led by a protective matriarch.

Kur bent and examined the tracks. If they found little else, they would probably have to pursue this group. He followed the tracks a little further and found the rest of the herd. Seven in all—four cows, one bull, and two young. The tracks were recent. The wind was coming off the glacier into their faces. That was a good omen.

Kur raised his hand making the fingers down sign for Kra to join him. When his deputy neared, Kur grunted in the direction the herd had taken—then he hand-indicated with a circular motion they should continue to comb the rest of the valley for spoor and prey. The wind picked up; telling them a storm threatened. The snow lifting into swirls as the hunters made their way along the valley floor, to the other side where wolves were howling.

Every member of the group kept a sharp lookout for animal movements. Anyone not accustomed to these conditions would find little sign of anything in such atrocious weather. To the little band of Neanderthal hunters, this was normal. This was the world they lived in—the world in which they trailed, stalked, and tracked the food they ate. The simple fact was; a lack of hunting skills equalled starvation. It forced their eyes and ears to attune to the wilderness, their senses to rise above the weather and their surroundings, pinpointing anything that moved. Like their spirit guide, the wolf, they copied the pack's tactics.

Gron punched his fist into the air demanding attention. He pointed his hand at a snow hare bounding over the permafrost to the left, in the distance, chased by an arctic fox. The two animals leapt across the snow, the hare twisting and turning through the sparse conifers, the fox trying to anticipate the hare's every change of direction. Gron jumped up and down in frustration, knowing it was futile pursuing such speedy animals.

A beneficial spin-off from watching the chased hare, was that Kur spied an Elk's head peering over a hillock from that direction, topped by one-meter long antlers. The barely visible dark head looked at them over the hill, and from that distance, only the trained eyes of one of his people could see it. Kur gave a low grunt that got everyone's attention. He looked at the giant Elk, which is all he needed to do. The other warriors immediately looked in the same direction.

As one, the warriors hunched down. Kur gave the hand signal for the group to split. Kur would lead two to the left and Kra would take two to the right. They would try to circle round the Elk. Gron would wait for a signal and then approach the Elk from the front.

Southwards, beyond the glacier, out on the open steppes, the cold conditions had reduced the pervasive dense cover of the earlier coniferous forests, enabling large herds to support themselves on the open grasslands. This summer had been difficult. The slightest approach from the hunters of the clan, and the herds they stalked, would make a crazed dash in the opposite direction. The summer had been short and barren—more than usual. Earth tremors had created panic amongst the herds, making them constantly skittish and restive. Glaciers shifted their enormous weight, the ground rupturing, creating fissures and crevasses. Gathering plants was made more difficult as some growths failed. Roots tended to be smaller than they could remember.

The clan had gone into the first snows with only half of their usual over-wintering provisions. Kur knew he would have to hunt throughout winter to give the clan a chance of survival. The dried meat stock would be insufficient. There was no choice. It brought more worry into his hearth, and his mate, Lina, knew their fortunes were slimmer than the previous season. She hoped her two young sons would make it without succumbing to afflictions. They'd had it tough before and the way through, from experience, was to gather closer to the fire, draw their belts tighter, chew leather and brace themselves till spring. They called to their spirit guides, danced into a trance, summoning them to give them strength. They begged the spirits for a kinder coming year—but above all relied on the daily hunt.

Kur's small group took a wide route round the giant Elk and from the distance saw Kra's group doing the same. The wind still in their favour was gusting down the valley. If they were lucky, there might be more than one Elk. That would increase the chance of running something down. A giant Elk would be a fine kill, plenty of good meat. More than one would give them an opportunity to secure a kill.

Kur knew that if it were a lone Elk, it would be trying to skirt the wolf pack. More likely, an old buck, thrown out of the herd, and on its last legs, trying to survive one last winter. Trouble with old bucks was, old age made them wily, cautious and smart. Witness it peeking at them almost out of sight, only the head showing over the hill. Staying quiet not to attract attention. Unfortunately for the Elk, there were more cunning animals around than itself. It had attracted Kur's attention.

Gron had stayed standing so the Elk could focus on him. Bent double, both flanking parties had reached an arc just behind the Elk, then spread out. Gron held its attention to the front and the two parties were positioned in a semicircle to close its escape route, either to the rear or to the side. Gron moved forward when Kur raised his hand. At first, the Elk, two and a half meters at the shoulders, was curious and simply watched the human approach. Then it began to back off a little. It looked round and saw humans behind it, to both sides. It panicked. Tossing its large palmate antlers to either side, it made a mad dash to its right on its long legs; its four hundred and fifty kilos pounding directly at Kur, fleshy muzzle open wide, antlers down and panting heavily.

Unnoticed by the humans, concentrating on stalking the Elk, a snow leopard had been watching and stalking them in turn. Watching—waiting to see if it could gain an advantage. It wasn't fussy. Initially it was after the Elk, but a human would do just as well. It had been camouflaged by the snow, lying flat, blending in. Now it decided to join the hunt.

Rag saw the snow leopard first and hurried from the rear, alerting Bor with a grunt. Both were in Kur's party and now saw the danger their chief was in. Rag threw his spear with all his might, missing the Elk. The spear landed near the snow leopard. Bor stared in horror as the snow leopard made a dash for Kur. The reddish brown Elk veered away from Kur, to the right where Rag had been waiting. Then the Elk twisted further right, then left, breaking through the human trap. It was off down the valley, loping through the snow as fast as its long legs would carry it.

The snow leopard reached the petrified Kur, who stood his ground; spear poised in readiness. From the other side of the semi-circular trap, Kra, Nim, and Derg were racing through the deep snow, trying to reach their endangered chief. For Kur the hunt had turned into a fight for his life. He wounded the snow leopard with his leading thrust but the leopard swiped him with its right paw; tantamount to being slashed across the chest with four large razor sharp knives, slicing through his thick fur. Kur had fallen back and the snow leopard pounced, holding him by the throat.

Bor was the nearest, reaching the struggling pair with his spear in hand. He thrust it into the ribcage of the snow leopard, mortally wounding it. Rag arrived, axe in hand, and threw himself on the dying snow leopard, hacking at the back of its neck repeatedly. Then Kra arrived with Nim and Derg; all three thrust their spears into the bloodied body of the snow leopard, half in anger, half in vengeance.

A stunned silence descended on the scene. The wind howled and the snow fell, swirling everywhere, tossing the snowflakes around in flurries. The six warriors stood in a semicircle, looking at their dead chief. They didn't need to check if Kur was dead—his throat was ripped out. Kra's short brow was crinkled on his low forehead, as if he was trying to work something out. Finally, he let out a blood-curdling yell at the top of his voice.

'*Aaaaaaargh!*'

The other five warriors joined in the dirge.

'***Aaaaaaargh!***'

The lamentation lasted some time, as the warriors grieved for their dead chieftain. The sorrowful lament joined the wailing of the wind, creating an eerie chorus drifting on the snow, down the broad valley. Even the wolves made themselves heard, as if in ritual sympathy for the death of the leader of the wolf clan.

Kra ceased his lament as spontaneously as he'd begun; he then held up his hand, taking charge. He pointed at the dead snow leopard's bloody carcass. Derg was standing the closest, and kicked the snow leopard with his left foot.

Nim knew what Kra wanted. Nim had been Kra's closest childhood companion. Nim bent over the snow leopard and put its front paws over his back—then he looked at Derg to take the back legs. Derg understood. He put the leopard's back legs over his chest and both warriors stood up. Although the leopard was large and heavy, the two Neanderthals' musculature was easily capable of dealing with the weight. Nim had the snow leopard's chest over his right shoulder and Derg had its crutch over his left shoulder. They would carry the carcass in this manner, back to the cave.

Kra looked sternly at Gron, Rag, and Bor. Then he looked at Kur's body. The three went over to Kur and quickly lashed three spears into a makeshift litter. One shaft held Kur's neck, either end carried by Rag and Bor; this was crossed lengthways by two more shafts supporting the body. They lashed Kur's legs to the spear shafts. Gron took the two shaft ends on both his shoulders. In short time, the pitiful column was making its way back towards the deep fissure crossing the valley floor.

Rag and Bor led; Kra followed behind Gron, then came Derg and Nim carrying the snow leopard. The order of march was intended for Kur's body to lead the hunting party back to the cave, at least symbolically. It was his head that was at the fore of the column. He had led them out of the clan cave that morning, and he would lead them back—he was still the chief. On the way back, the snow was coming down more thickly, obscuring the landmarks, blurring their vision. The snow was a fine powder, great clouds whirling and twisting with the wind. Instinct drove them unerringly towards the deep pit they had dug close by the fissure.

As they neared, they could hear a crashing and scraping coming from that direction. Then they heard the bellowing— and they knew it was the Elk. Somehow, it had stumbled into their deception and was making a desperate effort to climb out. Kra raised his hand, then lowered it meaningfully. The column halted, and lowered their burdens gently to the ground. Kra carefully led the warriors to the pit. Visibility was such, they almost fell into it themselves. Staring hard, they could just discern the outlines of the massive Elk. It had stopped making a noise, sensing the presence of the humans.

What passed for a smile broke on Kra's face, as he looked into the hollow. The sadness was now mixed with a blessing. Glancing sideways at his fellow clansmen, he distinguished similar cheer forming in their features. Life indeed was strange. It took away with one hand, and gave back with the other. Kra shielded his eyes and peered skywards, looking for the Giver of Life. The thick swirling snow obliterated any sign of the Sun. He made the sign of the circle above his head in thanks for this gift of food. The rest of the warriors followed his example.

What Kra needed to know was, whether the Elk could somehow escape from the pit. He desperately needed the Elk meat for the clan. But he also needed to observe the correct proprieties in dealing with Kur and his succession. He had to get Kur back to the clan so the ritual mourning and burial could take place. It was momentarily perplexing, juggling with the need to maintain ritual and the need to feed the clan. He decided the Elk couldn't get out. He turned and led the warriors back to where they'd left Kur. He put a burst of speed on when they resumed their march, intending to send warriors back for the Elk when they reached the cave.

In the midst of a ferocious snow blizzard, they finally reached the bottom of the hill that led to the cave mouth. By now, Kur looked like a long white parcel shrouded underneath a mantle of snow. His carriers resembled polar bears as they made their way up the hill. When they reached the cave mouth, Kra saw a boy disappear back inside. Someone on lookout had gone to warn the clan; the hunting party was returning.

Rag and Bor still led the procession, with Kur's inert head pushed just ahead of theirs on the shaft of the spear as if he was leading the hunting party back into the cave. The snow-covered cortège entered the cave, and the tragedy became glaringly obvious. Someone was injured, or worse. The improvised stretcher was lowered to the cave floor and Kra, out of respect for his dead chief, swiftly moved to brush the snow from Kur's body. The snow leopard was dropped on the ground unceremoniously. Then the warriors jumped up and down, shaking the fur as they did so, dislodging their snow covering.

People rushed to the entrance and surrounded the hunting party; then a great commotion broke out amongst the small community. Relatives searched the faces of the returning warriors to see who was missing. It wasn't long before Lina, Kur's mate; let out an all-mighty scream. Kur's two sons held their mother back, preventing her from pulling her hair out. Some whimpered; others gasped in astonishment, then howled in despair that such a catastrophe should befall them. Their chief was dead. Moans were followed by groans. Heaving breasts were followed by hysteria, then by sobs. Other women let themselves go, and in their grief, began pulling their hair out. Men beat their breasts. Some even had tears of rage at life's unfairness. Why them?

Gan came forward; large wolf-skin still concealing his features, and banged his ceremonial staff on the cave floor, trying to attract everyone's attention. He banged away until silence prevailed.

Kra helped to quiet the din by crying out loud, '*Bahnnna!*' The chief's often voiced angry invocation.

Gradually the uproar died, leaving only Lina sobbing over the body of Kur. All eyes were turned on Gan. When a death occurred in the clan, Gan officiated over the dead before the ritual burial took place.

Kra turned to the five warriors and imitated antlers on his own sloping forehead. They immediately understood. All five ran to get more spears, then followed Bor, rushing out of the cave—amazing the gathered throng. They had been ordered by Kra to go and collect the trapped Elk.

Gan told the women to pick up Kur's corpse, and solemnly led the way back into the middle of the cave—past the fire, back to where he normally dealt with the bodies of the dead. There was a low elongated boulder in a corner far to the right of the entrance. Near the low boulder, there was the clan shrine. This consisted of a number of flat stones built up into a Π-shape. Inside the Π lay two wolf skulls, male and female. A large flat square stone topped the shrine. This was covered by a black wolf skin, effectively making it an altar.

The women placed the body carefully on the low boulder near the shrine and began to strip Kur of his fur garments. His mate would normally lead this part of the ritual, but Lina was too distraught to tend to her duties. The wolf teeth necklace rattled as they took it off reverently. This was the chiefly insignia—to be passed onto the next chief. Gan took charge of it, placing it on the wolf skin on the shrine. When Kur was disrobed, Gan ordered the women to scrape him down. One of the women, Maga, Kra's mate, went to get Kur's summer fur wrap-round. She returned shortly and they gently girdled the lighter fur wrap round his waist.

Gan picked up a pelvic bone containing ochre paste and began to decorate Kur's hairy body with his finger. On the hairy torso, Gan painted delicate swirls, circles with dots in the middle. Parallel lines were painted on his upper cheeks and forehead—zigzags, and meanders on his hairy legs. Ladders drawn on his arms. The gathered women watched in awe, before being brusquely ushered away by the men. This was a part of the ritual normally only reserved for the men, the sacred decorations being applied. As he worked, Gan mumbled incantations to his spirit guide, low under his breath.

Back near the fire, Kra ordered the snow leopard to be skinned and the meat cut into portions. The skull and a large hunk of meat from the leopard's rump, were sent over to Gan. It would be included into the burial ritual. The leopard skin was saved for Lina—after all, Kur had killed the large cat before it tore his throat out. The original uproar had subsided, older men with prominent brow ridges, now argued fiercely over the succession, gesticulating vehemently, as if it were somehow open for discussion. A sense of excitement mingled with the grief. Children were subdued, sensing momentous events occurring around them. Three of the men began roasting the snow leopard portions, skewering them on long poles over the fire, broad blunt noses working overtime, absorbing the smells as they did so.

When the six warriors, led by Bor, got to the pit, they made use of a nearby tree trunk as a weapon. The trunk was normally used to get in and out of the hole. This time all six warriors rammed the trunk into the Elk with as much force as they could muster, battering the Elk to death.

Then they climbed into the cavity out of the wind, butchering the Elk on the spot, skinning and quartering down there for ease of transport. This made getting it out of the hollow much easier. They left the entrails and blood in the pit as a snare for other animals. With the Elk out of the hole, they covered the hole again, ready for the next animal. With their tremendous strength and endurance, they began the trek back to the cave, hauling their burdens.

A commotion at the entrance proclaimed the return of the six snow covered warriors. Four were laden with one quarter over each shoulder, whilst Gron and Bor carried the head with the enormous antlers. They laid their burdens near the entrance and shook the snow from themselves.

Kra sent the Elk's head with the antlers to Gan to be added to Kur's burial, together with a portion of Elk meat. A quarter of the Elk was put aside; the rest sliced into strips and hung on leather thongs at the back of the cave in an area that acted as a larder. Woe betides anyone who touched this. They would be ejected from the clan, into the arctic cold. Other such dried jerky meat was hanging on lines, but still too meagre a hoard to take them through winter without the daily hunt.

Nominally, Gan as the clan shamán was the temporary chief until a new one was elected. Yet, it was all a bit of pretence since everyone knew Kra would be the next chief. Custom demanded Gan act as the interim chief, so he decreed the burial of Kur would take place in a short while, when everything was readied. The inauguration of their new chief would take place the following day. All activity in the cave was directed to these ends.

A shallow trench was dug into the cave floor, into the white coloured marly soil, by Prag, Brin, Tun, and Gal, near the shrine itself. The calcareous mudstone proved tough to dig using only the implements they had. Animals' shoulder blades to shift the compacted earth, and spears to loosen it. The rectangular trench was one meter wide, one and a half meters long, and thirty centimetres deep.

When the grave was ready, Gan held himself erect in his wolf-skin and called the clan around the low boulder holding Kur's body. Firebrands were held high, so the scene was well lit with flickering light for the ceremony. Squat, thickset powerful people stared reverently, with craggy, beetled-browed faces, at the decorated body of their dead chieftain. Kra and Gron stood a little forward—Gron was to be Kra's deputy. Nim was Kra's childhood friend but Gron was chieftain material—at least Kra thought so.

Gan's long jaw spoke to Kur's spirit guide through his own spirit guide, asking the Life Giver to take onto him the spirit of the clan's chieftain. He asked for Kur's spirit to unite into the spirit council of the past chieftains of the wolf clan, to oversee the welfare of the wolf clan, to get them through their current difficulties. He made the sign of the circle high up in the air. Then Gan pointed at Kur's body. Rag, Nim, Bor, and Derg, gently lifted Kur's body and took it the short distance, to the shallow grave.

Kur was laid on his right side in the grave, the thick ridges over the eyes now at rest. Gan arranged Kur's right hand on the back of the head, his long right cheek resting on his elbow. Kra came round and extended Kur's left arm, such that his left hand draped over his mighty hunting club, placed to his front in the trench. His body was manoeuvred so that it curved into his usual sleeping position. The grave and body, were oriented east to west, head pointing west towards the setting sun. Lina knelt down and bent over Kur, long matted dark hair flopping over her dark eyes, and deposited a few dried flowers around his head, tears still flowing freely. His two young sons, trying to maintain a manly composure, each laid his beautiful hand axe and spear into the grave respectively.

Gan, firstly lifted high, the snow leopard's scull, and cursed the animal that had taken their chief from them. The scull he arranged at Kur's feet. Then Gan took the piece of meat from the snow leopard and laid that at his feet near the scull. The Elk meat, he laid near his stomach, as food for his journey. All the warriors came in turn and deposited a precious flint tool into the grave—the last one, picking up a shoulder bone to fill in the trench. The rest of the warriors helped, filling in the soil on top of corpse.

Thus it was, at the eve of that day; the Wolf Clan buried their chief. The Elk's head with its magnificent antlers was deposited at the top of the grave. Around the mound, many more skulls were arranged. Facing Kur, was a wolf's skull; at his back they placed a huge cave bear's skull. Crowding the area were Auroch, Red deer, roe deer, giant deer, and Saiga antelope skulls; all surrounding the grave. Mastodons, woolly rhinoceros, musk oxen, bison, reindeer, and horses—all were represented. In this manner the clan rendered their final respect for their dead chieftain.

Only when Gan was satisfied that all the proprieties had been observed, and all the skulls arranged to his satisfaction, and to the satisfaction of Kur's invisible spirit guide, did Gan lead the clan back to the main fire for the funeral feast. Women hurried to put Elk bones with bits of meat still left on them over the fire. Gan took Kra aside and they had a whispered gesticulated conversation. The earlier roasted snow leopard portions were handed out by Gan and Kra. The Elk quarter was portioned and stuck on poles over the flames. Slowly members of the clan relaxed, sitting in a circle round the roaring blaze.

Gron joined Kra's company, indicating to all present that Gron was being promoted to deputy chief. Such little things were noticed by the twenty-five-member clan, and were exceedingly important. The activity of eating took over and dominated the little community. Everyone used the occasion to gorge themselves on the leopard and Elk meat, not knowing when the next opportunity would arise. Bones were split with stone hand axes, and the marrow-rich fat given to the young, helping them to grow. Merriment set in, men banged stretched skins; women banged bone against bone. A sort of rhythm enveloped the cave with children prancing about. Drum sounds counter pointed bone sounds.

Gan looked at Kra and a smile broke on his craggy features. Kra returned the smile. Soon people began to get to the serious function of grooming. The bonding ritual that cemented the clan into a family unit, determining, reinforcing individual's status—dictating relationships with others. Teeth, tongue, fingers picked at ticks. Gan groomed Kra and Kra groomed Maga...and so on.

For Kra, life had become more complex, more burdensome, but it also promised to be more fulfilling. Soon people began turning in, bedding down. Some went into a small side cavern, to the latrine. Others squabbled over leftovers. Then—a hush descended.

Kra was sorry Kur was gone—sorry for Lina and the young boys. He lay on the fur bedding and cradled Maga, his mate, a satisfied smile lingering on his rough face. The momentous day had come to an end. The next day he would be ceremonially installed as the next Chief of the Wolf Clan.

Perdition

'*What are you doing?*'

The rope slackened—Colin dropped another meter.

'*Stop it!*' Colin yelled at the top of his voice.

The guideline tethering him to his partner above, loosened again.

'*You're killing me! Have you gone mad?*'

This time the guide rope relaxed substantially, and plunged him about 10 meters. Colin was now convinced Bert intended to kill him.

He yelled at the top of his voice '*Help! For God's sakes—someone help me.*'

A thousand meters up a mountain, who was going to hear him? Frantically, he searched the rock face, looking for a ledge or a hole where he could get a grip. He stretched out his left hand for a crack…just out of reach!

'*Bert! Why are you doing this? What have I done to you? For the love of God—speak to me.*'

For the last hour, there had only been a sinister silence from above. Half way up the rock face, Bert stopped talking to him through their intercom. The mike and earphones were dead. Clouds descended, cutting off any visible communication. The last fall had loosened the piton directly in front. He still had the piton-hammer in his right hand and took a swing at it. Missed! Another yank of the rope prised the piton loose and he swung precariously. More of the rope came loose, and this time, he plummeted 20 metres.

Bruised and battered, he'd gathered his wits, tried to force the right boot into the rock face, but to no avail. The crampon slid off the icy rock, having nothing to grip. The glacial wind howled, numbing his senses. The weather had taken a turn for the worse.

It dawned on Colin, Bert must know about Flora and him. Why else was he trying to kill him? He remembered the present from Bert *and* Harriet. So, Bert must have told her! His own impulsive, grabby nature had led him to this—.

The final plunging of the rope came, and it was almost a relief. Aware the end was close, Colin, in the time left, mentally endeavoured to put his affairs in order, make peace with his God.

On the way down he bounced off of a protruding overhang; setting off a flashback, focusing his mind on to what led to this catastrophe.

A few months before, Colin had a visit from Bert's mistress, Flora. He took a fancy to her—and she liked him right back. She was ensconced in nearby Soho, in a shabby flat Bert had bought for her.

She came to complain, Bert was ignoring her; could Colin do something about it, talk to Bert. Colin did something—for himself and for her. She ended up in bed with him.

He was now two-timing, his wife, Harriet, but also his business partner. Such was life in the 21st century. Egged on by the media, internet porn, morality had become a dirty word, both in the Church and in Government. In the short period of a hundred years, society had gone from Victoriana back to Caligula. True, some of the older generation still professed a moral outlook, attending Church from time to time, making an effort to believe. The rest of society, glancing over their shoulders at US inspired examples, was at it like dogs in a park, with not a thought for what, or why, they were imitating their four legged cousins.

Colin saw himself as a thoroughly modern man and saw no reason *not* to indulge with the rest. Flora, Bert's mistress, had needed consolation, and Colin made every effort to console her—in and out of bed.

It had been Bert, who'd suggested the glacier climb in the Alps.

'What say we head for the Rhône Glacier upstream from *Lac Léman*. When I worked in Switzerland, I used to sit on the shores of Lake Geneva, watching the huge fountain, *Jet d'Eau*, Europe's highest fountain, spurt 132 meters upwards, wondering where all that water came from.'

Incredulously Colin asked, 'You really sat there and wondered about the water in the lake?'

'Yes I did!' Bert's candid face told Colin he really did.

'Let me get this straight. Instead of lying in the Sun, you want to go mountain climbing?'

'That's it!'

'And you want us to climb a glacier?'

'It'll be fun, you'll see. We'll be able to climb Dammastock—it's so close to the Mer de Glace.'

'I need my head examining!'

'The high ozone of the Swiss mountains will make a new man of you. You'll come back healthy and invigorated. Think of the energy you'll be able to bring to your work. Come on Colin—say yes.'

'What about our wives? They won't like this.'

'It's already taken care of. My Dora has booked a place for two, at a health farm in Hampshire. Your Harriet jumped at the chance—she just hasn't told you yet.'

'What? All has been arranged—behind my back?'

'Don't get sore! She was only thinking of you. I told her you'd enjoy the climb.'

'You did what?....Ah! Hell! I don't know! I think it's crazy. You should have asked me first. All these sneaky manoeuvres. Well—if it's gone this far—I suppose I'll have to go along with it. Next time, Bert—ask *me* first.'

'Good! I'll tell the women. Now we can get on with business.'

The *business* in question was running an Art Gallery in Cork Street, just behind the Royal Academy. Twelve hard years of toil, flattery, shady deals, charming, and smooth talking. Colin as CEO and front man—Bert behind the scenes, running the finances. Both wives finalised the paperwork in the backrooms.

As Bert, travel brochure in hand, gave the wives the news, he winked at Colin, who had reluctantly agreed to the climb. Harriet then asked Dora what part of Switzerland their husbands were headed for.

'Ask Bert—he's the expert.'

Bert waved the brochure in the air, 'This is from the local Guide,' he read from the opened page. 'The Rhône originates in the Swiss Alps, upstream from Lake Geneva, or *Lac Léman* as the locals call it. It comes into being at an altitude of 1,830 metres, emerging from the Rhône Glacier, which descends the south flank of the Dammastock, a nearly 4,000—metre peak, close to the road below the Grimselpass. There are many paths in the area giving fine views of the glacier and surrounding mountains, or one can pay to go into an impressive ice-cave.

'The river then traverses the Gletsch Basin, from which it escapes through a gorge, and flows along the floor of the Goms Valley at an altitude of 1,200 meters. The second sector of the Rhône's course commences with Lake Geneva, large and deep—300 meters—and lying between Switzerland and France in a basin hollowed out of the less resistant terrain by the former Rhône Glacier…'

'Okay, I get the picture. You don't have to read it all.' Harriet interrupted, suddenly becoming jealous of her husband's holiday.

A week later, Colin and Bert landed at *Cointrin*, Geneva's airport. They hailed a taxi to their Hotel, *Les Armures*

in the heart of *Vielle Ville*, advertised as an archaeological treasure. Both taxi and hotel required real *treasure* to use them, but it was only for one night.

Over dinner, Bert told Colin, 'When we get halfway up the climb, I'm going to give you a present—from Harriet and me. She asked me to give you this present, from the bottom of her heart.'

'Can't you give me it *now*?'

'Sorry. *No!* I promised Harriet.'

Next day, they hired a car and set out on a fine June morning, heading east on the E25. Waved through at the border, they entered France, bearing north onto the N5, then east into the Sun alongside the river Rhône; high mountains to the left, back into Switzerland, going to Aigle, Salvan, Crans, and finally Gletsch. It had taken them nearly three hours to travel the 260 kilometres to the foot of the Glacier. High above the village of Gletsch, in the far distance, they could see the 3,630 high Dammastock, their destination.

Bert booked them into the village Inn and reported his proposed climbing route to the local gendarme. At dinner that night, Colin caught Bert looking at him in a strange manner— sort of distant—almost calculating. *I wonder what he's up to?* Colin thought. *Probably something to do with that present from Harriet,* he concluded.

They set out early next morning at dawn, fully geared up; to tackle what Colin presumed would be a hairy climb. They were told the weather might be changeable. Bert was the real mountaineering expert, and had checked Colin's outfit and equipment. Helmet, rucksack, rope, harness, pitons, ice screw, leggings, crampons. Bert ticked off each item from a list.

'Can't be too careful,' he told Colin. 'This is a serious pastime.'

'I thought you insisted it was a *sport*.'

Bert assured him, 'It is…it is. Don't worry—I know what I'm doing.'

Later in the morning, after a bumpy ride in a local cart, they reached the base of the glacier. They unloaded their gear. Bert took a moment, stood back and scrutinized the route he'd chosen to climb. Again, he checked the equipment, then roped Colin to him, and began to climb the rock face, followed by Colin.

Colin's flashback was over and done with; he'd bounced off various protrusions, then landed not far from the point he'd begun to climb from earlier that morning. Battered and broken, the body grounded in between two standing rocks, almost unrecognisable. It took Bert a long time to descend—he took his time, a smile playing on his features as he reflected with satisfaction of how he'd delivered Harriet's present.

A small piece in the morning *Journal de Genève* reported that, "An English climber had fallen to his death in an unfortunate accident. His co-climber was said to be devastated."

And with that, the body was flown back to the UK, the matter closed—to everybody's satisfaction. Well! *Almost* everybody's.

Sasha Garrydeb

FRANKENSTEIN SCIENCE

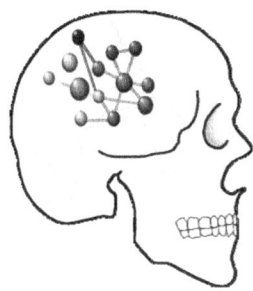

'*Dr. Pierce*! *I* booked the Electron microscope for ten this morning. May I be so bold as to inquire why *you're* still using it?' Hollis Jordan stood impatiently tapping his toe on the laboratory floor. He was staring at the growing bald spot on the back of Pierce's head, his rival for the promotion stakes.

'Just one more minute Dr. Jordan; just let me finish this scan.' Pierce hurriedly tapped the console keyboard of the computer directed Transmission Electron Microscope, staring intently through his gold-rimmed glasses at the Micrographs on the computer screen. 'There it is!' he exclaimed, 'I knew it was there.' Pierce got off the stool and stood up, looking down at Hollis with a condescending smile on his face. 'I'm sorry Hollis. Thank you for your patience. Do you want me to reset the machine?' Pierce half smirked.

'No! I'll do it. You've already held up my work.'

'Suit yourself,' and Pierce's gangling frame walked studiously away.

'You do that on purpose Ted, *don't bother to deny it.*' Hollis yelled at Pierce's retreating back.

Pierce gave a half wave with his right hand; all that was missing was the two fingers. It may have been missing, but Hollis *saw* them. Deep down, Hollis knew Pierce was the brighter of the two, and if there was a promotion, Pierce would get it. In recognition of this reality, Hollis was working on an equaliser. Any spare time he could squeeze in between his workload was devoted to his "equaliser project."

Hollis had hit on the idea of making use of a retrovirus carrier to enhance his own intellectual powers—increasing his intelligence quotient, all in an effort to outsmart Pierce. If he could boost his own intelligence, and come up with a brilliant conclusion to his "official" research, it would secure his promotional chances and forestall Pierce, once and for all.

Hollis had been hired as a genetic engineer, nominally working on retroviruses, also known as RNA viruses. They belonged to the same family of unique RNA viruses that were currently causing so much havoc in the world's population. They were exclusive among nature's reproductive systems; in that the RNA of the virus could indirectly replicate itself using the cell's ribosomal and metabolic precursor systems, then function as messenger RNA.

Hollis worked at the secretive government laboratory nestling amongst the beautiful Wiltshire countryside, seven kilometres east of Warminster, just outside the village of Chitterne on the southern side of Salisbury Plain. As a safety precaution, the actual lab was some two hundred meters underground.

It was partly involved in disease research, funded by the Ministry of Health, and partly research into bacteriological warfare, funded by the Ministry of Defence. Its location snuggled safely amongst the military encampments of Salisbury Plain, effectively camouflaging its existence.

The lab was far more secretive than Porton Down, the Chemical and Biological Defence Establishment eight kilometres further east, or the even more secretive Nancecuke site in Cornwall. The latter site was supposedly closed, as Britain *"officially"* concentrated purely on *"defensive"* chemical and biological weapons under the Biological Weapons Convention of 1972.

In Hollis' lab, they held the cryogenically frozen brain of one, Hans Adolf Vorting. An ex-Nazi German-born biochemist, who led the Nazi Biological Warfare programme. At the end of the war, he'd been spirited back to Britain—and put in charge of the lab Hollis now worked in, but died in 1961, aged 67. All this was kept hush-hush by the government and none of his research papers were ever published. Vorting was classified as a *bona fide* genius and would have deserved the Nobel Prize in Biological Warfare, had such a prize existed.

Hollis first became aware of the existence of Vorting's brain when it was used as an example in a lecture at the lab. He wished he'd half the man's genius, which got him to thinking how he might transfer some of the genius to himself.

He inveigled the lab technician nominally in charge of looking after Vorting's brain, to allow him to measure the brain's ventricles, and under this shallow pretext, had purloined a small fragment of the brain. He intended using a carefully constructed retroviruses he'd mutated and nurtured, to enhance his own brain with Vorting's DNA. The virus, like the Simplex Herpes virus, was constructed to sneak past the defences of the

Blood-Brain Barrier. His constructed RNA virus was intended to produce an enzyme that would synthesise the DNA from Vorting's RNA molecule. The fresh double-stranded DNA thus formed would be injected into Hollis' brain to act as a vector that would transform his lacklustre DNA by adding a few sequences of Vorting's genius DNA, nominally, without disturbing Hollis' long-term memory. At least, that was Hollis' theory.

Hollis spent an hour working on the Transmission Electron Microscope, carrying out final checks on every aspect of his newly constructed retrovirus. He'd already used the retrovirus in his own lab, but felt he had to check the nucleotide base sequences on the gene, to satisfy himself they were in order. The sequence of nucleotides coded for the particular polypeptide that was to change the amino acid in the target polypeptide chain, was where he intended it to be, in its correct position.

For this to work, only one nucleotide base in an amino acid, on one gene, on one chromosome, in all his brain cells, had to be changed to Vorting's; all else remained the same—that would produce a concatenating effect, Hollis hoped. Before he left the lab that night, he intended to inject himself with his "little baby." If all went well, he ought to notice an improvement within a week.

At the completion of his session on the Transmission Electron Microscope, Hollis reset the machine and tidied up his work folder, then retreated to the men's washroom. In the washroom, he hurried over to the washbowl and scrubbed his hands thoroughly, drying himself with the hot-air dryer fixed to the wall. Feeling in his inside pocket, he pulled out his toothpaste and toothbrush, went back to the washbowl and thoroughly scrubbed his teeth, all the time observing himself in the large mirror. It wasn't vanity, but a manic fastidiousness; he was checking his full dark hair was smoothed, that no ugly hairs protruded from his aquiline nostrils. He even checked the whites of his brown eyes were clear. He noticed a black spot on his chin, and squeezed it. That forced him to wash his hands again. There was no hint Hollis was aware of his obsessional behaviour. In fact he waved to the CCTV when he'd finished, watching him from the ceiling corner, before returning to work.

It was late in the afternoon when he returned to his own section of the lab. The luminescent lighting in the lab bounced off the pastel coloured walls, irritating his eyes. He nodded to Victor, who occupied the bench next to him.

'Anyone been chasing me?' he asked his colleague.

'Not that I know of,' Victor responded.

'I'll be in my office if anybody wants me.'

Hollis didn't mean to be brusque, but being an only child, he was stuck with a lack of social graces. He collected his newly produced sample of Vorting's DNA from his bench and went to his office. Hollis' office was neat and extra tidy, almost an insult to the name of research. In it, he pretended to get on with some paper work; but instead, he transferred the vile containing the fresh solution of recently RNA modified Vorting's DNA, into a hypodermic. He locked this into its slot in the helmet. The helmet had to be carefully positioned into the injection groove locator.

For the next stage, he needed to get access to the small room at the back of the lab. It contained the computer guided injection appliance holding the helmet in place. The contraption was a prototype he was testing for his Ministry, to be used on the general public during finicky precise brain stem surgery. It was the presence of this prototype contraption that had finally swayed Hollis in his decision to act.

Quietly he took the helmet and went to the small room at the back of the lab, desperately hoping nobody was intending to barge in on him. He closed the vanes of the blinds and locked the door, then set up the program for the injection. It would take only ten minutes to complete the whole procedure. He hurried, but took care not to make a mistake.

When the programme was ready, he wiped the target area of his scalp with a little alcohol. He set a minute's delay into the programme and pressed "ENTER," then sat his medium frame beneath the helmet, clamping the helmet into position on his head. He waited, and then felt the fine laser incision producing a minuscule fine hair width puncture in the area of the cranium giving the most direct access to the brain stem. It was swiftly followed by the ultra-fine injection needle.

Normally a patient would have had a local anaesthetic; but that was a luxury Hollis could ill afford. After the procedure was completed, Hollis felt a little nauseous, had a mild headache; otherwise, he was all right. The puncture hole was so fine his body's natural fibrinogen would seal it. All had been accomplished in the allotted time and Hollis dismantled any trace of using the machine on himself. He went back to his office and became introspective, pondering on how life would change if this element of private enterprise worked out as he hoped it would.

It hadn't occurred to Hollis there might be a side effect, or that the procedure was in itself dangerous. It had occurred to the professional in him, but his overwhelming desire to outdo Pierce had relegated the nagging warning to a small corner of his mind. He'd been working with retroviruses for nigh on seven years and an arrogance of familiarity had made him complacent. He was convinced he knew the retroviruses little secrets, their foibles and tricks.

Hollis saw Victor wave at him and then leave. It was time to go home to his wife. He went through the normal security checks before he reached the elevator. Hollis felt smug; he was bypassing security by smuggling something out in his head. After two journeys in extra grey elevators, he reached the surface and headed for his car. Sauntering over to his small white Mini, he got in and turned left along the narrow wire-mesh tunnel leading to the outer perimeter gate. There was a fine flurry of snow and he switched the windshield wipers on.

Hollis Jordan stopped at the gate, was scanned by the guard, and passed through the outer gate, where a large sign on the fence said

"**Government Property - Keep Out Trespassers May be Shot**."

This always gave him a comforting sensation, he was on the right side of order in society. It said to him, he was an insider; an elite member of the scientific community working for progress and a betterment of the human condition.

To his utter astonishment, there were a small group of scruffy protesters milling opposite the gate, held back by the MoD police, with placards against Frankenstein Scientists. *In this weather? How on earth did they find this place?* It was an angry thought upsetting his equilibrium. *There must have been a leak somewhere. It's that damned Freedom of Information Act,* he concluded.

He sped past them, forcing one poor anorak to jump for it. He pointed the Mini along the frozen B390 on his normal route back to Warminster. He hadn't really aimed *at* the protester; he tried to convince himself it was his damned headache. On a late January evening, despite being gritted, the roads were dark and slippery. He travelled the seven kilometres every morning and punctiliously returned every evening, never stopping.

Hollis arrived home just before eight that evening, to find his plain doting wife Jenny, waiting for him at the door. She had a Doris Day look about her, neat and tidy. Hollis believed in his family, in providing for them, in their proper upbringing and sustenance. He believed in the order of things as laid down to him by his disciplinarian scientist father, now long dead, bless him.

He could still sometimes hear, ringing in his ears, his father's erstwhile admonitions: *A little order in life goes a long way.* All was voiced to the rhythmic sound of a slipper crashing on his aching backside as his father sought to reinforce his message with the aid of a little "manly" pain. When he occasionally recalled the exhortation, he winced with the remembered pain accompanying the message, but he never questioned its wisdom, or its desirability.

Hollis reared his two teenage sons up in the same austere manner, enforcing obedience and discipline, trying to gain control over their souls. He maintained submission, moulded the mental faculties and instilled a moral character; for him, the prerequisite for an academic career. An outsider would have called him a "control freak," but Hollis never gave it a second thought.

Nursing a whopping headache from the self-administered injection, he greeted his wife, 'Hallo, darling. Dinner ready?'

'Just finished! Serve it now?'

He pecked her on the cheek. 'I've just got to lie down a bit—shocking headache.'

'It'll be ready when you come down, dear,' she whispered.

The little lie-down lasted until the next morning. When he finally opened his eyes, he looked at the painful daylight through the prism of a wavering multi-coloured rainbow. Nothing remained still; all danced before his flinching gaze.

'Do you want me to send for a Doctor?' Jenny asked in a worried tone.

'No,' he whispered dry-mouthed.

'But darling, you're not well. Let me call for a Doctor,' she urged.

'Please, *let me be*. I don't want a Doctor,' he moaned. He tried sitting up, but failed. He next tried getting his legs out of bed, and again failed. 'Jenny? You'd better call the lab and tell them I'm not coming in today. Tell them I'm okay and haven't caught anything from the lab. Tell them.....I've got a cold. Tell them *not* to send their resident Quack.'

Jenny stood listening to his instructions, counting off the points he wanted her to make over the telephone.

❀   ❀   ❀   ❀

Some three weeks passed since Hollis had injected himself with Vorting's DNA. After the first two days, the immediate effects settled, and he was able to return to his lab work.

Within a week, he'd thought of a few new ideas in his ongoing research that seemed glaringly obvious, and he couldn't for the life of him understand why he hadn't seen them before. He became excited, and took it for granted that it was his newly injected DNA working for him. By the third week, he'd written up his conclusions on the research project, and presented the results to his Departmental Head, Professor McLoud. The old man was visibly shaken at the swift conclusion of the protracted investigation Hollis had been carrying out. Worse was to come.

Hollis waited a couple of days for the conclusion to be accepted, and when McLoud asked him to come to his office, ostensibly to congratulate and promote him; Hollis handed in his resignation.

'Aren't you happy with your work? Is it the money? We can work something out,' McLoud's big frame was saying.

'No sir, it's not the money. I just want to do something different, something more challenging, away from a lab.' He looked at McLoud, and for the first time saw an old man, big in stature but past his research prime, given administration to eke out his days until retirement. That wasn't going to happen to him. He was going to make something of himself.

It was eventually clear to the anxious administrator, Hollis intended to go, and so he wished him well. Then promptly had security escort Hollis off the premises. Hollis wasn't allowed to take anything with him. Hollis passed Pierce in the corridor, and could see Pierce sneering at him, clearly pleased at his discomfort.

His car was thoroughly searched before he finally left the compound. On his way home he came to a number of firm decisions. Hollis arrived home and remembered, Jenny had told him she was going to the Supermarket, to do some early shopping.

Hollis went upstairs, packed a small overnight bag. He sat and wrote Jenny a small note on his laptop, printing it out, telling her not to worry, that he'd be in touch. He called for a Taxi on his mobile and told the driver to take him to London. The astonished driver couldn't believe his luck at getting a £150 fare.

In London, he booked into the Orion Barbican Hotel in the city, to be near the centre of financial power. He bought a lot of books on the workings of the Stock Market, and then settled to absorb them. He phoned Jenny, told her he had the urge to make some money for them. She was not to worry and if all went well, he would be back with a pile.

Within a week, he bought a small defunct shell mining company for a mere five thousand pounds. The shares of ESDO (El Sato de Oro), west of Durango, in Mexico's Sierra Madre Occidental Mountains, were trading at 11 pence when Hollis bought the company. He put out a false rumour on the Internet, that a new gold-bearing deposit had been discovered half a kilometre from the old mine workings, yielding one part gold to 3000 parts of rock. That was a substantial find.

Such rumours were always checked and substantiated by the professional Fund Managers and investors before they became financially involved. However, the speculators always tried to get in on the ground floor before the price rose, but then they were risking their own funds. The price of ESDO shares rose sharply, bought mostly by those Internet speculators. When they reached eight pounds a share, Hollis sold all his stock, and trading in the shares were suspended at £7 pounds, pending an investigation.

However, Hollis had taken the precaution of re-registering his shell company in Panama through Liechtenstein, disguising his involvement. On a simple five thousand pound investment, Hollis became a millionaire overnight; that's assuming the Stock market regulatory body didn't catch up with him. On the 11p share, he made a profit of £7.89p, over 7,000% profit.

He next speculated on a number of currency movements, rightly predicting the fall of the Japanese Yen from

¥113 to the dollar, to ¥121 to the dollar. He bought Yen "short" and then delivered at ¥120. More millions were made. He entered the Futures Market and began to deal in Derivatives, forecasting trends in Market movements. He bet on the fall of the Eastern European Markets, and was proven correct, mainly due to Russia's poor economic management and the consequent knock-on effect.

He bought a large Georgian house with some of the proceeds, out in north Herefordshire, near the Welsh border, and had Jenny and his sons join him. He now did his wheeling and dealing from the comfort of his mansion. Then one morning, three months after quitting his lab job, Jenny remarked on his greying hair.

'Hol darling! Have you looked at yourself in the mirror lately?' It was a casual remark.

He *had* noticed the grey hairs appearing. Wrinkles and lines, crowfeet, and even some aching in his joints. He'd put it down to tiredness and overwork. He had relapsed in his normal obsession with himself for a while, whilst he accumulated more money.

He'd been engrossed, busily arranging venture capital to fund various Biotechnology companies to counteract the effects of the financial community beginning to dissociate itself from any involvement with bioscience. The Market had the jitters over what the media was calling "Frankenstein Science."

As Jenny now mentioned his appearance, his brows knitted and he gave a limp smile.

'I'm just tired dear. Everything will sort itself out when we go away to Acapulco next month. A long needed rest and holiday. Think of it.' He looked wistfully into the distance.

'You're probably right.' She frowned as if she didn't believe it.

'Look darling. I'm going for a long drive to Wiltshire. There's something I've to take care of. I'll be back late tonight.'

'Fine, I'll be all right dear. If you must go, then you must.'

He packed an overnight bag and put it into the black Rolls. It took him a couple of hours to travel the 140 kilometres to Warminster, crossing the River Severn on the M4, bypassing Bristol, through Bath, and on to his destination. He pulled up outside Pierce's small bungalow on the outskirts of Warminster, parking the Rolls slowly, ostentatiously, and waited.

It was seven in the evening when Pierce got back from the old lab. He stared at the Rolls parked outside his house but couldn't see inside the darkened windows. When Hollis lowered the window and stuck his head out, Pierce nearly fell over.

'Yes, it's little ol' me,' Hollis said to the open-mouthed Pierce.

'Eh, yes, I see. Err, well—what do you want?' Pierce tried to regain his composure.

'I want a word with you,' Hollis said firmly. 'What do you say to earning a hundred thousand pounds?'

Pierce's jaw dropped. He stood dumbfounded, as if someone had struck him with a hammer.

'Is this....some kind of sick joke?' he finally managed.

'*Pull yourself together!*' Hollis hissed loudly. 'It's *no* joke. I just want you to do something for me.' Hollis got out of the Rolls and stood before Pierce, looking up into the angular face of the tall thin rake of a man. 'Can we go inside and discuss this?'

Pierce turned round and led the way to his door. 'I promise you'll regret this, if you're pulling my leg.' Pierce said half-heartedly in an effort to hide his confusion.

When they were inside, Hollis noted no one came to greet Pierce; the house was empty. He then remembered the place was probably bugged. It was a general tendency of MI5 to blanket bug all the houses of sensitive personnel, just to keep a "friendly" eye on them. Anyone working at the lab was definitely considered sensitive. Hollis put his finger to his lips and motioned Pierce back to the door.

'Stop acting the fool,' Pierce whispered, irritated at Hollis' antics. However, he opened the door and they both went out, Hollis leading Pierce back to his Rolls.

Only when they were seated in the seclusion of the Rolls, and each had a drink from the cocktail cabinet, did Hollis state his proposal.

'You remember Vorting,' Hollis looked at Pierce.

'Not personally. He was before my time. Why?'

Hollis opened his dashboard and pulled out a bundle of fifty-pound notes. He tossed it into Pierce's lap. Always let the punter feel the dosh; it makes it harder for them to say no.

'That's ten thousand pounds. Even if you refuse, that's yours to keep. Stay and listen to me, and there's more where that came from. I'm going to give you twice what I said at the beginning. That's two hundred thousand pounds.'

Pierce just sat staring at the bundle in his lap. Hollis could see he'd caught his undivided attention.

'*All* I'm after, is a copy of Vorting's file: no big national secret.'

Pierce's eyes narrowed, 'And how the hell do you expect me to smuggle something like that out? You know what the security is like at the lab.'

What Hollis heard was Pierce agreeing to get the copy for him. It wasn't "No," it wasn't "If," it was just a matter of "How?" Pierce was examining the logistics of obtaining what Hollis wanted.

'I have that worked out Ted.' Hollis took out a small spy camera quarter of the size of a matchbox, and held it between his finger and thumb. 'This is a miniature all plastic digital camera with an inbuilt DX sensor. The automatic reduction system in it takes it to microdot size. It must have a good three minutes for the electronic chip to carry out the complete reduction, which then pops out on a plastic 1 mm square tape. The camera itself strips to four flat component parts that can be taped to each of your limbs separately, reducing its exposure to the Security "sniffers." It's a use and throw item and only needs to be smuggled in—not out. You destroy the camera after use.' Hollis stopped to see Pierce's reaction.

'I...I...don't know,' Pierce seemed doubtful. 'Where did you get such a thing?' Pierce was sounding suspicious.

'In business espionage; it's the latest gadget for sneaking out Boardroom minutes. Got it from a friend of mine.'

'You sure it can't be detected? I know the security is stricter coming out. Even so!'

'You tape the microdot inside your mouth and, hey presto! You're richer by two hundred thousand.'

Pierce sat chewing his lower lip, weighing the pros and cons, thinking of the money. He gently scratched his right temple, and after what seemed a long time, came to a decision. In real time, it was four minutes. Hollis sat waiting patiently; letting the bundle of fifty pound notes do his persuading.

'All the payment to be made to a Swiss account *I* set up. I check the balance in the account before I hand over the microdot—agreed?'

'Agreed! I'll need *all* of Vorting's file in McLoud's office. That's only fair for the amount I'm paying.'

'I'll do my best,' Pierce nodded.

'*All* of Vorting's file.......Ted? Aren't you even curious what all this is about?'

'None of my business.'

'When?'

'Give me two weeks. If I haven't got it in two weeks, then I can't get it. Okay?'

'Right!'

Pierce got out of the Rolls and went into his house without looking back. Hollis sat for a moment, thinking—then started the car up and drove back to Herefordshire the way he'd come.

It was a frantic two weeks for Hollis. He seemed to be ageing at a frightening rate. He used hair colouring and hired a professional make-up artist from a film company, ostensibly for his wife. Every morning he had her make him up just to look his normal age—without Jenny knowing. He slept in a separate wing of the house, giving the excuse he needed to stay up late; it wasn't fair on Jenny to keep her up—he said.

He suspected the rapid ageing had something to do with Vorting's DNA, which is why he hired Pierce to get Vorting's file. He *needed* to see what the problem was, to see if there was a solution, if Vorting had found a solution.

His joints were the worst, clearly inflamed. He was keeping the pain under control with painkillers. He was getting irritable, and latterly, forgetful. Hollis Jordan was only thirty-six years old, but felt three times that. The additional problem was, he looked well over sixty.

A phone call from Pierce, right on schedule, lifted his depression. They agreed to meet in Bath, noon the following day, in the Abbey Churchyard. It was half way for the both of them. The view from over the Severn Bridge was breathtaking; both sides of the river were spread out in a panoramic spectacle. Hollis went through the Kingswood district of Bristol, skirting Bristol, on to the ancient Roman city of Bath.

He arrived early and sat listening to a young woman busker playing some Bach on a violin. The day was warm and heady, it being the late spring. Hollis closed his eyes and let the music pervade his essence. He felt someone sit on the seat to the right of him, and a couple of seconds later, to the left of him. Hollis opened his eyes and saw a burly man in a beige trench coat and brown hat standing before him.

'Dr. Jordan? Dr. Hollis Jordan,' the man said.

Hollis nodded. He guessed who they were. He looked to his right and saw another burly trench coat sitting looking at him: the same to the left.

'I wonder if you wouldn't mind coming with us. We'd like a quiet word with you.'

Hollis resigned himself to the inevitable, stood up and was escorted on either side by the burly men, with the fellow who had spoken to him, leading the way back to the Grand Parade. As they got into the waiting dark green Rover, Hollis asked them to confirm their ID. As he'd suspected, they were all Special Branch.

The Rover took him back to Chitterne, through the beautiful Wiltshire countryside, so vibrant this time of the year. He was taken to the Chief of Security at the underground complex, escorted into the BW Section. There, he was put into a bare room containing a table and chair. He was left to stew for over four hours with only a small spy camera peering at him from a corner of the room. Hollis twiddled his thumbs, watching the camera watch him.

BW indeed. What have I got to do with Biological Warfare? The thought kept going round and round in his head, in a sort of protective indignation. Simmering in his head was another more malevolent thought. *If I ever get my hands on Pierce....that bastard........*

Sometime in the fifth hour, the door opened and a middle-aged man, medium build, carrying a red folder, wearing a grey suit, had an underling bring in a chair, on which he parked himself.

'Sorry to have kept you waiting so long Dr. Jordan. We had some facts to crosscheck. By the way, my name's Evans.'

He placed the red folder so Hollis could clearly see it. The white label said in big black letters: **Hans Adolf Vorting.** Hollis sat still and waited for the question game to begin. Instead, the door opened again and three men came in. One was small and wiry, wearing a white lab coat, and he was escorted by two burly security men.

One of the security men grabbed Hollis' left arm; the other stood behind Hollis holding his shoulders. The fellow in the white coat rolled up Hollis' sleeve, removed the cover of a tray he was holding and removed a hypodermic. He put a tourniquet on Hollis above the left elbow, swabbed a little alcohol on the inner side of the elbow, and inserted the needle.

They wanted a sample of Hollis' blood and weren't bothering to ask his permission.

'You've been a busy man Dr. Jordan. We've been keeping an eye on you for quite a while now.' The trio with his blood sample left the room.

'Have you indeed,' Hollis said more loudly than he intended.

'Ever since you used Government property to inject yourself with something. So the first thing we want to know is, what was it you injected yourself with?'

If they knew that, then there was no point in hiding anything else. 'It was a sample of Vorting's DNA.' He said quietly.

'Yes, we thought so.' His hand went over to the red folder.

'And why did you do it, Dr. Jordan?'

'I was using it as a vector to transmute my cerebral DNA.'

'Yes. Again as we thought. And would you mind sharing the current results with us?'

'It made me rich,' it was a flat statement of fact. Hollis didn't feel like offering long explanations, not under this kind of pressure.

'Come now, Dr. Jordan. We know all about your artful gambling in the Markets. That's not what we're after. After you broke your parental conditioning, we had no qualms in you casting your entrepreneurial nets. No! What we want, is the confirmation of the side effects of your injection. Remember, we've just taken a blood sample and we're in the right place to analyse that.'

Ah! What was the point in delaying the inevitable, he thought. 'If you must know, I'm ageing rapidly, that's the bloody side effect,' Hollis said vehemently.

'And that's why you wanted to have a look at this file,' his interrogator asked, fingering the nearby red file.

'That's correct.'

'Well, why didn't you simply *ask*,' Evans said, pushing the file over to Hollis. 'I'll leave you for a while to get acquainted with Herr Vorting.' With that, Evans got up from the chair and left the room.

Hollis stared in disbelief at the red file. Just like that! What on earth were they playing at? But the *need to know* overcame the shock of what Evans had just done.

He opened the file, and after fifteen minutes of careful perusing, he came across the information he was dreading. Vorting had suffered from a premature ageing disease, brought on by working in near proximity to heavy-duty electromagnetic emissions and X-ray equipment during the war. He was working on some pharmaceutical-come-herbal delaying mechanism when the Allied soldiers picked him up after the war. According to his file, he was allowed to complete the work on an antidote in this lab, but had never written the results up, keeping them in his head. He died, still with the information in his head, taking it to the grave.

A scribbled note from someone, at the back of the file, said they thought the herb Vorting had used might have come from the ancient Belavezha Forest on the border between Belarus and Poland.

'Fat lot of good that is,' muttered Hollis under his breath.

At that point, the door opened and Evans walked back in and sat on the vacant chair.

'Well Dr. Jordan? Any good to you?' Evans looked bemused, as if he'd said something humorous.

Hollis sat shaking his head. 'I suppose you haven't found a cure for Vorting's disease?' he said in a quiet whisper.

'I'm afraid not. We were hoping you might have come up with something. From the look on your face, evidently not.'

'Well, what now?' Hollis looked across at Evans.

'The government has no interest in wasting its money on a prosecution. You're free to go.' Evans looked deeply into Hollis' face. 'You opened a Pandora's hypodermic when you went ahead with that injection. If it's any consolation, I'm sorry you've contracted this Vorting thing. The two Security Guards will escort you to the top. We have a car to take you back to Bath. You can pick up your Rolls there. Goodbye Dr. Jordan.' Evans left the room, leaving the door open.

Hollis was escorted up top where the car that brought him to Chitterne, still waited. He climbed in slowly like some cranky old man, joints stiff and painful.

On the way back to Bath, a thought kept reverberating in his mind; *I'm only thirty-six years old.* When he'd quietened a little, then the contents of a note he'd found in Vorting's hand returned to haunt him. The note was written in quivering German, dated 14th July 1961. There was a translation appended, burnt into Hollis' failing memory.

«The frontal areas of my cerebral cortex are deteriorating; at least that's my guess. It seems to be leading to the cerebral cortex flattening, causing me to be irritable, fatigued, and depressed. I've lost most of my motivation. I'm becoming irresponsible in my personal affairs, progressively callous and forgetful. I'm grossly lacking in judgement. There are periods of euphoria, accompanied by absurd and grandiose delusion of position, power, wealth, and physical prowess. My eyelids have developed a tremor, also my lips and facial muscles. I'm beginning to mispronounce and slur my words. Developing a wobbly gait. I hope this new concoction will save me—otherwise God help me.»

Night Visitor

The patient sat relaxed in the dentist's chair until her eyes fell on some ancient relics of the profession—then she visibly grimaced.

The dentist, an elderly observant practitioner, noted her anxiety and attempted to calm her.

'I see you've noticed some remnants of a bygone age. It's part of my collection. I promise not to use them on you,' he joked.

The patient forced a smile.

Murphy tried to change the subject to something more neutral. 'Nice weather for this time of year, Mrs. Doyle.'

'But why d'you keep them there?' Mrs Doyle persisted.

'I like to look at them,' Murphy said gently. 'I think they're beautiful. Such craftsmanship.'

'They give me the creeps,' Mrs Doyle said firmly, deciding instead to look at the dentist's flowery qualifications hanging in their simple frames, decorating the wall.

When Surgery finished, just after five, Murphy watched a little TV to unwind, then in the evening ate a light meal prepared by his wife, and again watched more television for an hour. Finally he listened to some Beethoven.

In bed, as soon as his head hit the pillow, he was fast asleep. His wife sat up, read for some time, before putting the light out.

Around 3.25am, the beeping of what might have been a clock alarm woke him. Almost as if Murphy was expecting it, he roused and swung his legs out of bed. He pressed the button that shut the alarm off, stretched himself and eased into his slippers. He got up and reached for his nightgown. A slight smile etched his face as he found the bedroom door. His wife slept soundly. Nothing would disturb her. Murphy opened the door and went downstairs; the evening's Beethoven suddenly sprang into his head. He hummed gently to himself as he made his way to the Surgery.

He lived in a large detached house on the main road, with the Surgery in one of the downstairs front rooms. He opened the door to the Surgery and found what he'd expected. Lying prone on his face, near the window, was a figure dressed all in black. Murphy put the light on and then turned the figure over with his foot. The eyes were wide open, a terrified fear blazing out of them.

'Now me lad, I know you can hear me—so be so kind as to blink twice, just to confirm that.'

The eyes blinked furiously.

'No. I said blink twice.' Murphy looked benevolently, the smile still on his face.

The eyes blinked twice.

'Good! Now I'm going to tell you what's happened to you. You tried to break into my Surgery—no doubt hoping to find some drugs. Trouble is—I've been expecting you. You broke an infrared laser alarm and have been shot with a hypodermic dart containing a carefully measured quantity of tubocurarine chloride. It's a curare derivative. I won't bore you with the details, but it paralyses you. You can hear me, and I'm told you'll feel pain.'

Murphy bent, and heaved the limp body to the dentist's chair. He searched the burglar, and found a small wallet with a few items in it. He glanced at the details and returned the wallet to where he found it.

'Over confident and somewhat careless, bringing ID on a job like yours,' he told his intruder.

The burglar's eyes held even more fear, if that were possible. Murphy then strapped the arms, as a precaution. He went to the antique drilling appliance, dated circa 1900 and moved it next to the chair.

'Using these new laser drills all day, gives me no *satisfaction* at all,' Murphy confided to the petrified burglar. 'These old drills have a nice zing to them. Let me show you.' Murphy plugged the antique into the wall socket and switched it on.

Zzzzzzzzz, sang the old machine, in the quiet of the night.

If you'd rather, I could use the old pedal drill, it's even older. Trouble is, it's a bit too much like hard work for me

The burglar's eyes shifted into the top corner of his eye sockets, as if his eyes were trying to escape.

Oblivious, Murphy continued, 'So, we'll settle for the old electric, shall we. There, don't that have a lovely sound.' Zzzzzzzzz. 'They knew how to make drills in those days—fine craftsmanship.'

He switched the drill off.

He reached over and seized a mouth clamp, inserting it in the burglar's quiescent mouth, then rotated the screw, forcing it to keep the mouth open, a bit like the jack of a car.

He examined the mouth and announced, 'You'll need some fillings my bucko. Just the two, but I'll have to drill *d-e-e-p*.' The mischievous smile finally asserted itself fully across his face. 'Mind if I use the slow drill?'

If the burglar could only have screamed, Murphy's fine house would have fallen around his ears—but of course, he couldn't. His eyes did the pleading for him.

Murphy put a large steel rosehead bur No. 10 drill into the antique contraption, and switched it on. Zzzzzzzzz, sang the machine. Carefully, Murphy began to drill into the mandible's left premolar. He prided himself on his skill—all his patients praised him for it. This was a measured approach, going centrally into the dentin, through the enamel and into the pulp, *and the nerve*. The slow drill wobbled in the tooth, shearing the nerve ending. The same procedure was used on the second premolar, again in the mandible, but on the other side of the burglar's mouth.

'Hmm. I do like the feel of this old drill. You know, normally people pay me for this—but as we're so close you felt you could drop in any time—I'm not going to charge you a penny. Don't you think that's generous of me?' And he began humming a part of Beethoven again.

'There, that should do it. Don't forget to drop in anytime, day or night. You're always welcome—*and expected.*' Murphy smiled sweetly at his captive patient.

The burglar's eyes were wide with pain, his face puffed and almost purple with strain. Everything about him suggested he was unlikely to take up the invitation to return.

'Now, since you can't yet walk, I'm going to be a gentleman and carry you to the door.'

Murphy unfastened the burglar's hands and lifted him onto his shoulder, fireman style. Then he went past his receptionist's desk, took a piece of paper from under a box on a shelf, wrote something on it with difficulty, placing it in the burglar's back pocket. He carefully opened the front door, looked around to see the coast was clear, and carried the hapless burglar to the front gate, sitting him with his back propped against the garden wall on the pavement.

'I'll leave you now and let the tranquilliser wear off. You should be okay in about fifteen minutes by my calculations. Go straight home now; and no more visits tonight. Promise?'

Murphy didn't wait for a response. There wouldn't be any point. He went back inside and returned to bed.

The next day, around 10.30 in the morning, Nora, his nurse, interrupted him whilst he was preparing an amalgam.

'There's a policeman asking for you. An Inspector Walsh. I told him to wait in the Hygienist's room. He was most insistent.'

'That's all right Nora. I'll take care of this.'

He went to see what the Police wanted of him.

As he entered the room, he noticed last night's burglar standing smugly behind the Inspector. The uniform approached Murphy. 'I'm sorry to trouble you sir, but we need to clear up one of the most bizarre stories I've heard in a long time.'

'And pray tell—how do I come into this?'

'Bear with me sir. This gentleman here,' he pointed at the burglar, 'insists he broke into your surgery last night.' The policeman stopped and waited for a response.

'What, Mr. Dibbings? Surly not.'

'You know him then?'

'I ought to. He was here only yesterday afternoon having a couple of fillings done. Isn't that right Mr. Dibbings?' Murphy looked at the burglar, smiled at him as if at a recent patient.

'*He's lying Inspector,*' yelled the cowering burglar.

'Have you any proof of what you say, sir?' The Inspector was firm but civil.

'Let me see now. Oh, yes. I'll bet it's still there. Look in his right hand back pocket—that's where I saw him put the receipt I gave him. Payment for the work I performed. They look like the same trousers he wore yesterday.'

The Inspector turned to the burglar. 'If you've been wasting Police time, I'll see you regret it my lad. Come on, turn your pockets out.'

'*Inspector, I tell you he's lying,*' shouted the burglar, backing away against the wall.

'Come on now, don't make this any harder for yourself—turn your pockets out.'

The burglar dropped his hands, hung his head and reached for his right hand back pocket in submission. Surprise spread on his face as he pulled the receipt out and reluctantly handed it to the Inspector.

Grim faced, the Inspector unfolded the piece of paper and scrutinised it. He scowled at the burglar and turned to Murphy.

'I'm so sorry to have troubled you sir. We have to check all these stories—no matter how outlandish they may sound. This is clearly your receipt—for work done; yesterday's date. All very correct. We'll be off now. Come on my lad, I want a word with you outside. Thank you for your patience. Goodbye sir.'

And with that, the Inspector marched the burglar out of the surgery.

Connor Murphy went into the corridor, smiled at Nora, then went back into the front room to look at his precious, recently exercised, antiques.

Sasha Garrydeb

A Wait in Vain

(Set in 1438 Aztec times near the end of the reign of Itzcoatl (1427-1440))

Hualco left Tetzcoco in the early hours of the night, paddling steadily for a long period of time—now he'd reached that precarious point where he dreaded, the instant just before dawn. His fingers hurt from gripping the paddle tightly—tension and fear ran through his body. *Please, let the sun rise.* Silently he implored the prayer, petitioning Huitzilopochtli to intervene. *Please make the sun rise.*

Although the Lord of Tetzcoco, *tlatoani* Netzahualcoyotl, had abolished idolatry, and had all idols removed from his Temple of the Sun—Hualco kept the old faith. He couldn't, wouldn't accept the new—"House of the

Single God." When he prayed at the Temple he always mouthed the name of Huitzilopochtli.

Now he was full of apprehension—that moment before dawn—if the sun should fail to rise, that darkness might become permanent. Would the sun rise? Did the priests in Tenochtitlán offer up sufficient sacrifice? Sweating in the cool night air—he was about to find out.

Slowly–ever so slowly—in the East, the horizon lit up. Light blue replaced the dark blue. Then a grey white with a red tinge crept over the edge. Finally—the deep red disc of Huitzilopochtli rose to stride across another day.

Hualco sighed deeply—a sigh of relief. He softened the grip on the paddle, then dug boldly into the blue waters of the lake. Another hour of hard paddling lay ahead. His destination—the mighty city of Tenochtitlán.

When dawn cleared the night sky, the brilliance of his surroundings became apparent. His canoe was painted vivid colours. The water was intense—glistening, alive with fish. The sun threw a blinding light across the surface. His feather cloak lay magnificent in the prow—vibrant green, decorated with a red border—covering the sack of cacao beans. Cranes and herons flew overhead, making a racket. Ducks floated on the misty waters, diving for fish.

Everything was alive, pulsing, like the blood coursing through his veins. His tension disappeared. He smiled at the world—and it smiled back at him—in his mind. It released the problem of the present, he intended to buy his father. He'd brought sufficient cacao beans to pay for a handsome gift. He didn't want to buy it in Tetzcoco—he was too well known there. His father was bound to find out. He wanted *this one* to be a surprise.

Hualco was of a noble Acolhua family, close to the *tlatoani* Netzahualcoyotl. His father was a *pipiltin* ("noble") war chieftain, commanding a whole regiment. He was expected to follow in his footsteps. Already he'd seized many captives—and earned the right to wear a warrior's feather cloak and feather headdress.

In the coming year, his father had arranged for him to marry the daughter of another *pipiltin* war chieftain, and with this in mind, he wanted to give him a suitable dignified recompense for this bountiful endowment to his son. Hualco looked forward to the marriage as a fulfilment of his manhood. He wanted to hear the patter of little feet—his future—running noisily around his house.

He looked up, and through the lifting early morning mist, saw the outline of the centre of the Empire, looming up at every stroke of the paddle. Even at this distance, the top of the central pyramid of the sun protruded from the island city.

On nearing land, he headed for the main canal leading through Aztacualco, sitting halfway on the western coast of the island. He entered the canal, keeping to the left. On either side of the thoroughfare were *champa* plots held with stakes, willows, and wattle fences filled with sediment dredged out of the water. The whole island was held together by *champa* plots on which crops were grown such as maize, dahlia, and amaranth. Over the years the plots had solidified enough to construct roads and buildings.

He'd been to Tenochtitlán many times, since Tetzcoco, his city on the eastern shore of Lake Tetzcoco, was part of a tripartite confederation together with Tlacopan, the city on the western shore. True, his city was only a fifth of the size of Tenochtitlán, but ever since the *tlatoani* Netzahualcoyotl came back to power, Tetzcoco was expanding its sphere of influence to the west. He was proud to be allowed to take part in the battles to bring greater tribute to his city. His was a city renowned for its art and poetry. Netzahualcoyotl was a man of poetry and music, and made great effort to encourage the arts and crafts in his small empire. As his contribution to the arts, Hualco was renowned among his friends and companions for playing the flute. At the many dances and festivals, he would be entreated to perform—and, he didn't need much persuading.

Paddling energetically along the waterway, on the watch for other traffic coming out of the smaller canals at the intersections, Hualco still hadn't settled on the type of gift he wanted to get. Maybe a grand cape made from fine hummingbird feathers, or an intricately carved statue of Huitzilopochtli—no, that wouldn't do—the king wasn't keen on idols. As he paddled, his mind was pondering these thoughts, when he almost ran into another canoe coming from a major canal intersecting at right angles. He back paddled furiously, narrowly avoiding a mishap. *Must concentrate on what I'm doing,* he chided himself.

After a while, he swung left into the canal leading to the Ritual Centre of Tenochtitlán. He arrived from the north at a spot where the canal paralleled the Great Ritual Plaza, allowing him to leave his canoe tied to a pole. Lifting the cape and sack from the prow, he draped the cape round his shoulders and began walking, holding the sack tight under the cape in his right hand. Theft was dealt with harshly in the Aztec Empire, yet where life was desperate, many of the outcasts felt they had little to lose.

He walked down the main avenue with a spring in his step, the Great Pyramid to his left, on top of which stood the twin temples of Tlaloc and Huitzilopochtli. He was heading for the great Market Square on the far right, held just on the outside of the ritual precinct to the right of the Causeway to Ixtapalapa. Through the magnificently paved great square, past innumerable bas-reliefs and statues adorning the great buildings and halls. People milled everywhere. This was a city of two hundred thousand souls—many here on formal business, pilgrims come to worship at the forest of *teocalli* pyramids, others rushed from one palace to another, promoting themselves to the nobles and officials. The place seethed like an ants' nest.

Finally he reached the edge of a sea of stalls. The great marketplace was adjacent to the vast ceremonial precinct and each kind of merchandise had a specially marked out place. Around fifty thousand vendors and buyers came to do business here. All regulated by Inspectors walking around, checking on fair prices, penalising rip-off merchants.

Dealers in gold, silver, and precious stones, feathers, mantles, and embroidered goods, tried to waylay prospective customers. Every kind of slave was for sale, men, women and children, tied to long poles—captives from far off tribes. Some traders had great pieces of cotton cloth, and articles of twisted thread. Others sold cacao beans in various states, from raw to foamy chocolate drinks, flavoured with vanilla pods or sweetened with honey. The beans were prepared on the spot by grinding roasted cacao beans, sometimes mixed with parched corn. In another part of the market, various kinds of beans, sage, herbs and vegetables were on sale. Fowls, cocks, rabbits, hares, deer, mallards, and young dogs. Cooked foods, dough, tripe. Pottery made in a thousand different forms and styles. Lumber, planking, cradles, beams, and finished benches. Paper, and scented reeds with liquid-amber. Obsidian knives, axes, clubs, were on sale next to salt merchants.

When he passed the food stalls, his stomach reminded him he hadn't eaten for a long period. All the paddling had left him famished. He stopped and bought a couple of large tacos filled with chilli and beans, then decided to include a frothy chocolate drink with his meal. He sat on a nearby stone bench, and soon demolished the tacos. While he drank, he noticed a young fellow holding out a superbly carved mahogany flute, clearly trying to make a sale. What caught his eye, was the number of stops. The usual flute had five stops, but this was so out of the ordinary that he nodded at the poorly dressed youth. The youth looked nervous and kept looking around. Hualco assumed he was eager to be rid of the flute so he could buy some food.

The young fellow ambled over, all the time looking furtively around, as if looking for someone.

'I'm trying to find my brother, he's somewhere round here,' he told Hualco by way of explanation.

'How much do you want for the flute?' Hualco asked.

The youth looked Hualco up and down, endeavouring to determine how much he could ask for it.

'A small sack of cacao beans?' he said hopefully.

'Sorry, I need all my beans for a present,' Hualco replied.

'What about that knife in your belt?'

Hualco was loath to part with it—it was made of fine obsidian with an elegantly carved handle. A gift from the battlefield. Yet he *wanted* the flute. He examined it—twelve stops! He took out his knife and grudgingly handed it to the youth. The young man quickly took the knife and gave him the flute, still looking around for his brother. Then he was gone.

Hualco turned the flute over in his hands, scrutinising every beautiful figure on its surface. He tried a few notes. The range shocked him—twelve stops! The most he'd ever seen was eight. He finished his drink, grabbed his belongings and sauntered over to a far wall. He carefully placed his sack of beans between his knees and sat on the ground—and started playing. He went up the scale then down, each time varying, struggling to get accustomed to the instrument. Then he clicked with the range and began a lively improvised melody. Unnoticed by him, a small crowd gathered and was listening intently. He played—and they swayed in time to the music. He soared ever up, and the crowd lifted their eyes to the sky— down the scale, and the crowd smiled with Hualco. He took absolutely no notice—he was alone, entranced with his music.

At the edges of the crowd, a small commotion— became louder as it pushed itself to the forefront. Soon the front of the crowd parted, and soldiers pushed the listeners back with clubs, clearing a path for a Notable. A nobleman walked forward attired in a fine eagle-head helmet and eagle feather cloak. A hush settled—Hualco stopped playing. He stared in astonishment at the Eagle Knight warrior and his retinue.

The Eagle Knight nodded, and the soldiers rushed forward and pulled Hualco roughly to his feet. In the process, he dropped the flute. One of the soldiers picked it up and handed it to the Eagle Knight.

'*Where did you get this*,' he demanded loudly.

'I just bought it from a young man,' Hualco explained.

'And where's this young man?' said the Knight sternly.

'He's gone—just now,' Hualco said boldly. He felt certain of himself as only a noble's son could do.

'Bring him,' the leader commanded, also pointing at the sack of beans.

'*But...but I haven't done anything*,' Hualco protested as soldiers dragged him after their leader. He'd had the wit to grab his sack of beans.

They took him to a nearby building where three judges sat to adjudicate on market disputes. This court was where the Inspectors who roamed the market on the lookout for vendors who cheated customers and felons with stolen goods were brought to be judged and punished. Both carried the death penalty.

Hualco was hauled before the three elderly judges—two priests and a presiding *pipiltin.* It was a long immense hall with the judges sitting at the far end.

'What is he charged with?' the presiding judge demanded, when the prisoner was brought before him.

'Theft of this fine flute—stolen today from the chief musician waiting to play for our Emperor.' This accusation came from the Eagle Knight warrior.

'Are you the accuser?'

'The musician is a member of the Royal Household—the accuser—for whom I speak—is the Emperor.'

It was evident the presiding judge's attention perked up at this information.

'What is your name and home,' he asked Hualco.

'I am Hualco, son of Maxtla of Tetzcoco, *tillancalqui* to Netzahualcoyotl.'

That brought a gasp from everyone. They were going to have to be careful. This Tetzcocan was a high born and not so easy to dispose of.

The presiding judge—paused—shook his head—then calmly announced to those present, 'This is beyond my power to deal with. He will have to be taken to the court for *pipiltin*—

brought before the *cihuacoatl* Tlacaelel, as the judge in matters of elite crimes.'

'*But I am innocent*,' Hualco shouted.

The bench ignored the prisoner and ordered the next case be brought. They washed their hands of this *pipiltin*.

The Eagle Knight warrior stared in amazement at his prisoner. 'The son of Maxtla of Tetzcoco, eh! Whatever next?'

But at least, he ordered the escort not to be too rough with Hualco. *If this* pipiltin *should turn out to be innocent, the Emperor will have me sacrificed instead.* The escort marched Hualco outside, and to the far side of the ritual plaza, with the Eagle Knight warrior marching out strongly in front. They arrived at the palace of the *cihuacoatl* Tlacaelel, but were ordered to wait until the *cihuacoatl* had finished his midday meal.

After a while, Tlacaelel, Prime Counsellor to the king, deigned to appear, preceded by numerous officials.

'Well, where is this prisoner?' he demanded loudly, being in a truculent mood.

'My Lord,' the Eagle Knight walked forward and bowed deeply. 'I have him here—he's accused of stealing the prized flute from the Chief Musician of the Royal Household. He's a Tetzcocan.' The latter was said in such a manner as to imply his guilt.

Tlacaelel sniffed and half looked in Hualco's direction. 'What has he to say for himself?'

'He claims someone sold it to him.'

'Has he proof—where's the vendor?'

'That's just it—there's no sign of him.'

'Likely story. Why do you bother me with such trifles? You know what to do with him!'

'But Lord—he claims to be the son of Maxtla of Tetzcoco. Only you can pronounce on his fate.'

Just then a rumble emanated from the *cihuacoatl's* stomach and he winced with pain. 'Let the *Quetzalcoatl totec tlamacazqui* deal with him. Go now, I have made my decision. He's to go to the blue heron bird.' With that Tlacaelel turned to his priest physician, and demanded he do something about his upset digestion. The audience was at an end.

Thus dismissed, the Eagle Knight motioned his retinue to follow him. The Knight thought the *cihuacoatl* had made a blunder. This could have serious consequences. But he wasn't going to contradict the prime councillor to the Emperor, not with *his own* life depending on the outcome. He would carry out the *cihuacoatl's* orders to the full—and let *him* take the blame if this went wrong.

The sack of cacao beans to which Hualco still clung, was taken from him by a guard. Hualco's feather cape was removed and he was given a fine cotton cape and leather sandals—a gesture of goodwill by the Eagle Knight. Hualco now understood what was to happen to him—and he saw no way out. In the manner of those about to be sacrificed, he slowly resigned himself to his fate—and his god. Given a choice—he'd rather live—but he wasn't given the option. According to Aztec religion, the sun, in the form of Huitzilopochtli, refused to move unless the priests gave him fresh hearts filled with blood; so they were compelled to sacrifice to feed the sun. The present world was the fifth sun, and the Aztec thought of themselves as "the People of the Sun." It was their divine duty to wage war, gather captives, in order to provide the cosmic sun with his *tlaxcaltiliztli* ("nourishment") in the form of freshly removed hearts. Hualco's blood would feed the sun, so it would rise the next day—it was the only comfort he had.

The small party made its way to back to the ceremonial plaza, and made for the huge steep twin stairways, where the steps led upwards to the Temple of the Sun. They began climbing the pyramid's right-hand stairway. On its west façade, four superimposed platforms rose in stepped-back tiers—the fourth tier formed a broad ceremonial level at the top. After a long climb with a disinclined prisoner, all were exhausted when they reached the broad level area at the top. Before them stood the dual temples of Huitzilopochtli and Tlaloc, devoted to the sacrifices needed to keep the solar disc in motion.

On the left of the broad platform stood the temple of Tlaloc, the god of rain; "he who is the embodiment of earth," painted with blue and white symbols of rain and moisture. Out front, he had a blackened recumbent stone figure of a ritual attendant with a raised platform on her stomach on which the sacrifices were performed.

On the right stood the temple to Huitzilopochtli, their destination, coloured with red and white symbols of war and sacrifice—and before it sat a conical sacrificial stone blackened with dried blood.

Waiting on the broad level, were six other victims ready to be sacrificed with Hualco. A priest nodded at another priest, who went and released one of the prisoners.

'You can go, we only want six in total this evening,' the priest told the confused man.

'*No—I insist. I want to go to Mictlan. I'm going to be a hummingbird,*' the prisoner shouted.

'Not today. The numbers are not propitious. Come back tomorrow. You can be a hummingbird tomorrow,' the priest tried to pacify him. He motioned for a guard to take the reluctant ex-prisoner back down the steep stairway.

The *Quetzalcoatl totec tlamacazqui,* chief priest to Huitzilopochtli, turned and pointed at Hualco. Four priests of Huitzilopochtli came forward, pulled off his cotton cape, grabbing each of Hualco's limbs, lifting him face up to the sky, and spread him with his back onto the blackened stone, whilst the *Quetzalcoatl totec tlamacazqui* tore open his chest with a ritual obsidian knife and removed his beating heart. The *Quetzalcoatl totec tlamacazqui* lifted the still beating heart above his head, dripping with blood, and offered it up to Huitzilopochtli in the heavens. This happened so fast—it was over in an instant.

The priests dismembered Hualco's limbs, handing them reverently to the Eagle Knight and his soldiers. The abdomen was cast aside, to be fed to the animals in the Royal Zoo close by.

At the end, Hualco went to his death stoically, convinced of a glorious afterlife in Mictlan, living with the gods. Hualco was of noble birth—his body was handed over to a noble, the Eagle Knight warrior, who would take the left honoured thigh home. He would have the flesh served separately, in an *olla,* atop of cooked grains of maize. No chilli was added—only sprinkled salt. He would invite all his kinsmen to the meal. All was governed by strict rules. Because sacrificial victims were thought to have become divine, their limbs were consecrated and were eaten with reverence, and ritual—as if it were something from heaven.

Meanwhile, in Tetzcoco, Hualco's father waited in vain for the return of his missing son.

𝔗𝔥𝔢 𝔉𝔞𝔩𝔰𝔢 𝔑𝔢𝔣𝔢𝔯𝔱𝔦𝔱𝔦

On a balmy autumn afternoon, Keefer sat staring out of his window, gazing over the choppy Juan de Fuca Strait, looking over towards the Victoria township, over the border into Canada. His office was on the fourth floor of ChronoCorps Inc. in Port Angeles, America, just north-west of Seattle. He was trying to complete an unpleasant task, and his mind kept wandering.

Keefer's tall muscular frame was naturally fidgety, inducing a thinning of his brown hair. The strong hazel eyes were set in a chiselled face. To relax, his thoughts jumped forward to having some time with his son and daughter, with Helen, his wife, and to having a family barbecue out on the veranda.

A voice near his ear interrupted his reverie; there was a call for him from the Curator of the Egyptian Museum in Berlin.

Currently, Keefer had set himself the task of trying to squeeze his Departmental budget into the constraints of the Corps' financial allocations for his section.

'Tell him I'll call him back, I'm in the middle of something.'

'Sir, he's most insistent,' his secretarial computer persisted.

'It had better be *important*. Put him through.'

'Hallo! Director Keefer?' a cultured voice with an English accent inquired.

'Yes, this is he,' Keefer's voice was somewhat abrupt.

'Of ChronoCorps?' the baritone voice continued.

'*Yes!* Temporal Safeguards. *How* can I help you?' Keefer's irritation grew.

'My name is Schröder; I must see you at once, it's urgent. May I teleport in to you—now?' and the baritone voice *did* sound urgent.

I suppose this budget thing can wait, Keefer thought. 'Well Herr Schröder, if you must.'

'It's not Herr, but Professor,' the link was broken.

A few minutes later, there was that faint whiff of ozone, giving the only warning someone was rematerializing from a teleport. The Professor materialised as an elderly man of medium height and build, grey hair, a walrus moustache sitting on a square face, and sparkling clear blue eyes. He stood looking austerely at Keefer.

'Please, have a seat,' Keefer pointed to a chair near his desk. 'What can I do for you, and why is it so urgent?'

'We have in our Museum, the famous bust of Nefertiti. This morning I was looking at the painted sandstone bust; I like to admire it from time to time, and as I gazed at it, it changed before my eyes,' the elderly curator became edgy. 'From the most beautiful busts of any of the Egyptian Queens, it has now changed to looking just *ordinary*.' He sat silently for a moment looking downcast.

'Do go on,' Keefer prompted gently—now alert.

'I mean, it now looks like so many of the other busts of Egyptian Queens. I went back to my office and searched out some holopics and ancient photographs. The holopics and photographs have also changed. Nobody in the Museum remembers her as anything *other* than what she appears right now, nothing special. That's *not* right. Ever since she came into our possession way back in the 1920's, she has always been considered an outstanding beauty. We gave her pride of place, and reorganised the Egyptian collection around her.' He stopped again.

'Please go on,' Keefer encouraged.

'The problem is, I'm the only one who remembers her as anything special. Every time I bring the subject up, my colleagues look at me as if I've gone crazy. I thought of the implications of such a thing occurring, which is when I thought of you. *Tell* me I'm crazy?' he sat back and stared at Keefer.

'Now let me get it straight. It changed *before* your very eyes. Is that right?'

'Correct!'

'I'm going to take what you've just said seriously, because of who you are. Let's see the implications of a time-line shift.'

'Just before you go on. How's your Egyptology?' Without waiting for an answer, he continued, 'Have you ever heard of Akhenaten?' Schröder tilted his head a little to the side.

'Wasn't he the ninth Pharaoh of the 18th Dynasty? Started his reign as Amenhotep IV, and then went out to destroy the power of the old priesthood of Amun by resurrecting a minor deity, making Aten the only god.'

'That's good and entirely correct of course. He was called Akhenaten, "servant of the Aten," and "hammer of Amun,"' Schröder was getting a grip on himself. 'Akhenaten is one of the most famous names in Egyptology. In the 20th Century, he was diagnosed as having had Cushing's syndrome, which caused his visible androgyny, due to a pituitary tumour that prevented the secretion of the luteinizing hormone, which in turn prevented the testes from secreting testosterone. It's evident in all the portraits of him. He resembles the female form, more so than the male. His six daughters must have been born before the onset of this Syndrome.'

'Okay, I'll bite. What's all this leading to?'

'The current portraits have also changed. He now looks like a robust picture of a vigorous male.'

'You mean that's corroborating evidence?'

'Of course! Here's another query for you. When did the Roman Empire end?'

'Everybody knows that, eleventh century,' Keefer felt uneasy.

'No it didn't. It was in the fifth century. Already your memory has adjusted itself to blend in with the new time-line shift.'

'By insinuation, your suggesting someone's tampered with a major event at source,' Keefer said cautiously.

'Most certainly! I don't understand why *I* remember the original events. Everybody's memories have adjusted to the new order, apart from mine. Have you ever heard of the Ptolemy's, Alexander, Cleopatra?'

'Who are these people you're throwing at me? I've never heard of them,' Keefer's unease was mounting.

'This false Nefertiti gave Akhenaten four sons, instead of the six daughters he should have had. It strengthened the dynastic line, and the *Egyptians* conquered Persia. Not the other way round. Because there was no threat from Persia, Sparta managed to conquer up as far as Illyria, and so Macedonia never produced the megalomaniacal Alexander. There was no subsequent Library at Alexandria, because Alexandria never existed. In this new time-line, it seems the Roman Empire fell to Bartek and his Mongol Horde.'

'That last bit I understood,' Keefer interrupted. 'That happened in 1043. Then they converted all those Christian loons to Hinduism, eventually spreading Krishna to all parts of Europe.'

'That's not how the unchanged time-line went. By the way, how old is ChronoCorps?'

'Coming up to a hundred and fifty years.'

'And if I told you it was set up in 3473, making it more like four hundred years old?' the man was relentless.

'Now that *is* serious.' The calmer the Professor became, the more Keefer became unsettled. 'If the changes centre on Nefertiti, then we're going to have to send a team back and restore the original time-line. That's our job, after all is said and done. By the way, what date do you estimate we need to return to, to catch the culprit?'

'Sometime during 1347 BC. Nefertiti is first recorded as appearing in the 4th Year of Akhenaten's reign, which is

1346, when she visited Akhetaten, the new city he was building half way between Thebes and Memphis. So, a year earlier is 1347. At this time, he was still living in Waset, Thebes to you, and he only moved to the new city in Year 6 of his reign. So, your team ought to be sent to Waset, prepared to pass off as Khemetians, Khemet being their name for Egypt, and get close to the false Nefertiti. Send them to the end of the season of *akhet,* the end of *Khoiak,* October, the end of the inundation of the Nile, or as the Khemetians called the river, *itr-da.'*

A bleeper sounded on Keefer's desk, followed by a gentle red glow. '*That* Professor,' Keefer pointed at the red glow, 'is *our* warning that a major temporal shift has occurred. You managed to beat it by half an hour.'

'You mean *that* confirms my story?' The Professor tilted his head in the direction of the glow, and seemed visibly puzzled.

'We have history files stored back in the Laurasian deserts of the Triassic. If a shift occurs, then the computers running the matching parallel history, throw out an alert to the present, and all hell breaks loose....like now.'

'And a red glow appears on your desk?' Was the Professor being facetious?

'That's what you've just witnessed.' Keefer looked for signs of mocking, but found none.

After a week of preparations, Amanda Mollon and Ron Bartel were ready to go through the annoyingly humming, temporal portal. Amanda ran her eyes over Ron and saw a powerfully built individual, medium height, dark complexion. He wore the dress of a Khemet Noble, a dark wig, a light electrum collar around his neck, a sheer blouse of white linen with elaborately pleated sleeves, a kilt with great panels of woven material hanging from the waist, and finely decorated leather sandals. There was a solid bronze dagger tucked into his kilt at the front. On his right wrist he wore a wide gold wristband, inscribed with his Egyptian name, Nebtwenef, and titles. Ron was the older of the two.

Ron noticed the gaze and returned her scrutiny, casting his eyes up and down, observing a woman of medium build, athletic, in her middle twenties, dark haired and alluring sloe eyes ringed with kohl. She wore a caplet and embroidered sash in gauffered sheer white linen, with a red girdle showing through. That was complemented with a shoulder length perfumed black wig. Round her neck she wore a beautiful necklace made of lapis lazuli and carnelian. There were various decorative rings on her fingers. On her feet, she had gold gilded leather sandals. The height of fashion in the New Kingdom.

Both had been in Temporal Safeguards for over five years, and were old hands at time travel. They'd just been through Programmed Learning to acquire the language and customs of ancient Khemet. Both were impatient to be off.

Their preparations meticulous, down to the local eating habits. They carried a small hoard of copper *debens*, barter trinkets of silver and gold, and a concise map of Waset and Akhetaten lodged in their heads. The later just in case they had to go there.

They were to be discharged into a ravine in the East Valley, of the Valley of the Kings. For that purpose, precise geographical co-ordinates were set into the

Temporal Peregrinator, as well as their temporal co-ordinates. This done, they were set to go.

'Professor Schröder and myself wish you luck and good hunting. *Immutable Time*,' Keefer ended with the Departmental motto.

'*Immutable Time*,' both Amanda and Ron chorused. They put their heavy dark visors on, and walked into the humming temporal portal, holding hands for reassurance.

The next moment they were aware of, they were standing in a cold ring of brilliant blue light, in the designated ravine, on a sunny afternoon surrounded by high cliffs and deep gullies. At least they hoped it was the right ravine. The visors were essential to protect their eyes from the cold blue light.

While they were removing their visors, Ron spied a dark head disappearing behind a boulder. *Damn*, he mouthed to himself and pretended not to notice it.

'Psst! We're being observed,' he whispered to Amanda.

'Where?'

'Ten o'clock, the large boulder. One dark head.'

They placed the visors in a plastic pouch and hid them in the red earth of the ravine in a shoulder high hole to their left. In the same hole, they deposited a small bag of essential fourth millennium goodies, marking the spot carefully with a nano sized invisibility holo camouflage unit. Part of their equipment included compact cloaking devices fitting neatly on their left wrists, camouflaged as thick decorated golden bracelets. Ron activated his and quietly walked to where he'd seen the dark head disappearing.

He came back to Amanda, 'He's gone whoever it was. We'd better make a move.'

The only contact with base would be a miniature portal opening noon each day, so if they needed to, they could throw a canister into the small portal, and receive a similar canister in return. Once more, they quickly looked around to see if they were being observed. They couldn't see anyone.

Leaving the ravine, they turned left into a gully, and soon came out on a well-trodden track in another ravine. For some three hundred meters, the track sloped downwards, with little gullies branching in on either side at odd intervals, and high cliffs on both sides. The whole of the west bank of the Nile, where all the tombs were built, was bordered by a chain of high sandstone cliffs set back some kilometres from the river. This sprawling rocky wilderness was the Necropolis of Waset, the *khert-neter* of the then capital of Khemet.

'There's someone up there, keeping pace with us,' he whispered to her, pointing to the red coloured hills above them.

Eventually they came out of the foothills onto a flat piece of ground, and in the far distance, way to the left, could see a gathering of people, who seemed to be performing some kind of ritual. Feeling inquisitive and wanting to bring their follower out into the open, they sauntered the distance over to the area of the gathering. This was to be their first encounter with the ancient Khemetians.

Here on the fringes of the *khert-neter*, in the *deshret*, two rows of pits had been dug in the red earth. Laid out in their "yesterday's linen" were twenty bodies covered by sackcloth in each pit.

'What's happening?' Ron asked a bystander.

'The poorest of the poor, who died a week ago in the city, their *kas* are being sent to the western horizon, accompanied by their *bas*. They are entering the gateway to eternity.'

Another chipped in reverently, 'Their *akhu* are soaring into the heavens to dwell as stars, protected by the arms of Nut, where they shall live in the houses of eternity.' He added quickly, 'But only after they have been decreed worthy, by the forty-two judges in the great Judgement Halls of Osiris, in Tuat.'

Ron noticed three rough ragged individuals had joined the milling crowd attending the funeral. He nudged Amanda and nodded in their direction.

'It's our followers. There's three of them.'

'We're going to have to deal with them,' she hissed back.

The three ruffians kept surreptitiously glancing at them from under grey rags on their heads. Then, seeing they'd been spied, they moved further back, sidling away round the crowd, trying to blend in with the throng.

The officiating priests were, one *hem-ka* and three *sem-*priests from the cult of jackal headed Anubis, God of the Dead. They were Lords of the Mummy Wrappings, dressed in plaited black hair pieces, white linen, and sandals, intoning in harmony to Wepwawet, the 'opener of the ways' who seeks out the paths of the dead. In unison they incanted, "Spirit to the sky, corpse into the earth. Show these sinners your mercy and allow them swift passage to Tuat."

Each priest had a leopard skin pinned over the right shoulder, the tail hanging down their fronts. The tall *hem-ka* priest in charge leaned on the staff in his right hand, looking down on the bodies in the pits. All the corpses had been laid on their left side, facing east towards the rising sun.

Because there was little in the way of embalming performed on these poor bodies, being simply eviscerated and washed, the *sem*-priests tried to refrain from breathing in the pungent smell of decomposing flesh, emanating from the pits.

A woman next to Ron muttered, 'They will have their hearts weighed by Thoth himself, on the divine scales, weighed against the Feather of *Ma'at*. If they don't balance, Amemait the Devourer will claim the *kas* of the unworthy.'

The *hem-ka* priest in charge then began to read from a papyrus scroll, *The Declaration of Innocence,* exonerating the deceased of transgressing the ancient commandments of the gods, to help the deceased before the forty-two Judges, to establish their moral virtue, and claim his or her right to eternal bliss.

'I have not stolen; I have not plundered; I have not slain people; I have not committed a crime; I have not stolen the property of a god; I have not said lies; I have not cursed; I have not copulated with another man's wife; I have not copulated with another's husband; I have not copulated with another man; I have not caused anyone to weep; I have not indulged in despair; I have not lead anyone astray; I have not gossiped; I have not slandered; I have not been contentious in affairs; I have not caused terror; I have not become heatedly angry; I have not eavesdropped; I have not made anyone angry; I have not made anyone hungry,' each of the affirmations was accompanied by an address to a particular judge.

As the *hem-ka* priest finished the affirmations, a small group of *kites,* hired mourners, dressed in blue-grey, the colour of sorrow, with their faces daubed in mud and dust, began to wail loudly. They pulled at their hair, demonstrating the tragic loss that the death of these people had brought onto their families, and the nation of Khemet as a whole.

Ron leaned towards Amanda's ear, 'Those villains are on the other side of the crowd, still eyeing us. We'd better make a move.'

'We need to catch that ferry to the east side of the river, and then we might have to find lodgings for the night on that side,' Amanda reminded him.

'I have a plan for our roughnecks,' Ron informed her.

'You can tell me as we go,' Amanda was eager to move on.

They continued down the track, now openly being trailed by the three ruffians, who seemed to be working up enough courage to make a move. Eventually Amanda and Ron came out into the open, and a little further on, they stepped onto a fifty-meter wide causeway lined with sphinxes, which fronted two enormous forecourts containing two tombs with their accompanying temples built into a high cliff.

The comparatively recent temple of Hatshepsut, daughter of Tuthmosis I, and fifth ruler of the 18th Dynasty was at the back of the right forecourt. They could see a ramp leading to a second court, where an imposing colonnaded frontage hid the cliff tomb itself.

Side by side, but to the left, stood the much older temple of Nebhepetre Mentuhotpe, fourth king of the 11th Dynasty. Again, they could see a ramp leading to the mastaba with the royal tomb behind it. The tomb itself sat on terraces of varying height, in the style of a pyramid.

The names and deeds of the dead pharaohs were proclaimed on the walls surrounding the forecourts in vivid beautifully painted hieroglyphs. A tiny temple of Tuthmosis III, tiny compared to the other two, stood on a separate causeway fronting the larger temples.

Amanda and Ron could see mortuary priests busying themselves in the distance, wondering in and out of both mortuary complexes attached to the temples, presumably reciting the rites to the dead as their assistants carried out the embalming.

Those following them, hung back, taking for granted those they pursued, would enlist the help of the priests.

'I wish we had time to tour the Temples,' Ron sighed.

'We *can't!*' Amanda cut in sharply.

As they reached the causeway of Tuthmosis III, sloping gently downwards, Ron suggested, 'Now, let's wait for our *friends.'*

They halted, waiting, and their pursuers stopped—waiting for them to move on. The stand-off was going nowhere and so the pursued moved on, following the causeway downwards for two kilometres, reaching the small temple of Tuthmosis IV. From there, they could see in the far distance, the mighty Nile, the great river, the *itr-da.*

Ron stared at the river, 'Under four kilometres, I would estimate.'

'I've been *waiting* for you to tell me of your plan,' she said irritably.

'Down there—see! When we get to the wooden bridge crossing the irrigation canal. The field where that farmer is,' he pointed halfway down the path to a bridge, and a farmer working his field. 'I'm cloaking and backtracking to our *friends,* and I'm going to put such a scare into them it will have them running all the way back to where they picked us up. What do you think?'

'Might work. Worth a try.'

The time was roughly five in the afternoon, judging from the sun's western position in the sky. It would take them a good hour at a brisk pace to reach the ferry. They followed the path Ron had pointed out, leading across the black earthen fields. When they reached the designated spot, Ron cloaked and quietly approached the three rogues. He let them go by and then tapped one on the shoulder.

'What do yea want?' the tapped man asked his neighbour.

'Nothing,' his startled neighbour responded.

'So why'd yea tap me on the shoulder?'

'I didn't.'

'You trying to be funny?'

Then Ron kicked the third scoundrel in the seat of his pants.

'Hey!' hollered the indignant scruff.

The first man hit the second in the face, knocking him to the ground, and then pulled out a vicious looking knife. The kicked man jumped back, pulling out his knife.

'What did yea do that for?' complained the man on the ground.

Ron decloaked, pulled a sinister face at them, and recloaked. He then kicked the first man; then the one on the ground, and finally the third man again. This was too much for their simple minds. The shock of seeing the object of their attentions appearing out of thin air, then disappearing, followed by a series of kicks from a demon, sent them fleeing back up the path from where they'd come. Ron watched till they were out of sight, before returning to Amanda.

He was laughing as he told her, 'They didn't know what hit them.'

'You think we've seen the last of them?'

'Most certainly!'

They continued down the path watching the busy farmers preparing their fields for planting with emmer and barley. On another parallel path far to the left, there was what looked like a funerary procession heading up into the hills. This was quiet a large procession. A priest bearing a canopic jar out front, followed by many slaves pulling a mortuary sledge holding an elaborately decorated coffin—then followed by a large cortege of mourners. Clearly someone important, someone with wealth, had passed away. To the southwest in the far distance, they could just make out the village of Djamet near the vast palace complex of the previous pharaoh, Amenhotep III. One of the few pharaohs who built his palace on the west bank, south of the Necropolis.

As they neared the shore of the *itr-da*, they passed long cavernous drying sheds, with tables outside long shed entrances bearing a gilded bust of Anubis, the jackal god of the dead. In the sheds, surrounded by the sweet smell of frankincense and myrrh, the priests washed the blackened dried bodies with *natron,* and then embalmed those who could afford it, on rows of concave alabaster tables, before bandaging and returning them to their families for entombing.

Stacks of salty oval *natron* cakes, brought up from distant Lake Chad, leaned against the drying sheds. Muslin bag packages of this natural hydrous sodium carbonate, *natron*, were used in embalming, placed inside the deceased body after the removal of their internal organs. The muslin bags were left in the body for forty days to absorb all the remaining bodily fluids. The seriously rich had the embalming done discreetly, in the embalming tombs of the extended Necropolis further up in the hills, in the causeway temples.

The closer they got to the shores of the *itr-da*, the greater the number of sheds, morticians, their assistants, and *sem*-priests presiding over mortuary rituals. The sheds closer to the shore contained the commoners and the poorer members of society who were simply washed and placed into sackcloth on long rows of wooden tables, then taken to nearby mortuary sheds for quick collection by their relatives. The smell of incense floated heavily in this sprawling *khert-neter*, the ancient Egyptian name for their Necropolis, but mingling with this, was the unmistakable underlying pungent smell of putrefying flesh.

When the sun began to dip at their backs, touching the western horizon, Ron and Amanda reached the dockside, where they encountered many tethered hearse boats. They were secured amongst clusters of reeds, shrine cabins adorned with flowers, and with the palm symbols of resurrection. They walked along the shore, rejecting the more flimsy reed boats, looking at the sun disappearing over the red limestone hills of the Valley of the Kings. Both deeply felt the magic of the time and place. Further along the dock, they found the ferry for the east bank.

Everywhere they went, people surreptitiously stared at them, and by the time they reached the ferry, it was clear they wouldn't be able to simply take their seats, and cross by it. The ferry was only a small papyrus barge, able to take no more than twenty at a time; two ferrymen were at the stern of the craft, leaning on their steering oars.

'Have you noticed how we're being stared at?' Amanda remarked to Ron.

'Yes. Look how they're dressed, and compare it to ours.'

'They think we're Nobles slumming it,' she said with a little disgust. 'We're also supposed to be escorted by bodyguards.'

'We're going to have to hire a boat to cross,' he said firmly.

'How about hiring one of those hearse boats?'

'Why not? They look okay, even a little plush. I'll talk to the one over there,' he half pointed in the direction of one of the sailors looking idle.

She waited a little way off, while Ron walked over and shouted into the boat. 'Hey there, on the boat!'

A neat burly boatman dressed in white mourning, appeared out of the shrine cabin.

'Yes Lord.'

'Is your boat for hire?'

'Most assuredly, Lord. Where do you wish me to take you?'

'Just across the river to the east bank.'

Ron threw the burly boatman a piece of white cloth, the four corners tied into knot.

The boatman undid the knot and looked inside. 'My Lord, you are most generous. When do you wish to begin?'

'Immediately!' Ron waved for Amanda to come and join him.

'He's only too happy to take us across. I've given him two *deben* of silver, and he seems to think he's got a bargain.'

They clambered aboard the ten-meter boat, helped by two of the crew, and the boatman invited them into the spacious shrine cabin. Around the central table, seats were covered with embroidered cushions where the relatives of the deceased would have sat guarding the coffin. Ron and Amanda made themselves comfortable.

Standing up Ron announced, 'I'm going topside. I can't miss a moment of this journey. It's a bit like a dream; I'm thinking I'll soon wake up.'

'Suit yourself. After all the walking; I'm going to rest a while.' She settled into a reposing posture.

He went on deck, just to see the last rays of the deep orange Sun disappear from where they'd come, going down over the western horizon. Ron made out two of the crew at the bow, two manipulating the ropes on the single large sail, and the owner sitting at the stern clutching the tiller. They had left the shore and were heading into mid-channel, the crew, two to port and two to starboard, grabbed an oar each and began to vigorously row.

The crew kept glancing at him enviously out of the corners of their eyes, at the fine clothing. The wind and current were pushing the boat down river, so the owner was alternately tacking from starboard to port, zigzagging the half a kilometre across to Waset, helped by the rowing efforts of the crew.

The city was bathed in near darkness, with occasional lights coming from the palaces and temple complexes. Stars sparkled like little jewels in the deep blue sky. Ron stared into the star encrusted night sky, then looking up river, where he made out to the left the constellations of Andromeda hanging overhead, next to Pegasus, followed by Aquarius to the south-west. The moon was in its first quarter, giving off sufficient light, so Waset could be clearly seen in an eerie lunar light.

The boat approached the landing quay through papyrus reeds after half an hour's journey. Ron called out gently to Amanda to come up and join him on deck, but got no response. He went down into the cabin, and found her fast asleep.

Gently, he put his hand on her shoulder and said, 'Amanda, we've arrived, time to go ashore.'

She yawned, stretched her arms, and stood up. 'I must have been more tired than I thought,' she mumbled apologetically.

The crew breeched the gap to shore with a plank and the passengers nodded to the owner as they left the boat, stepping onto the landing quay, behaving haughtily, trying to get into the character of rich nobles living in the New Kingdom. Quickly, they made their way upwards from the riverside, through the narrow alleyways, into the city proper. Following the slight incline, they soon reached wider streets, and finally the main thoroughfare, running parallel to the shoreline. Even in the dark, the Royal Avenue looked wide enough to take four chariots abreast.

They stood on the corner observing the evening crowd of people. Shops, lit by alabaster oil lamps, were still open for late shoppers, selling fish, grain, fruit, wildfowl, sandals, cloth, spices and various snacks of emmer bread filled with fish. There were chickpeas, lentils, onions, garlic, and all intended to be washed down with *henus* of barley beer. The people who bought on the streets could ill afford meat; that was reserved for the better off.

Ron and Amanda hadn't eaten since they arrived, 'Let's get something to eat,' she suggested, sniffing the aromas.

'The smell of the food is making my stomach rumble,' agreed Ron.

They swung left down the wide Royal Avenue, and stopped at a double fronted tavern.

'Just like the briefing; "Bakeries always have beer taverns next to them," she quoted.

One counter was selling fried fish in emmer bread, the smell wafting invitingly around their nostrils, the other counter selling *henus* of beer. They downed the barley beer and dug into the pita-like emmer bread filled with fried fish, onions and garlic. Ron paid with a *deben* of copper, and the beaming owner nodded appreciatively. However, he must have thought them touched in the head for eating like peasants. However, he had his payment from them, so he really didn't care.

They walked along the Royal Avenue, named in honour of the resident Pharaoh, towards Ipet-Isut, known to later generations as Karnak. Passer-by stared at the two Nobles walking along the street, eating food, and in the process, observing a behavioural time-clash.

'The people seem outraged we're eating as we walk,' Amanda said, obliviously stuffing her mouth. From one of the alleys, a far off donkey brayed in the night air, complaining loudly at the end of its day.

'We're supposed to be home, banqueting. That's how we're dressed. It's like watching someone back home, dressed in a full evening suite, eating pizza out of a box on the street.'

After five hundred meters, the poor solid dwellings gave way to Villas of the rich and powerful. Through the open folding gates, standing between lofty towers, they could see the luscious gardens with reflective ponds and lakes dotted with lotus plants, watered by canals fed by the Nile. Servants moved around inside. Every so often, a couple of Medjay city police sentries with spear and shield, walked up and down the Avenue, guarding this prosperous part of the city.

Further along the Avenue, they came to a walk shaded by sycamores and jujube trees planted in neat rows, lots of pomegranate and date trees, interspersed with clumps of oleanders. Other fruit trees peppered either side of the Avenue. They were heading in the direction of the Pharaoh's palace, where they hoped to find the new Nefertiti, and ascertain who the impostor was. They needed to determine what had happened to the real Nefertiti.

A cool breeze rustled the sycamore leaves above their heads. Amanda pressed a couple of sweets into Ron's hand. She popped a couple into her mouth. Afters would have to be a 4th Millennium affair in 14th Century BC Khemet.

'You were supposed to put those in the hole with the rest of our modern stuff,' Ron scolded her.

She simply shrugged and kept walking.

As they neared Ipet-Isut, they passed a group of priests heading the other way, towards the city. All three raised their hand in friendly salute to them, and Ron thought it wise to ignore the greeting. Seeing their greeting was ignored, one of the priests came over and barred their way. He seemed angry they had not returned their greeting.

The priest wore a leopard skin fitted over his linen robes, denoting a senior rank, and he commanded, 'Adhere to your *ma'at*, reflect on the divine harmony. Your spirit is noisy, your behaviour unreasonable. Be more considerate of the eternal qualities of existence,' he swept his hand in the direction of the earth, then pointed at the sky. They both stood astounded at this admonition.

'We are all humble before Amun,' Ron quickly offered. 'Take no offence at our weary ways, we were distracted by the beauty of the night sky.' This poetic explanation seemed to satisfy the priest, and he inclined his head, and ran to catch up with his fellow priests.

'That was quick thinking,' Amanda told him. 'I'm glad he was so easily appeased. The priests must be extra sensitive to snubs, since the Pharaoh started persecuting them.'

'You can say that again. I thought he was going to bite my head off,' grinned Ron.

She added, 'Better to not antagonise the locals.'

They turned right onto the Avenue of the Sphinxes of Nectanebo and were approaching the broad avenue that led to the Pharaoh's palace. The Precinct of Mut, bearing the temple of Amun's wife, was half a kilometre further on. Half a kilometre beyond was the Precinct of Amun himself, at Ipet-Isut.

The palace they were headed for, was built a little further back from the Avenue of the Sphinxes, to the right. It had its own broad causeway leading to its gates.

'That's the current palace of the Pharaoh, am I right?' Ron pointed at the imposing building.

'That's what we've been led to believe,' she confirmed.

'Right! I think it's time we made use of our cloaking devices. I'm engaging mine,' and with that he disappeared to eyesight.

'I'm right behind you,' and she disappeared from view as well.

Ten minutes later, they approached the gateway of Pharaoh's palace, known as the House of a Million Years. The two storey sandstone building extended a considerable distance to the right and left—forming an outer approach from two lodges at the entrance, occupied by guards and porters. Some of the upper chambers looked down on this passage, whilst the whole building itself was crowned with battlements, like the walls of a fortified town.

Cloaked, they passed through the entrance without fuss, and took the right doorway, where a wide stairway with beautiful hieroglyphed walls led to the second landing. They slipped past numerous guards holding spears and wicker shields. At the top of the stairs, there was a long elaborately decorated corridor leading off to the left and right, with walls painted in low relief, or in intaglio, representing the Pharaoh's household—including lots of sacred lotus flowers.

Guards were stationed at equal intervals along the whole wide corridor, lit with translucent alabaster lamps; and according to their intelligence, from which the Pharaoh's apartments led off the corridor to the left. To the right they heard music, and went to investigate. Further along, a large double door was open, with a group of guards milling around the doorway. They were smiling and pointing at something inside, but remained outside, peering in.

Amanda and Ron, protected by the cloak of invisibility, looked inside. There was a long large decorated hall, with what looked like festivities in progress, and the Golden Hawk, Akhenaten himself, sitting on his alabaster throne, studiously enjoying a group of naked dancers performing in the middle of the hall. Finely dressed courtiers were milling around on either side of the throne, enjoying the dancing. Ron wanted to go inside, but Amanda indicated there was no sign of either of the Nefertitis, and continued down the corridor.

The next doorway along, led to a smaller room, a dressing room, where other dancers were preparing to go on. It was where they found their target, in a corner, nonchalantly doing her warm up *portes de bras* with her arms, followed by a pirouette. She was dark haired, slim, with a dark complexion.

They'd had good simulated holo pictures shown to them before they set out, burned into their brains, made from the miscellaneous busts in the various museums. Unmistakably they recognised this would be *prima donna* as their target.

'The sneaky so-and-so, she intends to charm the Pharaoh with a modern ballet performance,' Amanda hissed to Ron.

'Clever little bitch. With that routine, she's clearly not of this era,' Ron hissed back.

Amanda rapidly went over to their target and before she realised what was happening, swiftly attached a patch to her arm. It left her conscious, but paralysed. Ron simultaneously grabbed her by the waist, and they both walked the startled limp body, the few intervening steps over to a hard bench parked against the near wall of the room. Nobody had taken the slightest bit of notice that this single visible figure wanted to sit on the bench. A youth sat on another bench in the corner, head nodding in a silent rhythm, oblivious, nibbling lotus petals, getting a psychedelic high from—the much venerated flower.

A pre-prepared *sotto voce* audio tic was attached to her right earlobe, this requested her to stay calm, not struggle, and asked her to blink once if she understood. The figure blinked. The tic continued......she was to keep quiet whilst they released her vocal cords, any attempt to summon help would result in her death. Blink once if she understood. She blinked.

The language of the tic was English, not Khemet. Amanda and Ron watched, knowing this impostor was not of this time, and the impostor realised her captives knew. Ron took out a tiny zapstunner and held it to their captive's throat with his right hand. Amanda attached a small patch to the throat of their captive. The prisoner kept quiet. She was aware cloaked operatives had her, and there was little she could do.

'Okay, let's have it. Who are you, and when are you from?' Amanda whispered fiercely into their captives ear.

'My name is Mary Cooper, I'm from 3873.' She said this quietly with no hint of defiance in her voice.

'Mary, you must be aware you've *messed* up the time lines causing a major temporal shift,' Ron hissed this at her.

Amanda motioned for him to lay off. 'How did you get here Mary, and are you the only one?' Amanda played the good cop.

The rest of the room went on with their preparations, ignoring the sitting figure gently mumbling to herself.

'I waited till the maintenance crew left for the night, set these time co-ordinates, and walked through the portal, *alone.....*' she whispered this in a matter of fact way, as if she was talking to a cat. There was no regret, and no defiance. She was in the hands of determined operatives from her time, and she might as well come clean. She knew they were dangerous.

'But how did you get into the building where the Temporal Peregrinator was housed?' Amanda pressed her.

'I worked in the building.' Dismayed, Amanda and Ron gaped at her.

'*You worked for Temporal Safeguards?*' Amanda hissed. She simply couldn't grasp such an elementary plot.

'Yes. On the calibrating console. I input the temporal cohesion matrix figures and ran the calibrating dimensions against the probable entropic interference.'

For some moments, Ron and Amanda were speechless. An inside job! They couldn't believe how easy this lone woman had screwed up a trillion credit operation, and bypassed all the precautions specifically designed to prevent such an occurrence.

'How come you weren't missed from your post the next day?' Amanda continued.

'I hacked into personnel records, assigned another operative for my position, and erased all traces of myself.'

'You're lying,' Amanda knew deep down she wasn't. 'There's no way you could've hacked into the system. There's neural guardians to prevent that.'

'Over time, the system's got lax, it's nowhere near as tight as you seem to think.' Just like that, she dismissed the almighty neural guardian.

'*Aww damn!* There's gonna be hell to pay, after this little escapade,' Ron broke his silence.

'That part we'll sort out later when we get back. *Mary*, what did you do with the real Nefertiti?'

'I took her into the next room on a pretext, drugged her, gagged her, and put her in a closet, rolled up in a carpet. I got the idea for the carpet from the Cleopatra story,' she looked pleased with herself for having thought of the carpet.

'And what were you going to do with all the people who knew the real Nefertiti?' Amanda asked.

'I was going to send them to Nubia, into a comfortable exile,' Mary replied off handedly.

'Mary! I'm going to say this once only, so listen carefully.' Amanda said through clenched teeth. 'If you co-operate fully with what we have to do, then I promise you, I will try and help you when we get back. Do you understand?'

'I know your right,' whispered the captive, 'But I did like it here.' That she'd used the past tense, suggested she was going to co-operate.

'I'm going to put another patch on your arm, which neutralises the paralytic drug. I expect you to be on your best behaviour...otherwise.' Amanda nodded to Ron.

Ron pressed the zapstunner harder into her neck, for emphasis.

'Do you promise to behave?' Amanda now talked to her as to a juvenile offender. She positioned the patch.

'I promise,' Mary looked downcast.

'I want you to get up quietly, and go to the next room. We'll be with you all the way.' Mary got up, stood still for a moment to check her muscles after the paralytic, and then walked quietly out of the dressing room.

In the next room, they found the closet; unbundled the real Nefertiti, but left her gagged. They both decloaked, and Amanda used an antidote and woke the young Nefertiti. She really was beautiful, and could have passed for a model in the 4th Millennium. The kohl-rimmed eyes indicated a fierce intelligence. She was none the worse for her ordeal.

They explained to the haughty young noble lady—Mary would be taken away and put to death, after much torture. She would have expected nothing less. Furthermore, they hinted it was all part of a plot by the angered priests of Amun; a plot that had got out of hand. It would now be taken care of. It sounded plausible, taking the present antagonisms between the priests and the Pharaoh into account.

Nefertiti was invited to go back to the dressing room next door and continue her preparations, readying herself for the dance that was to captivate the Pharaoh. This was the night Akhenaten would take special notice of her, and ask her to join him for a walk in the gardens, where they would establish a rapport. After that it was history; the *real* untampered history.

Ron lifted his heavy ring on the left hand, and snapped a quick unobtrusive holopic of Nefertiti, as a memento, and they all left the irate noble lady, her anger clearly written on her face. Because it was hinted it was a priestly plot, she kept quiet for the moment. Amanda and Ron each took one of Mary's arms, stepping into the corridor, cloaking the trio as they went, and hurriedly left the palace.

They rapidly made their way back to the Nile, and this time they changed their clothing, swapping their beautiful outfits for cheap peasant attire. It wasn't too difficult to talk some poor locals they'd come across, in the alleys leading to the quayside, into doing the swap. They found the ferry, and all three climbed aboard. The ferry cast off and headed for the Necropolis on the west bank.

The time was near four in the morning, when they finally reached their ravine. Although tired, they sat awake to watch the sunrise coming up over Waset, to the east. Ron kept an eye on Mary, still distrustful of her. After a while, Amanda began making their report out for Keefer.

It would be noon when the miniature portal engaged next. They prepared a canister requesting abstraction for the next day, at the same hour. When noon arrived, the portal engaged on the hour, and the canister for Keefer was sent on its way. There was little else to do but prepare to settle for the rest of the day, and another night. Despite Ron's mistrust of her, Mary had accepted her lot, and was as quiet as a lamb.

The next morning, a boulder landed near Ron, launched from above. Then another landed near Mary.

'Quick, *cloak*,' he yelled to Amanda.

As he ran towards where the rocks were being thrown from, a large rock landed where he'd been sitting. The rocks stopped as soon as they had cloaked. Ron reached the top of the ravine hill, to see the same hoodlums they had dealt with earlier, running to the bottom of the other side. He drew his zapstunner and hit two in quick succession. They crumpled to the ground. The third was half way up the next hill when Ron zapped him; he rolled back to the bottom. He tied the wretched rascals up and left them in the next ravine.

'Was it the same lot?' Amanda asked when he got back.

'Yes! Persistent tykes! I've left them tied up over the hill. When we're ready to leave, I'll untie them.'

Ron held no grudge against a group of poor wretches trying to survive in this hostile environment, in the only way they knew how. The following day he went back, untied them, and the group of time travellers were abstracted as scheduled. All three returned to the 4th Millennium. ChronoCorps went lenient on Mary after Amanda intervened as promised, on her behalf, but they tightened their procedures and upgraded the neural guardian on the computer.

'Herr Director! Herr Keefer wünsche sprechen mit sie von Temporal Safeguards, von Amerika,' the curators secretarial computer informed him.

'Ja danke, verbinden sie mir.'

'Hallo! Professor Schröder?' Keefer's voice asked.

'Is that you Dan,' Schröder inquired.

'Look, has the bust of Nefertiti returned to normal?' Keefer was eager to know.

'Tut tut. You know it has. It's sitting on my desk right now, as beautiful, if not more beautiful than ever,' the curator gazed lovingly at the statue, *and* the holopic by its side. 'Ahh! But the holopic! In me, you have a friend for life. There are no words to thank you enough for the holopic.' The curator's eyes glazed over with a sense of well-being and contentment.

Death in the Caucasus

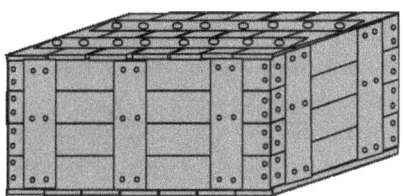

A green signal light flashed briefly from shore, breaking into the darkness of a moonless night. Waves lapped gently against the sides of the motorboat, prompting helm to steer in the light's direction for what seemed an eternity. It was just after 3 am, and the tension in the boat was palpable. They'd just spent ten hours in the launch, speeding a gruelling five hundred kilometres across the Black Sea from Kerch, on the Crimean peninsula. Helm cut the engines and the crew paddled the rest of the way silently, the half a kilometre towards shore. All on board were eager to offload their illicit cargo and head back to where they came from, before the regular sea patrols spotted them. They beached on the open side of the headland, separating it from the small village of Bichvint'a in Abkhazia. Two of the crew jumped onto the pebbly beach, burdened with a large heavy wooden box from the boat, which they hastily dumped onto the pebbles.

The sound of approaching feet coming down the beach made them jump.

'Is that you Kostya?' one of the crew whispered.

'Who else you expecting,' replied an irritated gruff voice. 'Have you brought the stuff?'

'No. I came all this way for nothing—course I got it.'

Three men in black gear emerged and crowded round the box lying on the beach.

Kostya spat out, 'Anton—I'll have you one of these days, you pimp. You got a bad mouth on ye. You can push off now.'

Without a further word, the crew jumped back into the boat and proceeded to "push off" as instructed.

From off shore came a quiet voice. 'Hey Kostya— you're a son of a bitch.' Then silence.

Kostya didn't reply, but made a mental note to deal with Anton the next time they met.

'Grab the box,' he told his dark garbed companions.

They lifted the heavy object and struggled back up the beach carrying the cargo between them to an army issue Gaz jeep. They dumped the box in the back, jumped in, switching on the engine. With the lights off, they pulled away, veering leftwards away from the town, that sat over the rise. Half a kilometre inland they halted. The silhouette of a of a black squat helicopter sat outlined against a dark sky, barely visible. The Gaz stopped and the occupants jumped out. They lugged the heavy box towards the chopper with lots of curses, puffing and shoving it inside the open bay.

Whoosh—whoosh—whoosh, the rotors whirled as the machine readied for take-off.

The pilot shouted from his seat, 'Vlad, close the bloody door, will ye.'

Vladimir Botnin was tying the box down for flight. He shouted back, 'Give me a minute. I'm securing the cargo.'

Vlad closed the bay door and returned to the co-pilot's seat. 'Listen Yura, we've got time—don't get so jumpy.'

Yura Gusinsky looked at his co-pilot and blew a raspberry with his mouth. 'Up yours,' he shouted above the noise from the rotors.

The Kamov 25 lifted without lights and skimmed close to the ground heading inland for Vladikavkaz in Ossetia. Both had done the journey over the Caucasian mountains many times and Yura knew the route like the back of his hand. All went as usual—without incident, as the pilot made a point of avoiding habitation. The chopper was an old Search and Rescue machine the Russian Mafiosi had appropriated from a corrupt Naval Officer. How the Officer explained its loss was his business. Its main benefit was its range, 650 kilometres. The distance from Bichvint'a in Abkhazia to Vladikavkaz in Ossetia was 350 kilometres—and if needed, it could even make it deep into Chechnya. That's where the profitable arms and drugs business lay.

Vlad pointed to his left, 'Look Yura, *there*, its old Mount Jangi Tau. Five thousand meters—right on the Ossetian-Georgian border. Once we're over it, we're home and dry.' Vlad then stared hard at his VDU display, shouting above the noise, '*Hang on Yura;* I've got a blip on the radar. *Shit*, it's the border patrol. They've sent a Sukhoi after us. You'd better try and land. We'll never get past that bloody thing now. Ossetia's out. Just head down. See if you can lose it. Go along the base of the mountain range. Maybe it'll confuse his rangefinder.'

Yura pushed the controls forward, sending the Kamov into a steep dive. At around a hundred meters he jerked the controls back hard towards his chest, lifting the nose barely twenty meters from the ground. The machine screamed in agony as the g-forces tried to tear the machine apart—but it straightened—and followed the mountain range southward skimming along the base. Yura was hoping to out manoeuvre the Sukhoi-24 jet chasing them. If the pilot of the Sukhoi was determined, he'd have his quarry at all costs. Yura was relying on a moonless terrain, on the many valleys rifting the range. His knowledge versus the Sukhoi pilots. In the end it was all just a game—a deadly game—but still, only a game.

The Sukhoi dived at them repeatedly trying to force them down. In the last dive he'd opened up with his machine guns. That was their final warning. Next time he'd send a missile at them. This *game* was getting out of hand.

'Vlad. Go and jettison the cargo—*NOW*.'

Vlad climbed into the back and undid the strapping restraining the box, pulling it to the bay door. The Kamov lurched just as Vlad opened the bay door—and the box flew out into the night. Vlad managed to hold onto the webbing near the door, preventing him joining the cargo. At the same instant the Sukhoi pilot loosed his air-to-air missile at the chopper. The missile followed Vlad and Yura for a short distance—then a bright fireball lit up the night sky. The Sukhoi pilot didn't notice two ejector seats shooting out sideways from the chopper. Sideways and upwards, propelled by small rockets built into the seats—then the parachutes opened.

The box didn't have far to travel and crash-landed, disintegrating on the Georgian side of the border high in the Caucasian mountains—spilling its contents into a dense mountainside thicket.

'The grazing's still not lush enough. We've got to get further up,' Tenghiz shouted across to Lado, urging his companion on.

Lado Akhmeli pulled the brass horn from his belt and blew a series of blasts, calling the goats to him. '*Up-up-up*,' he encouraged his flock. One hand held the horn; the other pulled the mule with their provisions.

Tenghiz Guruli was *shooing* the laggards from behind, higher up the mountain, waving his jacket at them in a circular motion. Both shepherds were tired and looking forward to the evening meal and a nights rest. It was late in the day and they hoped to reach the high pastures by evening.

The men had left Chargali, their mountain village in the upper reaches of the Aragvi River the day previous. They'd left families and friends for a week of hard hiking—needing to get to the high pastures to fatten up the flock. Their family's winter survival depended on it. As villages go, Chargali was a typical Georgian community and had no more than a dozen houses. Self-sufficient in most things—if they needed any luxuries they had to make the long trek down to Ghebi, with a population of twenty thousand. Ghebi was only ten kilometres away but might as well have been fifty—there were no roads.

They pushed the goat herd as fast as they could, both sprightly tough forty year olds, fit as only mountain people can be. Only when the light began to fail did they stop to build a fire. Lado unpacked the mule whilst Tenghiz went in search of firewood. At this height it was usually shrubs and thickets. Lado started the fire and Tenghiz searched for fuel to keep it going for the rest of the night. Even in summer the high mountains were bitterly cold.

Tenghiz went further than intended, captivated by a slight glow from a thicket that drew him. He reached into the thicket and found a couple of canisters—and was surprised to find them warm. *That's lucky,* he thought. *I wonder what's in them.* He picked up both canisters and carried them to where he'd left the firewood. Heavy but just manageable—the brush wood he'd gathered over his shoulder—he headed back to camp.

'Hey Lado, look what I've found. We won't be cold tonight.' Tenghiz dumped the canisters by the lit fire.

Lado left the roasting meat, came and stared at them—then touched them. 'Well I'll be. They're warm. You're right—we can use them to warm ourselves. He took one and upturned it. 'This will do to sit on,' he said parking his backside on it.

'I've tried opening them but they seem to be locked. I wonder what's in them.' Tenghiz upturned the other and copied his friend. 'Backside feels nice and warm,' he added.

'Meat's done. Here, take this!' Lado handed Tenghiz an aluminium army plate with a slab of roast goat and a hunk of black rye bread. 'Tuck in. I want to get an early night—I'm exhausted.'

'Me too.' Tenghiz yawned, then broke off a piece of meat and munched happily. 'This is good,' he complimented.

'*Mmmm!* I'm so hungry I could eat the whole flock,' Lado responded.

After the meal, Lado cleaned the plates with grass and put them away. He hobbled the mule and tied it to a bush with a long rope. It could graze but not wander off. Then they settled for the night. Each cuddled a canister for warmth.

During the night, Tenghiz began to moan in his sleep. Lado woke feeling sick to his stomach. He turned, pushed the canister away and vomited, unable to keep the meal down. He managed to sit—and heaved up more of his meal. Stumbling, he got to his feet and went to wake Tenghiz.

'Hey, wake up. I don't feel to good...wake up will you. *Tenghiz*...damn you! I tell you I don't feel well.' He looked at Tenghiz, whose eyes were open but in great pain. His canister lay glowing at his feet. He was sweating liberally. '*Tenghiz*...what's wrong with you?'

Panic rose in him. He was sweating badly himself and knew it was dangerous this high up.

'We've got to go back,' Lado groaned.

Feeling weak, he went to find the mule. Sighed with relief when he found it still hobbled. He pulled the beast to Tenghiz and began to hoist his friend onto the mule. He knew he'd never walk all the way back himself. He wasn't too sure *he* could manage the trek down to the village, but he had to try.

Throughout the night, stumbling into dawn, he pulled the mule ever downwards, Tenghiz slumped across its flanks, thanking the stars that gravity did most of the difficult work for him. The mule wanted to go back down—and that helped. It took him all the next day. Down was quicker than up. As they neared, someone from the village saw the state he was in, and rushed to phone the next village for the Doctor. By then Lado was vomiting blood, as was Tenghiz. Lado collapsed near the first house he came to.

Dr. Sandro Abuladze arrived in his Gaz jeep, took one look at the pair and knew there was little he could do. It was obviously radiation poisoning, and both men had suffered a huge dose. Lado was still just coherent, but slipping fast. The Doc asked them where they'd been and Lado managed to blurt out the story of the canisters.

It was an old story—well documented by the newspapers. The Soviet Army had pulled out in '91 but left

151

numerous radioactive materials from various medical laboratories and missile sites. Some found their way on to the black market, whilst others were found by children and innocent people who had no idea what they were dealing with.

The Doctor did his best. He loaded his jeep with the two dying shepherds and headed for the nearest large hospital—at Ghebi. It was the quickest solution. Waiting for a helicopter ambulance would mean they'd be certain to arrive too late. Time was of the essence. Driving like a maniac he reached the main hospital in Ghebi three hours later.

The Consultant diagnosed Strontium-90 poisoning. Tenghiz died that night, pumped full of painkillers. The following morning—Lado joined him. The dose they'd been exposed to was far too large. There was nothing to be done. Even Doctor Abuladze had to be given the anti-radiation treatment simply because he'd been that close to them.

Dr. Abuladze rode back to Chargali with tears running down his face, sad and angry at the same time. He railed at the criminal negligence that allowed such things to happen—swore and cursed at the stupid criminality of the Soviet system that lied to them and killed them even now. When he got back to Chargali, the news of their deaths hit the families of the shepherds badly. The wailing went on all night in the small community.

Dr. Sandro Abuladze made damned *sure* the Ghebi newspapers were full of the tragedy. The news even travelled as far as Tbilisi, the Georgian capital. He wanted his countrymen to know of the "presents" left them by their kind protectors. The article by Shota Pshavela pinpointed the spot where the canisters were found; 42° 47' N 43° 36' E, high in the mountains just below the snowline on this side of the

Georgian border. Fragments of a lead-lined box were found nearby. An obituary lamented the demise of Tenghiz Guruli and Lado Akhmeli, two innocent shepherds trying to get on with their lives, trying to support their large families—and now alas, leaving orphans and widows to struggle on as best they could.

A smaller column in the same paper noted that two bullet riddled bodies, likely to be Russians, were found by the Border Police high near the frontier with Ossetia. It concluded they were executed and dumped into Georgia by the Russian Mafiosi who frequently carried out such punishments. Thus ended the infamous careers of Vladimir Botnin and Yura Gusinsky. There would be no one to shed tears over them!

Sasha Garrydeb

The Tourist

Who's out there?'

I heard more crackling coming from the corridor. Reaching out to my right, I switched on the bedside light. A flash of grey and white fur made a run for her hiding place in the huge cupboard near the bedroom window.

'Psyche! What's the matter? Why are you hiding in the cubby-hole?' My cat only did that when frightened.

I listened. There it was again! That crackling! It had woken me; coming from down the corridor. I jumped out of bed and cautiously looked into the corridor, in the direction of what seemed like an electrical crackling. The sound reminded me of two live wires touching together.

It was near six in morning and the dawn light was just coming through the corridor skylight. I noticed a sort of shimmering to the left of the toilet door. It was then I saw what was making the sound. It was a spark, *crackling* in mid-air. The light from the spark lit up the faintest suggestion of a small cloud of fog hanging over the battery charger, opposite the toilet door.

I'd left the charger on, charging some batteries overnight. As I watched, mesmerised by the phenomenon, the cloud moved back from the charger, stopped, and gave a little crackle. It was as if it was checking its charge level.

I'm sorry! Did I startle you?

'What?' I couldn't hear anything, yet the *thing* spoke to me; in my head.

Don't be alarmed. I mean you no harm!

I stood paralysed. *It,* whatever it was, was talking to me, in my head. I'll bet I'm dreaming. I haven't really woken up; I'm still asleep and only dreaming I'm awake. That's it! I've had this before, not often, I admit, but it's happened before.

That's simply self-delusion. I am talking to you and you're hearing me: well not exactly hearing. I didn't realise it was going to be such a shock to you. I apologise again.

'Stop that! Will you get out of my head!' I was close to shouting.

I'm sorry! I should go.

'No! Wait!' I wanted *it* to go; but I also wanted some answers. If I was dreaming, it would sort itself out when I woke up. But what if I wasn't dreaming...? 'Look! Give me a moment to collect myself.'

Take your time. If you want me to go, just say so. I'm told most people just go into denial. They insist they're dreaming and go back to bed. That's if they see our kind in the first place. I haven't talked to any people; it's so difficult. It gets lonely like this: no one to talk to.

'Who are you? No! That's not right: what are you?'

I'm with TDT. I became separated from the main tour. Now I'm lost.

'TDT? Separated? Tour? You're not making any sense.'

Trans Dimensional Tours! I'm called Xerol from Ynsi. I don't want to alarm you. I'm a transcendental life form from another dimension—the forty-third, if that makes any sense to you.

'A tour? Are you telling me you're a tourist? I've been woken in the middle of the night...by a tourist? Now I know I'm dreaming.'

Have it your own way: why not go back to bed and forget all about this?

'Hang on! Who are you ordering around in *my* flat?'

For a few seconds I stood there, facing this insubstantial cloud, hanging there, the occasional low-key sparkle crackling from it. Ahh! To hell with this! I decided to go back to bed. This silly conversation wasn't going anywhere. Wait a mo! I can't go to bed and leave this *thing* floating around in my flat. 'You said you're on a tour; right?'

Yes! I stopped off to have a look inside a human home. Next thing I knew; I was alone. I've been looking through the houses for some food. I'm sorry for consuming yours without asking.

'Is that what you were doing when I first saw you?'

Yes. I hope you don't mind?

'You eat electricity?'

Electricity? The food is coming from the machine here.

'That's my battery charger. Look! This tour; how many of you are there?'

Oh! Not many! I thought they would come back for me when they found me missing. I suppose they're too busy having fun. I should go back to the antennae.

'You're rambling. I don't like rambling in my head. What antennae?'

We have a focal point for assembly just to the West of here. There are many large dishes collecting waves; and a lot of wave generators. It's our gathering cusp for this zone.

I stood puzzled, thinking.....then it dawned on me, 'You must mean the BBC complex at White City. That's to the west of here. There's a powerful group of receivers and transmitters there.'

There followed a sort of mental shrug, or so it seemed. *It could be,* it said. *You and I have different reference points. No.....wait! It seems from your memories it* is *the same place.*

'Is there no privacy? You're rummaging around in *my* memories. Do you mind!'

I'm sorry! Are you offended when I look into your mind?

'Your damn right! You're messing with my private thoughts. You ought to ask permission!'

I won't do it again. I will go.

'No, wait. If I'm dreaming then I'm getting my beauty sleep as we talk. If I'm not dreaming, then it's too late to go back to bed. You said earlier you had nobody to talk to. Okay, why don't you stay a while and talk to me?'

The little cloud hung there for a couple of seconds before responding, as if it was thinking over my invitation.

All right! I will stay for a short while. Thank you for asking me. What are you called?

'Me? My name is Alex. You told me yours was Xerol.'

That's right. You're not really dangerous...are you?

'What makes you say that?'

In our Guide to this planet, the natives are described as aggressive and dangerous.

'What "Guide"?'

We are supplied with an Information Guide to all the places we visit.

'And we're in there as being dangerous? I don't feel dangerous! What else is in this "Guide"? Oh, by the way; feel free to help yourself to some more..."food".'

That's kind of you. I might have a little bit more in a minute. The Guide says your species are at an early stage of its civilisation: you're not yet ready for first contact.

'Hold it there a moment! What do you mean "not ready for first contact"? Do you mean by other species, like yours?'

That's correct. Your species are too suspicious; too aggressive, and far too primitive as yet.

'I think I've just been insulted. The trouble is; I think your right. We're certainly suspicious: definitely aggressive; but primitive? That's what we call our Chimp cousins. I've not really thought of myself as primitive!'

Compared to all the other species in the Universe, and in all the other dimensions! Take my word for it;

you're primitive. I'm only a child, but I'm a lot cleverer than you.

'What are you saying? You're a *child*? How old are you?'

I suppose converting it to your life span: I would be about five of your years old. But in reality I'm about three hundred of your years. We live longer.

'This is ridiculous! I'm woken in the middle of the night by an apparition of a lost alien child. Surely this **must** be a dream?'

Your doubting reality again; just because I'm young? That's silly!

'Yea! I suppose your right! So what else is in this "Guide" of yours?'

Your science is still at primary level. You've just managed to begin space exploration. You have little understanding of the laws of Physics, clinging to some fantasy about a 'Big Bang', mainly due to the lack of a unified theory of physics. Your society is riddled with fanaticism and bigotry.

'Hold on a moment! Are you being honest with me?'

There goes that nasty suspicion again.

'All right! I take your point. It's just I find it difficult to see why a "tour guide" would mention the "Big Bang" and all that stuff about a "unified theory".'

What do you expect the Tour Guide to say? That your planet is pretty—it's a paradise of enlightenment? The Tour Guide has to be realistic and truthful. It goes on to describe the destruction of your environment. That you have little respect for the home planet you live on, dumping your waste products all over the place.

'I can't argue with you there. That's true enough, but we are beginning to clean things up. People are becoming aware. It's like the open sewers in earlier centuries, eventually put under ground. It will take a while for us to become planet proud.'

Your transport is in a mess; your seas are polluted. Three of your large cities have air that is cancerous; Mexico City, Beijing, and Calcutta. Because you're unable to control your business conglomerates, the heat pollution is creating havoc with your planetary weather, leading to global warming. Even then, your scientists are arguing over if global warming is real or not. Pack a hundred of your species in a small room and watch the temperature go up—global warming is self-evident. Not so?

'Your right! What can I say? We are getting round to fixing it. Come back in a thousand years and you'll find your paradise of enlightenment.'

If you survive? You're just getting started on genetic manipulation! All that needs is a few mistakes, a few rogue releases into your flora and fauna, and the fatal flaws could damage your planet just as effectively as any nuclear bomb.

'No advances are without risks. Where you come from, you must have gone through something similar; back in your past? My ancestors risked their lives every day just to get enough food to feed themselves. Now our supermarkets are stuffed full of food. Worst could happen to me now, is I might get run over by some drunk driver!'

Then there is this growth of planet-wide religious fanaticism. My Guide says intolerance is growing. It says you eventually mature into not believing in Father Christmas, but still insist in believing in someone no one has ever actually seen. Another religion has fanatics who you call suicide bombers, who kill themselves so they can have 49 virgins after they're dead? That seems pure lunacy to my poor mind. How can you have sex with virgins if your dead—and what would be the purpose. Sex is for procreation, not useless fun. Your species simply refuses to take full responsibility for their own actions. It says you have a long way to go before you grow up as a species.

'It's strange listening to someone criticising the whole human race, picking out all our faults. Trouble is; I tend to agree with most of what this "Guide" of yours says. Go on; what else does it say?'

It says if you were contacted by another species, you would panic and try and destroy the Ambassadors. That you react violently to anything you don't understand. That most of you believe in ghosts, astrology, and futurology. That most of your leaders are corrupt, selfish, and greedy, grabbing power for power's sake. That these power hungry people control most of the planets' resources, whilst the majority are deliberately kept in ignorance and poverty.

'That's got the nail on the head. Whoever wrote this "Guide" of yours did a thorough job of analysing us humans. Go on.'

There is an increasing UFO culture spreading through your species. The trouble is; those running some of the cults are totally insane. So many are living in pure fantasy worlds of their own making. They think they can get rides on comets by killing themselves. There are millions of humans who claim they've been abducted by aliens, experimented on, cut open, and then returned to

Earth. That puts onto the alien species, the worst motives of the humans. It suggests aliens are monsters. Why would any technologically advanced species want to experiment on another species? If a species is capable of intergalactic travel, it surely has the technology to observe without kidnapping anyone. If they wanted to know how a human is put together, why cut them up, why not simply scan them with a scanner? The current fascination with virtual reality and computer games is taking you people further away from reality, than ever. Soon, you won't be able to determine what is real and what isn't.

'Well, well! You seem to have one hell of a "Guide?" I mean it sounds about right. But I don't have anything to do with those virtual loons, personally. I'm always a bit sad when I hear what they get up to; most of their thinking ranges between the neurotic and the psychotic. Go on! Let's hear more from your "guide".'

You have no planetary Government to speak of. There are currently 46 wars going on your planet. I'm going to stop there. Don't you want to hear any of the positive things my Guide says?

'What? Oh! You mean there are good things about this planet in your "Guide"?'

I'm not sure, but I think you were being cynical just then. Of course there are positive things in the Guide. There is a phenomenal energy in your race. Humans have come far in a short time. It's only fourteen thousand years since the end of your Ice Age, and the beginning of human civilisation. If the race becomes calmer, more rational, unlocks the potential of all *of your population—then you ought to have a bright future. Many species take a great interest in you humans, seeing a vigorous contribution from this planet to the Universal sentient civilisation.*

'That's nice to hear! If we survive our development, we'll have a rosy future. How long is this going to take, does your "Guide" make any suggestions?'

The Guide says the next thousand years are going to be crucial. If your species can get through the next thousand years intact, it will take you to the boundaries of your Solar system. By then your Physics should have enabled you to build an intergalactic warp drive, and that will be your passport for an invitation to join the other species, lifting your quarantine.

'What quarantine? Does it have anything to do with why we can't pick up any other life signs from the cosmos?'

Everything is being screened. Nothing gets through to your planet except that which is allowed to get through. All the electromagnetic spectrum is screened by the cloaked devices around your Solar system.

'Well I'll be damned!'

It's quiet straightforward. The Guide says humans quarantine other countries for political reasons. Our quarantine is far more important. It's for your own protection! Wait...I think my companions have come back for me. Yes. I'm sorry! I have to go. It's been nice talking to you. Oh! Thanks for the food!

'Oh! Yeah! It's been an education...I hope you stop off again sometime.'

With that, the little cloud disappeared into the kitchen. I followed it, and saw it go through the glass of the kitchen window. In the light of day, I could barely make out the little apparition. I heard the chime from the lounge strike nine. 'My goodness! Is that the time?' I mumbled to myself.

During the day, I sat at the computer and tried to remember what happened. This is the story. It's all true; I *swear* it!

Sasha Garrydeb

Journey to the Spirit World

I stared fiercely into the fire, as tears welled up in my throat, choking me for the umpteenth time, and just as fiercely I clutched the clay urn of my beloved dead mate. Resting against my left boot, emotionally burning into my leg was the clay urn of my departed son, Ab. My muscles were tight—aching. I forced back the tears so the shaman, sitting across from me, would not see my weakness.

I put the mother's clay urn down gently next to her only child's urn, and pulled the sheepskin coat tightly round me, pretending the shivers were caused by the biting wind. It would not do to have the chief's son shedding tears on this joyous occasion. It was fortunate the shaman was preoccupied with keeping warm, sipping at his hot beverage cupped by his hands. He did not notice my grief. The others sat silently round the fire, each with their own thoughts, each sipping their own hot brews, chewing on dried deer.

The fire blazed into the clear night sky warming our little band of travellers. This was the fourth night we had spent on the road on our way to wood henge to celebrate the winter festival. It was said to be a joyous occasion. Even the urns we carried were said to be joyous, for we were taking the spirits of the departed to rest in their permanent ancestral place.

We had camped in a small clearing in this never-ending forest, listening to the night sounds all around us. Due to the moonless night, we could see little into the pitch darkness even though the trees were bereft of foliage at this time of year. The darkness promised untold terrors, were it not for the roaring fire that kept the beasts at bay. Wolves howled in the distance; bears rustled in the undergrowth not far inside the skeletal forest. It was close to midwinter, and in three days, it would be the midwinter festival when the sun would be at the lowest in the sky, and the night would stretch into the next day—according to the ancient knowledge of our revered shaman.

My thoughts, ever wandering, drifted back to the end of the summer past, when our son had been gored by the boar sow protecting her litter. It had been a tragedy that had destroyed our lives. Ab was always a bit mischievous, but this time his impishness had led him to depart this life prematurely. When news was brought to his mother of the tragedy, she tore at her hair and her clothes, wailing so loudly that the next world would be forced to acknowledge her grief. I, being the man and father, did what was expected of me and called the warriors together. We raced into the forest to find the sow, and soon had our revenge for my son's death—leaving the sow's litter motherless. Only later did I regret the action. Was the sow not doing what came to her naturally? Had my child been threatened—would I have reacted any differently? We live in brutal times—but then we are only the reflection of the harshness of our environment.

Within a month, the grief had also taken my wife, for she simply refused to accept that her little Ab was no longer with her. One afternoon, at autumn's end, she was found in the forest with the remnants of a poison mushroom still in her lap, sitting, leaning against a thick oak tree. The grief on her face was so evident that no one thought badly of her for deserting her bonded mate. It took an effort of supreme will for me not to go to pieces. I was the chief's son—the next chief in waiting.

We dug the pit, and cremated my poor son with due ceremony—and then we did the same for my wife—in the same trench. Staying behind—staying sane, was the hardest part. After we had gathered the ashes and placed them in the urns, I escaped deep into the forest and hunted for the entire month—at least I thought that was my intention. Eventually, worried at my absence, my father sent some warriors into the forest to find me—I was half-mad and starving when they discovered my whereabouts. My heart was not in the hunt. I would not have lasted another week.

'Nam…Nam! Come now! Time to rise.' The bellowing voice of the shaman rang in my ears. I shook myself beneath the sheepskin and opened my eyes. Dawn was well into her stride, and I could smell the fresh porridge being made ready on the fire. I threw off the sheepskin blanket and sat up, rubbing my eyes. The thick woollen trousers and feet wraps had kept me warm next to the fire. Rank has its privileges. I tied my belt and pulled on my sheepskin boots, then jumped to my feet, running on the spot for a short while, limbering up.

We had eight warriors in our party and twelve other members of my tribe carrying clay urns to the wood henge with the remains of their dear departed—twenty-two in all. After the morning meal, we set off in our ritual procession; the shaman in the lead, four warriors flanking both sides and the urn carriers following the shaman. Each was carrying their personal bundle over their shoulders. I, being the chief's son, was immediately behind the shaman, clutching a clay urn reverently in each hand. Thus, we had begun the journey, and thus we would arrive.

'Have heart my children,' boomed the shaman. 'We should see the white earthworks by this afternoon and be at the enclosure by nightfall.'

At this, our footsteps became lighter; knowing that the journey's closing stages were not far ahead. We were gradually joining with others making the same passage, all led by their shamans, many more numerous than our little band. Death had been busy this year. A mood of expectation and excitement descended on our group, and a quickening of our steps propelled us towards journeys end. By midmorning, we could see the final hill; southwards in the distance where the landscape appeared more open, and where the forest had been cleared.

When we penetrated the last hill, we came across many more processions converging on the imposing white earthworks from all directions. There were parades in front of us—and many more behind, travelling on a wide flint roadway. This mass of humanity, all reverently merging into the mightiest gathering I had ever witnessed anywhere or any time. The vast, potent, white earthworks, spanned a dry valley—and to my eyes, almost filled it. It was said to be nine hundred cubits in diameter. Those white imposing ramparts were twice the size of a tall man, and sixty cubits long. It was the holiest fastness in all the surrounding landscape—and it promised a grand celebration of midwinter, with festivities going on for days. Many would arrive purely for the festivities.

What I had to keep in mind, was the vital reason I was going to the impermanent dead wood henge—to the portal of the dead. It was to enable my two urns to be scattered in the moving river of life so that the spirits of my dear wife and son could journey to the henge of stones half a league away, where they would find permanent rest along with the other spirits of our ancestors.

Soon we were approaching the North West entranceway, where the gate was flanked by many warriors, and by two imposing upright carved totem poles—guardians of the sacred henge. Once through the gate, the internal ditch structure—over twelve cubits deep and fourteen cubits wide—made for a formidable defence, if it was ever necessary. We kept moving further into the enclosure, passing the dead wood on our left. Many upright trees had been stripped of their bark and planted in two massive concentric circles to signify the impermanence of life. It really did look like a wood subject to decay and it clearly denoted the land of the living, whereas the permanent and unchanging granite at the henge of stones embodied the world of the ancestors.

We moved in awe through the enclosure towards the southeast exit. Our warriors were to remain in the main enclosure, whilst we urn carriers, led by our shaman, continued to the enormous covered wood henge right outside the main enclosure. What my eyes befell was a roof so large—such that I had never seen in my wildest dreams. I walked through the entrance in the embankment with my sight raised upwards in amazement—and I only stopped when I bumped into the shaman, who had stopped in front of me. He had found a spot near the exit and we all settled down in a circle, unfurling our bundles on the ground, sitting cross-legged on them and placing our urns in front of us. The shaman sat in the centre and began intoning a prayer to our tribal ancestors, praising the gods for our safe arrival.

Thus, it would be throughout the rest of the night under the enormous roof, fasting and meditating, saying our final farewells to our dearly departed, while our tribal shaman officiated and observed. For me, this was the hardest part—the saying of the final farewell. This was the time to let go of my dear Lin, and my sweet son, Ab, whose life had been so short. He would never see his twelfth summer. I had to do it convincingly—meaning I had to believe it—I mean really believe it. If I held back any reservations about letting them go, then their spirits would not be able to cross over, and it would be my fault. I struggled with myself all night, and only when I felt the dawn nearing, did I suddenly release them to the other side. It occurred to me in a flash of insight, that if I really cared for them, really loved them, then as a final act of love, I should let them go to join with our ancestors. I felt a huge relief when this happened—a lifting of the great burden inside me that had weighed me down ever since it had happened.

When the shaman rose and beckoned us all to follow, I noticed many had had the same release as I. There was lightness in their step that had evaded them on the journey here. Just before dawn, we left the roofed wood henge and returned to the main enclosure where many roasting beasts were turning on spits over many wood fires at the outer edges of the dead wood. Here we faced east and watched the rising winter sun bringing in the New Year. All the shamans cried out in unison welcoming in the New Year and then we all roared our welcome in such a mighty shout, as to make it plain to the old year, that its time was over—banishing it into oblivion forever.

There then came, at least for me, the most important part of my journey, the solemn procession out of the south eastern exit, along the sacred causeway, made of compacted chalk, down to the eternal river which led to the permanent abode of our ancestors at the henge of stone half a league further south. We slowly gathered in one enormous spectacular parade following our shamans and solemnly marched down two hundred cubits to the water's edge. There, each urn in turn was uncovered and reverently emptied into the bosom of our eternal mother, the blessed goddess of nature, so the remains of the living could make their journey to the land of the dead. All the time our shaman deeply intoning, pleading chants of acceptance to our ancestors—so that they would not turn these fresh spirits away.

Then it was back to the main ditch-enclosed earthworks where the festivities began. Honey fed pig—which sweetened their meat—were roasting next to deer, making the stomachs of those who had fasted, rumble. These were the main meats. There were also many large pots of gruel being stirred on mighty fires. These were to be seen in great profusion. Although it was the middle of winter, the enclosure managed to stave off most of the wind and the numerous fires gave a feeling of warmth. Neighbouring fires had cattle and bear rotating over them, but there weren't many of these and had large groups of people surrounding them. Flutes and drums produced the music while those that could, danced in an exaggerated manner. There were also many jugs of fermented grain being emptied, with consequent rowdiness accompanying that particular activity.

With the lifting of the burden from me in the wood henge, I made merry and joined in with the rest of my companions. For the first time in a long time, I felt that I would survive, and be able to face the future. When midsummer came, I promised myself I would make a special journey to the henge of stones, bearing gifts for my departed wife and son. It gave me comfort knowing they were now at one, residing with their ancestors.

With acknowledgement to Professor Mike Parker Pearson's theory.

Gamblers Unanimous

"**W**arning! Warning!" The proximity speaker somewhere above his head yelled. "The Imperial Kingdom of Monaco," it announced, "welcomes careful drivers."

A huge screen above his head blared at him, "No unlicensed smoking. No unlicensed drug taking. No unlicensed gambling," and "Absolutely No Littering."

The beaming face of his Imperial Majesty, Maharishi Mahesh Yogi IV thanked visitors for politely conforming to his wishes. "Have a nice visit!"

Gusov sat in the queue, his ears ringing from the assault, and fumed. The morning sun warmed his face. *All the way from Siberia and snagged here by...by...by these Euro-*

bureaucrats. The "itch" was getting at him. *So close yet...so far.*

'*Get a move on!*' he yelled in frustration at the bearded face on the huge screen.

That caught the attention of the nearest *gendarme*. He scowled at Gusov and sauntered over aggressively to the bright red Merc convertible.

'Monsieur has perhaps something to say, *n'est-pas?*'

Gusov wasn't going to be put off. 'I'm here on serious business. What's the delay?'

The *gendarme* smiled icily and took in the black evening suit, black bow tie nestling on a white shirt. 'I don't need to ask where *you're* going.' There was scorn in that comment. 'Can I see your Health Insurance?'

In a double-take, Gusov knew if he didn't behave, the long arm of the Law would thwart him in the urgent task of scratching his itch. He decided to play it straight. He reached into the glove compartment and pulled out a stack of plastic cards held by a clip—handed the lot to the *gendarme*. He tried to grin.

Without lifting the scowl, the law took them and slowly began to sift each of the cards.

'Health Insurance...Drug Insurance...Drinking Insurance...Gambling Licence.' The *gendarme* ticked off each card in a droning voice. 'I see Monsieur's come prepared. Even Debit and Credit cards, eh!'

'Officer, can't we move any faster?' The itch was getting worse.

'If Monsieur wants to get to Monte-Carlo, Monsieur will *curb* his impatience—*and* his tongue!' The *gendarme* handed the stack of plastic back.

There it was. The gruff voice of authority. Always the same. Do this! Don't do that! All the time he was losing precious moments—moments he could be scratching the itch. Resignedly, Gusov kept his mouth shut and returned the cards to the glove compartment.

It took him another half hour to clear the border controls. Schengen, everywhere else in the EU—except in Monaco. *It wasn't even a real country,* he sneered to himself.

Ever since the Grimaldi family sold out to the Transcendental Meditation movement and moved to the Ascension Islands—the border controls had become ferocious. Health Insurance to contain SIDA (AIDS to the Anglos.) Drinking Insurance to mitigate damage by over indulgence. Drug Insurance to compensate for outrageous behaviour. Gambling Licence to prevent bankrupts and defaulters sneaking through. And the State got all that nice revenue from the sureties.

So that's what they dream up in TM, thought Gusov with spite. Nice number if you can get away with it oh "Great Sage"—and a Government always could.

Monaco, situated on an escarpment at the base of the Maritime Alps along the French Riviera between Nice and the Italian border, was the centre of TM's gambling empire—and home to Gamblers Unanimous. The latter was a creation by the industry to counter the pervasive influence of Gamblers Anonymous. The former invited committed gamblers to any number of Casinos worldwide—at a discount—so they could indulge in their passion.

Gusov had always wanted to "*do*" Europe and the GU had given him the opportunity and excuse to put his career on hold—onto a sabbatical. He continued down the steep incline of the "the rock" along the N98 into Monaco proper.

Destination—undoubtedly Monte Carlo. He turned onto the boulevard du Jardin Exotique and followed the winding road down towards the sea. On some curves, the glint shining off the azure blue water, blinded him, forcing him to find his sunglasses. Intermittently along the boulevard, sitting atop tall poles, cloud shaped neon signs with "MT travaux," told the travellers—TM works.

Bloody brainwashing, muttered Gusov.

He turned right onto the boulevard de Suisse and ended up in Beaumarchaise Square—then swung a right onto the avenue d'Ostende and a left into avenue de Monte Carlo. Finally he reached the place du Casino—his destination.

Gusov drove the red Merc up to the north side steps and jumped out, adrenalin pumping. A uniform parked his car. Gusov's long legs took the shallow steps two at a time and passed through the large glass doors, held open by more uniforms. The voluminous vestibule was adorned with evergreens. He negligently eyed the entrance of the grand-opera ahead—but greedily drank in the gaming-room to the left. To the right was the American Room, full of one arm bandits. Not for him!

Two uniforms guarded the doors to the left and, as he approached, he expected them to hold the door open for him, instead they barred the entrance.

'No one is admitted to the gaming-rooms without a ticket,' said the uniform barring the entranceway. He pointed to a bureau close by.

Gusov was almost tempted to push past—almost—but *that* route led to trouble. He was well built and reckoned he could take them, but as quickly as he flared, he subsided and approached the ticket-seller.

'What is your nationality?' the uniform asked in French.

'Russian,' replied Gusov in English, flourishing his plastic GU card at the man.

The uniform peered at the weather beaten blond man in the photograph. 'Thank you,' the man's manner changed on seeing the card. He handed Gusov a ticket and said, 'Monsieur, please enjoy your game.'

The final hurdle—and…Gusov headed back to the entrance of the gaming-room and now the doors were held open for him whilst the uniforms relieved him of the damned ticket. Through the swing doors, into a vast hall supported by massive pillars. Brilliant colours, lots of mirrors—not unlike Versailles. A hubbub of voices mingled with the click-clicks of chips being laid—or raked in. Seven huge green gaming tables—with three croupiers and an inspector to each table.

Bankers called out above the noise, "*Messieurs, faites vos jeux!*" Sweet music to Gusov's ears.

Now for that itch. He went to the booth to get some chips—showed his GU card to get the discount, and then with his hoard he turned to the nearest table. The crowd was hot, excited—the tension palpable, hovering. Gusov revelled in it—drank it up as though nectar. His adrenaline was up. He fingered his chips—oh the itch…almost. He jostled others to get nearer the action. Then he looked hungrily on the green *tableau*, the thirty six alternate red and gold numbers. He reached out and placed a hundred Euro chip on the end of the 33 line, a *transversal*, covering all three numbers, 33, 32, and 31. The odds were 11-1. He always liked to start with a "street." All gamblers are superstitious, and Gusov was no exception.

Le tourneur spun the core, and sent the ivory ball around the static part in the opposite direction, under the lip overhanging the edge of the wheel. Gusov followed the ball, eyes going round in their sockets. As the little white ball slowed, it fell across the sloping lip, hitting small inset metal buffers, then shot towards the spinning wheel. It reached the wheel and hit a fret, bouncing off—and—here it came…with a few more bounces, it landed in a numbered pocket……fourteen black.

Gusov' heart missed a beat—then flattened—as he realised he'd lost. It made him angry at the table. He knew the house always had a 2.7% advantage on the numbers—even so. His advantage was—he had a system. That was the difference between him and the other suckers. He'd revised the "Martingale System," with an addition. He was going to win— this time. He'd saved and scraped, sold the family summer house for this trip. He told his wife he was going to a conference in London. He knew she didn't believe him. It hadn't been the first time the "itch" had grabbed him— possessed him.

She'd told him, "If you want to ruin your life—go ahead, but don't expect me here when you come back— penniless."

Still—he went. It's not as if he'd had any choice. He had to get it out of him—so he could continue with his life. He knew deep down he was caught in an adrenaline trap, but like any addiction, his conscious mind refused to acknowledge the destructive nature of the obsession. Denial had set in. Sneaky slippery denial—able to produce any excuse that would enable him to pursue the itch. He'd have to hit rock bottom before he could admit its destructive power.

For the moment—he had to scratch.

"*Messieurs, faites vos jeux!*" the Banker intoned.

He tried *à cheval* next, the "split." Another two hundred Euro chips between 32 and 33. The odds, 17-1, but the house advantage was the same as on a single number. Again the core was spun and the ivory ball sent in the opposite direction. He held his breath——and the ball came down on......23 red.

"*Messieurs, faites vos jeux!*" as the croupiers raked in the chips.

Again he got angry. Determined—he tried a *carré,* to change his luck—a "square." He put down four hundred Euro chips in the centre of four squares, in the middle of the intersection of 33, 34, 35, and 36. The odds were 8-1 but the chances *had* to be greater of winning.

The ball went round—his eyes followed, mesmerised—and it landed in......four black. He fumed. He had to get to the top of the table, nearer the wheel. The three seats in the middle were reserved for heavy betters.

He backed away from the table, through the pressing crowd. Then stood for a moment looking over their shoulders—and realised he was extremely thirsty. Waiters were circulating with full champagne glasses. He grabbed one as a waiter passed nearby.

He ambled over to where a dark haired woman was scribbling on a piece of paper. An off-shoulder glittering silver gown draped her curves. She stared at the spinning wheel, and then scrawled with her pen. The *permanence* was encouraged by the casino to record winning numbers and make calculations. The house knew it was a futile enterprise.

She'd noticed his approach from the corner of her eye.

He stopped at her left elbow, hoping to catch what she was writing. She shifted her position, blocking his view. Then she stopped—and eyed him. Hazel green eyes scrutinised his weather beaten features.

'Yank?' she ventured.

'Ruski,' he corrected.

'Hmm!' she mused. 'Be a darling, get me a drink.'

He shrugged and caught a waiter's attention. He lifted a glass from the silver tray and handed it to her.

'Here you are dear. Can I be nosy? What're scribbling?' His curiosity got the better of him.

'Oh, just a few calculations.' She still held the paper away from him. 'What do you do—you know—in Ruski land.'

"*Messieurs, faites vos jeux!*" he heard the Banker's cry.

'I teach—snotty nosed kids.' He looked at the wheel—getting anxious. 'Byzantine literature—Irkutsk University.' His attention was wandering back to the table. 'Igor Gusov,' he half introduced himself.

'Laura Lowry—Physics—McGill University, Montreal,' she responded. She furrowed her brow—then showed him the paper.

He looked at a series of integral calculations and shook his head. 'Can't make head or tail of that,' he gestured with his empty glass.

She lowered her voice, 'It's the only way to get an advantage in this game,' she nodded at the roulette wheel. 'The spin of the ball and wheel have to obey the basic laws of physics. No point in working the odds in roulette—they don't stack. You got to pick a fixed point and record when the ball and wheel pass that fixed point. Then you can roughly predict the quarter the ball will land in.'

'But why not use a system?' Gusov was getting uncomfortable. 'You know—even money bets, doubling up if you lose.' He wasn't going to divulge his variation.

'Because all progressive roulette systems are based on the gamblers' fallacy, sometimes called "the doctrine of the maturity of chances." If I'm losing you, say so…' She stopped.

'Err! No! Go on,' he wasn't sure what she was getting at, but wouldn't admit it.

'Also called the "Monte Carlo fallacy." Appropriate here, don't you think?' she swept her hazel eyes around the room. 'It falsely assumes that each spin of the ball isn't independent of the others and that a series of spins will be balanced in the short run by the law of averages. That's true in the long run—at infinity. In the short term you're looking at a string of unconnected spins. The ball and wheel have no way of storing what the last number was, and so, what the last number was, cannot have any effect on the outcome of the next spin. Do you see?'

She waited for him to see the light. All she saw in his eyes was discomfort.

'Each spin is independent of the previous spin,' she continued, 'so there can't be any system—except one governed by the laws of physics.'

He was gazing at the table and she knew she'd lost him. Silently she slipped round him—and was gone. She knew his type. She knew his "system" was based on a fallacy; and that casino operators were happy to encourage the use of such systems—and to exploit any gambler's neglect of the strict rules of probability and independent plays. As such, he was entirely beyond her help.

Gusov wasn't even aware she'd gone. His itch held him in its grip. Compulsively, he moved closer to the wheel.

"*Messieurs, faites vos jeux!*"

Over the next twenty hours, Gusov used his system, and doubled up his bet each time. At the end—he'd lost a hundred thousand Euros. He couldn't believe his bad luck. His bloody "system" *had* to work. He was sure of it. He'd forgotten the Canadian woman—pushing her out of his mind—with a little help from denial. He was exhausted. Worse—his money was exhausted.

He went to the chip booth.

'I need some credit,' he informed the uniform bluntly. He laid the GU card on the desk and tapped the counter nervously with his right hand fingers.

'And how much would Monsieur wish to borrow?' the uniform inquired.

Gusov almost demanded, 'A hundred thousand Euros.'

The uniform tapped the computer and brought Gusov's file up. 'This is over your limit, Monsieur.'

'I don't bloody care—I need it.' Gusov was desperate.

'I see Monsieur has sold one house—and you will now lose the other house if you continue,' the uniform told him. 'You will be destitute!'

'I don't care, I tell you—I must have the money.'

'Very well, Monsieur, but that is the last advance I can give you. I will not be able to help you anymore.' The uniform had seen it all before and would be immune to further pleas. The uniform got Gusov to sign away his last house, leaving him homeless, and advanced him the hundred thousand Euros in chips.

Gusov with his modified "Martingale System," lost the hundred thousand Euros in six hours. He just wouldn't accept his system didn't work.

A psychiatrist in Irkutsk told him he'd got a disorder of impulse control. He was in with the shrink as the final ultimatum from his wife. See the psychiatrist or she would leave. So he'd given way. The psychiatrist told him gamblers usually had a personality disorder—known as an Obsessive Compulsive Disorder. It was a failure to resist desires, impulses, or temptations—the gambler insisted on carrying out an act that was harmful, both to the individual and to others; to their nearest and dearest. The gambler experienced a feeling of tension before indulging in the act, and then a feeling of release tinged with gratification upon completing it. His behaviour was diagnosed as pathological gambling. For Gusov, his course of action was obvious and simple—he stopped seeing the psychiatrist.

Back at the booth, he demanded more money. He wanted two hundred thousand Euros this time. He'd do anything, sign anything, as long as they gave him the money.

'But I told Monsieur last time—there was no more advance.'

That just made Gusov mad. He threw a tantrum, thumping the desk, shouting, 'I don't care—I want more money.'

Two burly uniforms grabbed him by the arms and frog-marched him to the exit. They pushed him down the steps none too gently.

'*Where's my car?*' he screamed back at them.

'Monsieur lost that at the tables,' the larger of the two informs threw at him.

To add insult to injury, the loud siren of a *gendarme's* car came screeching into the plaza, halting at the bottom of the stone staircase. Two *gendarmes* jumped out and advanced on Gusov.

'I'm glad you're here,' he told them. 'They've stolen my car.'

The *gendarmes* ignored his comments and grabbed him—snapping handcuffs on his wrists. Gusov was outraged—

and struggled. Big mistake. They clubbed him, and threw him into the back of the car none too gently. In the process, he lost his shirt, when he kneed one of the *gendarmes* in the crutch. The *gendarme* tore Gusov's shirt off with spite. Gusov kept kicking out, and so they took off his trousers, and tied his legs with them.

He was driven away from the gambling casino, through La Condamine, the business district on the west of the bay, with its natural harbour, sirens blaring his disgrace.

He arrived at the frontier, bruised and foaming. The *gendarmes* hauled Gusov out of the car, removed the restraints, and pushed him towards the barrier. At this point, Gusov was still reluctant to leave. As an encouragement, Gusov felt the *gendarme's* boot in the small of his back, and he was forcibly propelled back across the frontier, into France, dressed only in his underpants. He half turned to argue—stopped—shrugged, and resignedly threw a hand into the air—two fingers raised at the *gendarmes* as a farewell gesture. They hadn't even left him the shirt on his back.

The Envelope

Mr. Edward Eliot,
Apartment 3B12,
Level 15,
Lunar City,
The Moon

The last time I saw Harry, was a brief glimpse of his back, as he disappeared over the rim of our mining crater on Mercury. He was scrambling on all fours, trying to save his own skin—at my expense. He left me short of air, having grabbed the only spare air tank, and absconded. What a partner to have chosen for mining Hermian crystals with.

Later, I prayed the day would come for a chance to even the score. How I hated that spineless rat. Now, this treacherous son-of-a-bitch wanted my help—called me out of the blue after three years, as if nothing happened. How in all the stars did he track me to the Moon?

Harry asked for a meet, and like the sop he thought I was, I agreed. *You bet I'll meet him; I've got a present to give him.*

At short notice, for the evening, I've managed to hire an "oxygen thief." It's hiding in the room cupboard. I was in a typical hotel room, bland, beige cream colours. Plastic everywhere. It had to be made "thief" escape tight—and that cost a pretty penny in bribes. I've had to retreat into my protective transparent cocoon, just in case the "thief" decided to take us both.

There was a knock on the door; it opened cautiously. A head peered round the corner.

'Is it safe, Ned?'

'Safe for what?' I queried.

'Safe for me to come in.'

'Don't be so shy, Harry—come in, come in.'

'You're not gonna hit me?'

'Is there any reason why I should?'

'Look, I'm sorry about Mercury. I don't know what came over me. I panicked.'

'It's all in the past,' I assured him.

He walked into the room clutching an envelope in his left hand. It looked like a *paper envelope.* I mean we're talking *real paper* here. Harry looked prosperous. On his large overweight frame, hung an expensive elegant suit.

'You brought me a present?' I cast my eyes at the envelope.

'That's the reason I'm here,' he said nervously.

'Really?' My anger was rising; I couldn't wait any longer. I pressed the button in the palm of my right hand.

The beige cupboard door eased open, a fraction, the gossamer spectre of the "oxygen thief" came floating towards Harry. He really didn't know what hit him. The "thief" floated to his startled open mouth, and swiftly slid down his throat. I stood safely in my transparent cocoon, mesmerised by the performance.

Harry slid to the brown-carpeted floor, clutching his throat, gasping his last breath. As I saw his lights go out—I breathed a huge sigh of relief. Finally, I had tasted the cold dish of revenge. I really had no other alternative, not if I wanted to live with myself.

I saw the "thief" float over to the plastic container standing on the laminated sideboard. It floated inside; I pressed the second button, closing the container lid tight. That was the contract. It was now safe for me to come out of my cocoon. I degraded the cocoon, walked over to where Harry was lying, and picked up the envelope. It was addressed to me. *Real paper!* I couldn't get over it. How extravagant can you get?

I opened the flap gently, and pulled the sheet of paper from the envelope. I looked on one side, then the other. Nothing! I was holding a sheet of blank paper. What the hell was this?

Maybe I had terminated Harry too soon. Maybe I should have let him tell me what he wanted to give me. Maybe tomorrow the Sun won't shine. Maybe—maybe. I looked dumbfounded at the blank piece of paper. I couldn't imagine anyone *not* wanting to write something on *real* paper.

Then a thought struck me. *Maybe* it was trick paper? The type you read about in the old historical spy novels. *Maybe,* if it was heated, or soaked in some kind of chemical?

I had a friend in a forensic lab, here on the Moon. I was well overdue in contacting her, and this would be the ideal opportunity. If anyone could get to the bottom of this, she could. First, I had to get rid of Harry's body. Waiting in the bathroom for the job, I had readied the grey floating laundry bag. I put the sheet of paper back in the envelope and tucked it away in my inside jacket pocket. I pulled the floating laundry bag from the bathroom, and after a little effort, stuffed Harry's overweight body into it. The one-sixth gravity was a big help. Nice of Harry to look me up on the Moon!

More bribes, and Harry went into a recycling vat in an underground cavern, just outside Lunar City. Next, I gave Brenda a call—asked her to meet me in the Café just across from where she worked. She told me she was too busy, and I'd have to wait.

'Look Brenda,' I pleaded, 'I'm sorry. I've been busy myself. Don't get at me for *me* being busy?'

'It doesn't take much time just to give a friend a call. You lift your wrist, tell your wrist-vid the number; that's all there is to it.' She was angry; I could see her small livid face staring at me from the tiny screen of my wrist-vid. I'd forgotten how pretty she was.

'All right! I said I'm sorry. If you're too busy, forget it!' I was just about to order it to disconnect.

'Wait! Where do you want to meet?' Her voice had softened.

'In the French Café, across from you.'

'Half an hour,' and she disconnected.

Was that *in* half an hour, or was she going to give *me* half an hour? Women! You can't live with them, and you can't live without them. I was in the Café within half an hour, sitting, waiting. The Café was run by a real French couple. The smell of warm croissants and real coffee wafted throughout the authentic French decor.

'Hi Ned! Waiting long?'

I'd been preoccupied. Didn't even notice her come in.

'Hi Brenda! You're not still cross?' The turquoise jump suit she almost wore, caressed her body.

'Tell me you called, just to see me. Tell me you don't want to pick my brains.' She sat at my table, tossed her blonde hair back and ordered a *café complet,* followed by a *parfait.*

'Dearest Brenda! You know me better than I know myself. We should never have divorced.'

'Whose fault? You and your mining ventures. If you'd stayed with me, instead of gallivanting off with your mining buddies, maybe we'd still be together.'

'*Mea culpa.....mea culpa.....mea maxima culpa*,' I intoned.

'Don't! You know I don't like you taking the Mickey out of my beliefs. So, what brings you here?'

'To be honest with you...this,' I pulled the envelope from my pocket, and got the blank sheet of paper out for her. I handed it to her.

Ever the professional! She looked at it without touching it; got out a pair of disposable gloves; put them on, only then, took the sheet of paper. 'So?' she said, looking composed. 'What am I supposed to do with this?'

'Can you analyse it? Is there a message on it?'

'Should there be? Are you expecting there to be?'

'I got it from Harry.' I wasn't going into details.

'The bosom pal who left you to die on Mercury?'

'The same! I can't imagine him sending me a blank piece of paper. There must be something on it. Can you run some tests in your lab?'

'If this thing is impregnated with some kind of slow acting neurotoxin; I'm afraid you've already handled it. You sure you want to know?' Good old Brenda! Always the quick wit, the sharp tongue. I began to sweat. Others perspire; I sweat.

'Yes, I'm sure. I still think there's a hidden message in there somewhere. *Maybe* a map?' I had to get a grip on myself. Stay calm; think positive. 'Look sugar; you can name your price. All I want is the information on that piece of paper.'

I imagined her mental calculator whirring inside her head, notching up the cost. *Maybe* I should have gone to a quack dentist and had all my teeth extracted without anaesthetic; it would have been less painful.

'If I agree…to do this for you, you're going to owe me *big*. Agreed?'

'Okay—okay! The hook is tearing my mouth apart!' What else could I do? I was desperate. 'How long?'

'If I go back now, and start straight away…should have an answer for you in an hour. Soon enough?'

'You're a darling!'

She got up to leave.

Her parting shot, 'You've aged since I last saw you.'

She got in the last word, as always. I stayed and finished my *cappuccino*, pulling the strong liquid through the straw. In one-sixth gravity, every meal was an experience. Everything had to be done with care. That reminded me; I had better return the "oxygen thief" to its owner.

After returning the "thief," I sat and waited in the domed plaza with its artificial sunlight, surrounded by the genetically altered jungle, relaxing. It was exactly an hour later, Brenda called me. 'Do you want the bad news first, or the good news?'

'Let's have the bad.'

'There's *no* slow acting neurotoxins. But it's still going to cost you the most lavish meal I can think of at the Lunar Excelsior.' She smiled so innocently through the wrist-vid.

'*Ouch!* But I'll stick to the bargain,' I said. 'What's the good news?'

'What's appeared is the Last Will and Testament of one Harry Minter.'

'You're joking? You're pulling my leg?'

'You haven't heard the best part yet. This "Will" leaves everything to one Edward Eliot.'

'Now I know your toying with me. If his only possession was a case full of rattlesnakes, I might believe it.'

'Suit yourself. So you want me to throw the paper away?'

'Hold on! What I want is, to know *exactly* what's on the paper.'

'*I just told you!* You're an exasperating man; ex-husband or no ex-husband.'

'You mean, you were giving it to me straight?'

'You question it once more and I'm ordering a disconnect.'

But why'd he do that? Why leave his stuff to me?'

'The Will says something about compensating you for the wrong he did you on Mercury.'

'I'm sorry love; I'm having a hard time taking this in.'

'Meet me in the Café.' That sounded more like an order than a suggestion.

When we'd settled at a table and ordered two *cappuccinos,* she handed me the letter.

'I'm sorry I questioned your competence.' I was trying to make amends.

I stared at the piece of paper; horrified. I'd just killed the son-of-a-bitch—fully justified in doing so, in my opinion. But here he is, giving me everything he owned. He had a pang of conscience? It just didn't fit his character.

It then dawned on me—I was never going to find out what he'd left me. Harry had vanished, as far as officialdom was concerned. They didn't know yet, but that's how it would come out. No Harry, no legacy! I couldn't admit I was the last one to see him alive. I stared again at the piece of paper.

Last Will and Testament

This is the last will and testament of Harry Minter of Io Biosphere, Jupiter, which I make this 12th day of January, 2389 and whereby I revoke all previous wills and testamentary dispositions.

1. I hereby appoint Bulgarov & Belinger of Lunar City to be the executors of this my will.

2. I give all my property real and personal to Edward Eliot, my former partner, in compensation for the wrong I did him on Mercury.

Signed by the testator in the presence of us both present at the same time who,

at his request, in his presence   Harry Minter
and in the presence of each   *Signature of*
other have hereunto set our   *Testator;*
names as witnesses.   *Harry Minter*

William Jones *William Jones* of Io Biosphere, Jupiter, Dome Technician.

Henry Morgan *Henry Morgan* of Io Biosphere, Jupiter, EVA Charge Hand.

There was no way of presenting myself to Bulgarov & Belinger, saying, "I've got Harry Minter's Last Will and Testament. What have you got for me?" Not without implicating myself in his disappearance. I couldn't even tell

Brenda; not without making her an accessory after the fact. So now what?

'Brenda! Is there any way for me to find out what his estate is? I mean, what Harry left me?' I was clutching at straws.

'Why don't you go and raid the executor's offices?'

'You joking, right?'

'You could try hacking into their computer system.'

'Now, that's an idea.'

'Ned! You wouldn't? You know how severe the penalties are for that sort of thing?'

'I know. No, I wouldn't do that.' *Like hell I wouldn't. It's the best goddamned idea dear Brenda has come up with.*

'Look! I've to get back to work. By the way; it was simple invisible ink.'

'What was?'

'On the paper!'

'Oh...yeah...thanks.'

'I'm holding you to that meal. Don't forget!'

'Yeah...yeah...right.'

'Ned! You're off on a tangent. You're not *listening* to me.'

'Course I am honey! It's just...I'm thinking. Run along now, and I'll call you for that meal—real soon...I promise.'

She looked at me with those sad eyes of hers; got up and walked out of the Café without a backward glance, across the brightly lit walkway back to her lab. I had to get back to my place and start hacking. If there were too many encryption gates, too many fancy passwords, I knew a friend who was an expert at getting round that sort of thing. First, I'd have a go myself.

Back below, on Level 15, where my apartment was, I settled at my console and began by logging onto the Mining Network, then going through the Lunar Maintenance Network. I linked into the Meton Crater Space facility and came back to Lunar City from there. I'd done that a number of times before. I was trying to lay a false trail. Only then did I go for the Legal Network. It didn't take long to bypass all the low-grade encryption gates. I was using a neat algorithm, an encryption-busting programme to decipher the simple passwords people still insisted on using. Then I went straight for Bulgarov & Belinger's access point. Amazingly, that's where I got stuck.

No matter what I tried, I just couldn't get past their encryption. What had they got to hide? I was furious. Some pip-squeak lawyer's firm had me stumped. Loath as I was to involve more people in this thing; it seemed I'd have to.

I looked around the apartment, soothing pastel colours; tranquillity. I ordered a meal; something spicy, a Dahi Wala Gosht with Bombay Duck, it arrived down the tube. I ate, listened to some Bach. Finally, I stopped dithering and went round to Drago. His voice alarm announced: "I'm in; please wait."

When the door slid open, he was sitting on the liquid silicone sofa. 'Hi Drago. Ehm! You got a minute?'

'Hi! Sure, come in.'

'I need a favour.'

'Where...and what's in it for me?'

He knew exactly why I'd come. Like any professional, he wanted to know how much he could take me for.

'It's some lawyer's office. I need to look at a document they've got.'

'Sure, no sweat! Take a pew.'

I eased into the indicated liquid silicone armchair. 'I had a go at hacking into the lawyers myself; only I got stuck at their gates. They've got something they don't want others to access.'

'Lawyers, huh! You've just upped the price; I hope you realise.'

'Whatever,' I said glibly.

'Right! Let's have a go,' and we both sauntered over to his terminal.

He was at the encryption gates of the secretive lawyers within a minute. Then he hit the same problem I had. From a biochip, he uploaded a neural encryption buster. It took him another five minutes to get past the lawyers gates. There were five encrypted serial gates, all interlinked, which is why I failed. There's no stopping the experienced hacker. In the four hundred years since computers became ubiquitous; hackers challenged the most sophisticated fail-safe gates the software community had been able to come up with. Each time, by sheer persistence, they'd overcome the protection designed to keep them out. Every time the protection moved forward; so did the hackers.

I was watching a master at work. He was into the office files, swiftly rejecting the mundane everyday files. He got into the private personal files of Belinger; *oohed* and *ahhd* over them, deleting some, amending others. I got the impression he didn't exactly like lawyers.

'Nothing in Belinger's files about your friend Harry.'

'What about Bulgarov?'

'I'm trying him next......look at this! He's up to his neck in insider dealing with the bonanza on Pluto. Wait...his diary has your friend visiting him a couple of times. He's got a note about Harry—it says "Harry's not to be trusted," then adds, "...he's clever."'

'He's got that right! I can vouch for it.'

'There's a cross reference to another file. Where the hell is it?' He began to swear gently under his breath. 'Ahh! Here it is—well I never! Your Harry is quite a lad. In three years of heavy drug dealing, he's amassed a fortune. There's a list of his assets......with ticks and crosses by them. Some have "yes" and others have "no" by the items. I imagine the "yes" means Bulgarov'll let you have the items, and the "no" means he's gonna keep whatever it is for himself. My guess is; this lawyer is going to shaft you, but good.'

'Let me see,' I looked closer. 'You're right! Can you download this file?'

'No problem! This seems to be what you're after. There's a Safe Deposit box in the Bank on Jupiter. There's a "no" by the side of it. He's bought a lot of stock in the Company behind the Pluto bonanza. That's in the Safe Deposit box. A "no" against that underlined. A condo on Mars. There's a "yes" against that one. There's even a SpaceCruiser standing at Lunar Spaceport. A "yes" against that. Oh...and a full tank of oxygen. A "yes" underlined against that.'

My eyes and brain were overloaded. I could have been a wealthy man, if *only* I'd waited.

'Say Ned. What's all this about?'

I shrugged. 'Don't ask. You don't want to know. Take my word for it.'

'Your name's in there! There's a note against it saying, "Use force if necessary." That probably means if you present the Will, and if you don't like what he gives you, *and* you try and make a fuss; he's prepared to set some heavies onto you.'

'It's no longer a problem: believe me. I wish it was!'

'Well okay! Here's the downloaded file you wanted,' he handed me the optical data cube. 'If there's nothing else? I'll work out how much you owe me, and I'll let you know next week.'

I stood up and headed for the slide door. Out in the brightly lit corridor a phrase kept thumping around in my head like pair of heavy gravity boots.

"ACT IN HASTE—REPENT AT LEISURE"

Sasha Garrydeb

A Foul Desecration

Tiwantinsuya in 1532 (Inca Empire)
All Inca spellings herein are Quechuan.
A glossary is supplied at the end

I heard a loud cough behind me, followed by, 'Sir, the General has sent me to fetch you.' The messenger stood in the doorway looking apprehensive. A young lad, hardly old enough to be a soldier, but already with a hint of toughness behind that uneasy stare.

'Where is the General? And why this time of the morning?' I grumpily demanded, grabbing my feathered cloak, and plumed feathered officer's helmet. I rushed past him into the fresh air; then was forced to halt, squinting at the strong spring morning sunlight, before my eyes adjusted to the light.

'Follow me, Captain, Sir.'

The young lad led me up a flight of stairs onto the next platform, while I hastened to fasten my cloak and don my helmet. We continued ever higher into the stronghold of Saksaq Waman, the huge fortress built on a hill overlooking the city of Qusqu, the empire's capital—situated up high in a mountain valley. The heart of Qusqu was built to resemble a giant Puma, a sacred symbol to our people. The ancient fortress of Saksaq Waman was built on a large plateau above Qusqu, while the key citadel itself, resembling the cat's head, stood on some higher ground inside a north facing triple enclosure at the south eastern end of the plateau. The citadel's immense triple walls were fashioned to withstand *Pachakuti,* the Earthshaker, and resembled the jagged teeth of the Puma. From this area, runners ran relay messages to any of the four quarters of the immense empire controlled by the Sapa Inka.

After two more flights of stairs, up the spiky triple enclosure, we came out onto the top platform, where three tall towers stood amid other buildings on a large rectangular ground. The lad leading me, stopped at the massive entrance to the top platform, not daring to go any further. Now a member of the General's bodyguard, nicknamed "big-ears," in their red and white tunics, took over, and led me past golden statues of llamas, many exotic plants, and even butterflies decorating the elaborate gardens. We passed the two nearest round towers to our right, named *Pauqar Marqa* and *Saqllaq Marqa,* which were used to house soldiers of the garrison, composed only of privileged "big-ears," ordinary men not being allowed inside this citadel that housed both the arsenal and the temple to *Inti,* the sun God.

We were headed towards the third round tower furthest away, and largest of them all, called *Mayaq Marqa.* It was built over a clear lavish spring, fed by underground canals. The massive entrance to the royal tower was guarded by more "big-ears." The warrior leading me nodded to his colleagues, and we passed through the massive doorway, bypassing a circular stone staircase going upwards; instead we went down a short corridor at the end, leading into a small hall.

It was only natural that the commanders of the victorious armies, Generals Kizkiz and Challku-chima, had installed themselves in the Sapa Inka's royal residence in the absence of 'Ataw Wallpa, *our* Lord Inka, for whom we fought. Only now 'Ataw Wallpa's top general had arrived, and Cusi Yupanki had installed himself in the top hall above. Our Lord 'Ataw Wallpa was still up in Cajamarca waiting for news of the battles. He wasn't aware that the last battle had resulted in our total victory and the capture of his enemy, Washkar, Lord 'Ataw Wallpa's half-brother.

The enormous round tower we were in, contained rooms whose walls were all panelled with gold and silver, on which animals, birds, and plants figured plentifully in relief, as though they were many tapestries. It was here that the Sapa Inka lived when he was in the fortress. Also inside the *Mayaq Marqa,* in the enormous top hall, was the golden Temple of *Inti*, Lord of the Sun. That drew my attention like hot peppers—just being so close to the golden temple. *Inti* was represented by a giant golden disc, surrounded by golden rays hanging high on the wall, in the hall above me.

Inti

I would dearly have loved to see that. My "big ears" entered the small hall and I spied the two generals sitting in the middle of the hall on cushioned divans, deep in conversation.

The bodyguard tapped his mace on the floor and stated in a loud voice, '*Sir, Kuraka* Anka is here.' His broad shoulders and big-ears carried the confidence of the elite forces, well-practiced to talking with generals.

General Kizkiz looked at me, and beckoned me to approach. I stared wide-eyed at the gold and silver panelled walls as I neared the General. I could see the tiredness on both their faces. Months of battles had taken their toll, and the weariness was evident—it was the same with the rest of the army. All I could think of as I approached my General was—thank *Pacha Mama,* it's all over.

I halted and straightened my back out of respect—and waited.

'Well, *Captain* Anka, how are you? Have you and your men settled in to this peace?' The general look quizzically at me.

'Yes, Sir. The men thank you for their quarters; they're very comfortable—*and* the extra ration of *aqha* beer.' I shuffled my sandals on the stone floor.

'Don't get too settled. The man upstairs has given me a task. I'm passing it on to you. I need you to do a job for me. Are you ready for a short trek?' Both Generals stared at me to see my reaction.

'Give the order, and we will willingly obey.' I gave the standard response. How else could I react to General Cusi Yupanki's task? Clearly, he was "the man upstairs."

'Good!' General Kizkiz looked pleased. 'We have Washkar in custody, but we need to make sure his *royal cabal,* is destroyed—this is where you and your men come in. Take fifty of your best warriors up to the royal *sacred village* above Qusqu—locate the *mummy* of Thupa 'Inka Yupanki in the mortuary complex, and destroy it. That should put an end to the *royal cabal.* Without that Qhapaq, Washkar's finished forever. The people will soon forget him. General Cusi Yupanki has *dealt* with his family and their relatives, and now we need to destroy the cabal's *mummy.* Make sure all the *priest attendants* are dealt with—put them to the club. Burn the *mummy*; leave nothing that can be recognised.'

I stood, shocked, not knowing if he was serious. Cusi Yupanki had already ordered the killing of Washkar's entire family, wives, and children, while Washkar watched. All of them were strung up on poles along the highway leading out of the capital—left to rot as a future warning. Cusi Yupanki also ordered his *big ears* to kill the two infamous priests, and then scour Lower Qusqu to seek out and hunt down Thupa 'Inka Yupanki's *cabal.* They were to kill all they found, their priestesses, servants, and any others they found because they had supported Washkar during the civil war. *Now,* if I understood them, they wanted me to locate and burn Thupa 'Inka Yupanki's *mummy*—the ultimate desecration of a *cabal.* Without the *mummy,* Washkar's *cabal* would never be able to revive. My open mouth must have said it all.

The general stopped talking and looked at me keenly, a hint of anger in his eyes. 'You seem to be dumbfounded, Captain Anka. Are you capable of carrying out my order?'

I closed my mouth, pulled my shoulders even further back, 'I'm yours to command!' I barked in my best military fashion.

'Good! For a moment, I thought I might have to assign another commander to the task. I *trust* you Anka—so don't let me down.'

'No, Sir!'

'That will be all. Dismissed!'

I turned and marched out, my head buzzing with the idea of burning a sacred *mummy*, and damning myself in the eyes of *Inti*, the Sun God, *Wiraqocha* our creator and *Mother Earth*. I would carry out the order, but I resigned myself to eternal damnation. I'd best keep the mission entirely to myself until the last moment; otherwise, I would have a mutiny on my hands. My ordinary warrior is a good soldier, but a country bumpkin at heart. Superstitious to the core—but then that's why he obeys without question. They leave the thinking to me.

On my way out, I turned, and took one last look at the golden disc hanging high in the tower. I bowed in obeisance to *Apu-punchau*, another name for *Inti*, and begged forgiveness for what I was about to do. I quickly descended from the platforms and went to find Usqha, my second in command. He was bound to be helping to dispose of the *aqha* beer ration with some of his cronies.

I found Usqha outside the jagged teeth walls of the fortress. He was sitting with some others in a circle round the embers of a dying fire, in the far left hand corner of the large ceremonial plaza facing the entrance to the citadel, passing round the *aqha* gourd. The air, richly fragrant with the smell of spring, was more intoxicating for me than any *aqha* could ever be. With spring in the air, it was a pity there was this gruesome work to be done.

He saw me coming from the distance and waved. As I neared, he shouted, 'Hey Captain, come and have a drink with us.'

Usqha was a huge fellow, dark hair standing upright, held in place by oil, fat, and a large coloured headband, calculated to frighten any opposition which he faced. Standing above him, I scowled at him, 'Get your head together, Usqha—we've got work to do.' I sounded angrier than I should have done in the circumstances, but I knew it was just nerves from the mission I'd been given.

'Oh, no,' he moaned. 'Not now, Sir…. We've beaten them; four hard fought battles, victories at Cajamarca, Bombon, Ayacucho, and now Apurimac; we finished them. No more fighting, Captain, not *today*.'

'Usqha, listen to me carefully. I need you to round up fifty of our best warriors—sober them up if you have to, but we have to be on the road by midday. We'll be away for about three days max, so make sure everyone is provisioned for that length of time. Now get to it. Oh, and don't waste your breath arguing. Just *do* it.' I turned and went back to my quarters to collect what little gear I had, including my favourite bronze battle-axe.

When I arrived later at the front gate to the citadel, I found Usqha, looking more daunting than ever with his quilted cloth armour padding round his girth, lecturing to the rest of the squad in the middle of the plaza. They in turn were talking amongst themselves in whispers, leaning on their fearsome maces or clubs, shields leaning against their legs, speculating as to where they were going—at least that's what I assumed they were doing. It's what I would have done in their sandals. When Usqha spotted me, he brought the squad to attention. They looked a splendid sight in their wraparound multi-coloured skirts, the circular copper armour on their backs and chests, guard-protectors hanging down from the necks, helmets, clubs, and square wicker shields.

I stood in front of them, trying to look imposing with my plumed cane helmet and said, 'Right, listen up! The quicker we're off, the quicker we'll get back. It's not a long journey, and there may be some fighting, but nothing you can't handle. I'm confident you will do your duty. Now, let's get moving.' I nodded to Usqha, and took the lead. I heard some muttering from some of the warriors as they shouldered their weapons. We skirted the huge grey stone fortress walls and found the road leading up by the side of the fortifications towards the mountains, and all talk ceased as they needed to save themselves for the steep climb ahead. They all had their coca pouches at the ready.

The rhythm of our march brought my thoughts round to why General Cusi Yupanki seemed so intent on destroying Thupa 'Inka Yupanki's *mummy*. I could see the general's logic, but those had to be balanced against the sacrilegious consequences—were they worth it? Obviously, the general thought so. Had it anything to do with how Wayna Qhapaq had died seven years earlier? The stories that were told from that time were horrendous. It had been a time of terrible carnage—but not carried out by humans. Over a third of the Inca nation had succumbed to a horrible epidemic that had travelled rapidly from the east, simple by contact. Everyone knew the story.

It was a time of war, when Wayna Qhapaq was campaigning in the north of Chinchaysuyu against a minor uprising of the northern Caranqui tribe. Subsequently, he received word that the south-eastern Kollasuyu frontier had also been crossed by the Chiriguano on yet another raid against his frontier settlements, looking for bronze tools and ornaments made of precious metals. The Chiriguano were more of an irritant than an actual threat to the empire, but Wayna Qhapaq dispatched General Yaska, with a force large enough to drive them from the area, and orders to build forts along the frontier.

Wayna Qhapaq continued with his campaign to wipe out isolated pockets of Caranqui resistance, confident that the Chiriguano were contained by General Yaska down in Qusqu. However, messages soon arrived that told of a great epidemic that was ravaging Qusqu and the surrounding territory. It seems the Chiriguano had brought a highly infectious disease with them, and infected General Yaska's forces. People began to get confused, develop fevers, vomiting, body aches, and chills. Then a rash would appear a couple of days later, developing sores, and scabs. In about two weeks, the dead began to pile up in their tens of thousands.

I curbed my thoughts, and looked around to make sure all was well in the ranks. I noticed Usqha, who seemed to be busy with his own thoughts—a smile playing on his rugged face. All looked as if it was in order, so I continued with my own train of thoughts on the epidemic. Wayna Qhapaq marched his forces back down the highroad to Quito without delay, intending to speed on to Qusqu to deal with this disaster, but unfortunately he managed to arrive in Quito about the same time the epidemic did. Wayna Qhapaq reached Tumibamba before succumbing to the disease, and died there seven years ago, without naming his successor. At that point, his death set off a free-for-all fight over the royal tassel, and the *panaqas* cabals lined up behind their respective candidates.

According to custom, since Wayna Qhapaq's principal wife, *Koy-Ya*, was childless, he should have appointed one of his sons as his successor, as long as his chosen successor had "heavenly" approval from the augury of a sacrificed llama's lungs. The choice was from six of his sons: Ninan Cuyuchi, who was in Tumibamba with his father; 'Ataw Wallpa, who was in Quito; Washkar, who was in Qusqu; Thupa Wallpa, and

Pawllu Thupa Manqu 'Inka, whose mother belonged to 'Iñaqa, the royal cabal of Pachakuti 'Inka Yupanki.

My thoughts continued to mull over our recent history, while my sandals slapped the road automatically with military correctness. Our military road system covered the empire. We were on one of those roads right now, leading us straight to our destination. Anyway, back to Wayna Qhapaq—he was aware of his imminent death, and had asked the augurs to perform the ceremony to determine if he should name Ninan Cuyuchi as his successor. If the signs turned out to be unfavourable, then Washkar was next for the augury. Wayna Qhapaq died before the ritual was performed. Despite the lack of an augury, the two priests of the sun, Apo Challqo Yupanki and Rupaqa, notified Ninan Cuyuchi that he was to be the next ruler; however, Ninan Cuyuchi managed to contract the same disease as his father, and died not long after. However, again without an augury, the same priests took it upon themselves to name Washkar as the new emperor. The other sons naturally took umbrage and immediately sided either with 'Ataw Wallpa in Cajamarca, or Washkar in Qusqu, and the scene was set for civil war. Washkar himself had no more right to the royal tassel, than his half-brother, and Washkar felt the need to have an elaborate ceremony in Qusqu, where he had his mother, Rawa Oqllu, married to Wayna Qhapaq's *mummy,* in a bizarre attempt to legitimise himself and convert the Upper *hanan* cabal of Qusqu to his cause, but without consequent success.

Had 'Ataw Wallpa not been Wayna Qhapaq's favourite, the story might have been different. As it was, the union of the Emperor and his Cara princess, Toqtu Kuka, was a love match, and the son was much cherished by the people. Although not the legitimate heir, 'Ataw Wallpa felt he was the rightful heir to his father's throne, and he was not going to share it with anyone else—and the northern army was in agreement with him. More to the point, 'Ataw Wallpa had the backing of the 'Iñaqa *panaqa* of Hatun *ayllu* cabal—and so we won! So that was the end of the matter.

Now here I was, marching with my squad, all set to smash a social taboo in carrying out the task before us. I had a real worry, as I plodded up the road leading to the cemetery complex. What was to happen to me afterwards? How was it going to affect my standing in my own *village?* Would I be able to ever live it down? Would I be a hero, or would *people* point at me and whisper behind my back? *"There goes the desecrator of a mummy."*

What, with me deep in thought, I hadn't realised, but we'd been on the road for quite a while, and I suddenly thought it might be better for morale if I took it easy on the men, so I raised my hand. That halted the column, and I turned to Usqha, 'It's about time for a short rest, don't you think. Fall the men out for a break.'

Usqha looked at me quizzically, 'You're not getting soft, Sir, are you? We don't normally rest while there's daylight. Anyway, how far are we from our destination?'

I took Usqhar's arm, led him out of earshot of the others, and sat him down. I sat next to him. 'Listen carefully. It's time I let you in on the mission—and don't interrupt until I've finished. We're heading for the mortuary complex above Qusqu. When we get there, I need you to keep our men busy, and their attention off me. I've been ordered by General Kizkiz to do something that will revolt the men—and you. Even now, I'm not sure I ought to tell you... Oh, hell! I'm going to tell you anyway, and then you'll see why you've got to keep the men's eyes off me. I've been ordered to destroy Thupa 'Inka Yupanki's *mummy*—to burn it. You know what that means?

We'll have to kill all the *priest attendants*. If there's any guards, they will have to be dealt with. That's your job. Use our men to deal with the guards, any opposition, and the *priest attendants*. I'll do the dirty job of getting rid of Thupa 'Inka Yupanki's *mummy*. If there's any damnation to be incurred, then I'll incur it—not you or the men. That's it. Well, what do you say?'

Usqha looked horrified, and kept shaking his head. 'I can't believe what I've just heard.' Then he added as an afterthought, 'Sir.' He continued to sit there and shake his head with that horrified frown on his features.

'Is that all you have to say?' I asked. I expected him to refuse to continue—or something, but he just shook his head.

'What can I say? You drop this club on my head from nowhere. I'm shocked. Why do they want you to burn the *mummy*? I mean—did they give you a reason?'

'They want to make sure that Washkar's *royal cabal,* the Qhapaq *panaqa*, is eradicated for ever. Cusi Yupanki has killed all of his family—and most of the relatives. The *mummy* is his final act. It will mean the war is finished. Washkar will probably be killed—I'm still not sure why the general is keeping him alive. Maybe he's been ordered to take him to Lord 'Ataw Wallpa up in Cajamarca. Anyway, are you with me?' I looked down at my sandals, then into his face. He'd stopped shaking his head and now looked determined.

Usqha smiled, 'What do *you* think? Of course I'm with you. We've come a long way together, and you've been more than fair with me. But I think you're right. We should keep it from the men. I'll make sure to keep them busy, when we get to the mortuary complex. All I ask is you find a quiet room in the complex, and burn…you know what, out of sight. If they get a whiff of what's going on…well, I don't know what they'll do. I mean it's sacrilege.'

'Thanks, Usqha. I knew I could count on you. Right, I think now we'll push on. We should get there by dark. That'll give us the cover we need. I want to see if we can do this job as cleanly and as quickly as possible. Get them on their feet and get them moving.'

'Yes, Sir.'

Usqha busied himself with the squad, who got up with a few grumbles, and I led them on our way. We weren't on the road for very long before I saw a couple of warriors sitting by the roadside, in the far distance. I could have sworn they were waiting for us. Then I noticed a number of plumes of smoke coming from far to the right. I pointed them out to Usqha.

'What do you make of those?'

'Campfires by the look of them,' suggested Usqha.

'Yeah, but who are they?'

Usqha nodded ahead at the two waiting warriors, 'Maybe we're just about to find out.'

As our column neared the waiting warriors, they stood up, and I raised my hand to halt the men. 'Greetings,' I shouted at them. 'Are you waiting for us?'

I could see that one of them was an officer like me, and the other must be *his* second. The burly officer approached us, followed by his second.

'Hail, we come in peace.' He unsheathed his axe, and laid it at my feet. His second laid his mace beside the axe. 'We are the guardians of the mortuary complex, and I assume you're headed up there?' The leader asked.

'You're Washkar's men, aren't you?' I asked—just to hear it confirmed. Having it out in the open meant both parties knew where they stood.

'We were. We are now, loyal members of the new Sapa Inka, 'Ataw Wallpa, and we place ourselves under your command.' It was said with an open face, without any scheming glint in the officer's eye.

The question for me was—did I believe him? I nudged Usqha to pick up the weapons. 'Are those your men round their campfires out there?'

'Yes,' said the officer. 'They're good men, loyal to my leadership. They've agreed to what I'm doing—so they're yours to command.' He stood waiting to see how his words would affect me.

'In that case, I want you to collect your men and march them down to Saksaq Waman, and present yourself to the commander at the gate with my compliments. I'm called Anka, Captain Anka. Tell him I sent you. He'll fit you and your men into the rest of our army.' I gazed into his face, looking for deceit. I found none. 'Are your orders clear?'

'Yes, Sir. Saksaq Waman—Captain Anka sends his compliments. Thank you, Sir. May the *Mother Earth* speed your journey.' With that he turned and was about to walk away—but then remembered the weapons.

I nodded to Usqha to return the weapons to them, and he did so. I hoped I'd done the right thing. I didn't know how many of them there were, but there couldn't have been that many guarding the mortuary complex. Let the officers down in Saksaq Waman sort them out. At least I'd managed to get rid of the mortuary guards without a fight. I wondered who else was up there. It couldn't be that easy, surely?

'Right, let's get moving. See that dip in the road, up ahead a fair bit?' I asked Usqha, but I noticed he was distracted and taking little notice. '*Usqha!*' I raised my voice. 'Are you listening? What's up with you?'

'What puzzles me,' Usqha frowned, 'Is why Thupa 'Inka Yupanki's *mummy* is still up at the mortuary complex. How come Washkar didn't have it moved for protection? That's what I would have done.'

I could see that Usqha, faced with this enormous desecration, was trying to work the ins and outs of highborn tactics. He was using his brains, which is what I liked about Usqha, but I wished he'd listen. So I tried to explain. 'I think the defeat outside Qusqu was unexpected for Washkar, and I think he simply didn't have time to move the *mummy*. I mean, he must know the effect on his *royal cabal* if the *mummy* is taken—which suggests that our victory came as a surprise to his advisers, as well as Washkar.'

'Yeah, that's the direction my mind was leaning towards,' Usqha sighed. 'Still, I wish he had moved the *mummy,* then we wouldn't have to be doing this.'

'That's as may be—but back to what I was saying earlier. See that dip in the road, a fair bit up ahead?'

He nodded.

'Well, I think the mortuary complex is just past that. We'll stop just below the dip, and rest. The men can have some *jerky*, and then some coca leaves. That'll pep them up before we take the mortuary. Right?'

'Yes, Sir.'

As we did before every battle, we observed the ritual of the coca leaves. Every warrior carried a quantity in his pouch, and chewed them using their lime sticks. It gave the warriors that little extra bit of energy to fight—and this high in the mountains, it was not a luxury stimulant, but a necessity—we needed it. A little more marching, and we drew close to the dip in the road—then I halted the men and told them. 'A short rest and use the coca. Over that rise is the mortuary complex. Strictly follow Usqha's orders, is that clear?'

I sent a couple of scouts to spy out the complex. See what we were up against. We settled in the dip, and after a while, two of our men from the company came and sat before Usqha and me.

'May we have a word, Sir?' the older man asked.

'Yes, what about?' I was curious. It looked like a deputation. I'd seen both men before—they were *good* men. But—were they getting ready to mutiny? How did they get to know?

'We've been talking amongst ourselves,' said the younger of the two, 'And we've concluded we're here to torch the cemetery. That'll mean the *mummies* as well. We just thought we'd let you know we're with you, Sir.'

I was stunned. 'You know? How?'

'We worked it out, Sir,' said the older man. 'I mean, why else would we be coming up here? It had to be to torch the place. After all, it's Washkar's cemetery.'

'Well, thank you for the vote of confidence.' And I meant that. 'I must say, it's going to make the job a lot easier if you don't have a problem with what we're going to do.'

'Oh, we have a problem with it,' said the younger man, 'It's just that we're with you come what may. That's all.'

'Tell all the men, I'm extremely grateful. It makes me feel a lot better. Now re-join the rest.'

'Yes Sir!' Both spoke quietly in unison, then crept away.

'Well, what do you make of that,' I asked Usqha.

He was smiling in a smug way. 'That's *my* men! I keep telling you they're good lads. You can't get better. Warms my heart to hear them like that.' Usqha looked as proud as the father of a new-born.

My attention was with what was over the dip. 'Have they eaten? Time is getting on. The sun's almost set. Get them up, and let's see what we're facing.' I unhooked my battle-axe and felt the edge. I always check if it's sharp enough. A blunt axe can cost you your life. The two scouts I'd sent earlier, reported back that it seemed quiet up at the mortuary—maybe too quiet. Every warrior was now busy chewing coca leaves, getting hyped up, and ready for a fight.

Usqha raised his hand—and lowered it gently, telling the men to crouch, ready for an advance. I gave the signal to move and we slithered over the dip in the road. Ahead, to the left, stood the squat building of the mortuary complex, carved into the side of a rocky outcrop. The road veered towards the entrance, which seemed to be blocked with a wall—or was it just the dusk light, that was playing tricks with my eyes?

'Is that entrance blocked, or am I seeing things?' I asked Usqha.

'Yes, Sir. They've thrown a wall across the entrance. Well now we know!' Usqha sighed. 'We're going to have to fight our way in.'

'Whoever's in there, is expecting us.' I told Usqha. 'No point in crouching. Get the men into battle formation. Shields, maces, and advance.'

I got up and strode out in front to lead the charge, steadying the silver plate on my chest with my left hand, battle-axe at the ready in my right. Five rows of ten abreast. We moved forward towards the walled entrance. Two hundred paces from the entrance, and the defenders used slings. Stones began to rain down on us. My men used their shields to ward off the stones. I shouted loudly, '*Spears!*' and watched as my men loosed off their javelins at the defenders behind the wall. Then I yelled, '*Charge!*'

Some of our men went down, where the missiles had evaded the shields. The men in the rugged terrain off the road, on either side, fared better because of the uneven landscape. The defenders had a superior view of the road looking down. A hundred paces, and we made a mad dash for the wall. As we closed, I began to discern the defenders more clearly. Some seemed to hesitate as we came rushing at them, screaming our war cries. Then we were upon them, over the wall, wielding our maces, axes, bronze swords, and spears—pushing them back with our shields. Usqha was beside me parrying and thrusting with his spear, felling one after another—then stomping over their bodies to get to the next priest. The majority of the defenders couldn't take the pressure, breaking and running back down the narrow passageway, towards the inner recesses of the mortuary complex. I swung my axe repeatedly at the heads of *priest attendants*, some still holding their ground, and wanting to fight to the end. Fanatics, all of them. Blood spurted everywhere from huge gashes and wounds we inflicted. A big strapping fellow with a shiny baldhead fancied himself a match for our warriors, and was wielding a bronze sword with a zealous determination. I parried his sword on the head of my axe, while Usqha darted round my right side and thrust his spear into the big man's left side, twisting it inside him for more effect. Surprise burst onto the priests face, as he realised he was finished—yet he made one last mighty effort to press his sword onto my head—but then the life left him, and he crumpled onto the floor. The warrior behind me smashed his skull in with his mace, as he leaped over him, just in case.

Still breathing heavily from the effort, I forced my lips to mumble to Usqha as he turned to face me, 'I've never seen a bald priest before.' Usqha just shrugged.

Then, as suddenly as it had started, there were no more defenders to kill. The passageway was clear. I halted the men, fearing a trap. We waited for a hundred heartbeats, and then I crept forward cautiously. Then I beckoned to two of the men behind me, and sent them ahead to reconnoitre.

They returned shortly and one of them looked grim. 'You'd better come and see this, Sir. There's no danger.'

I followed the two scouts down the passageway, and as we turned the left corner, I came across a number of the priests with their throats cut. A few more steps, and one of the priests lay with a knife in his guts, both of his hands still round the handle. 'Seems this nasty rascal cut their throats, then killed himself. What do you think?'

'I'd have to agree with you, Sir,' replied the older of the warriors.

We went further, and the same story unfolded. Dead bodies everywhere! I winced at a thought that came to my mind. *How appropriate, after all—this is a mortuary complex.* 'What a waste,' I mused aloud, to no one in particular.

Usqha came briskly towards me. 'I see you've found the priests. It's the same story down the right tunnel. Everywhere we go—nothing but bodies. They've all committed suicide. At least it saves us a job, eh?' Usqha winked at me.

I nodded at him. 'Right! Let's find Thupa 'Inka Yupanki's *mummy,* and get this thing over with.'

We sent out warriors to search every nook and cranny of this royal mortuary complex, and all came back shaking their heads. There was no sign of Thupa 'Inka Yupanki's *mummy.*

'This can't be right,' I told Usqha. 'It's got to be here somewhere. They can't have moved it—although they should have done. Why waste their time defending this place if it isn't here?'

'There was one place that looked a little strange to me.' Usqha told me. 'It's where I would have expected the mummy to be—but to me, the place seems too small. Come and have a look.'

We went to the end of a tunnel, which came out into a large room. On the walls were the symbols of *Inti,* the sun. A large golden disc with a sombre face and rays radiating from it. On another wall was the smudged outline of a royal tassel—as if someone had been trying to rub it out. There was a cove where a royal mummy should have been, but it was empty.

'Look over here,' called Usqha. 'This wall seems not right, somehow. Look at the floor, its worn, as if there's a passage to another room. And the wall seems deliberately dirty, as if someone was trying to age it with muck and dust.'

I stared hard at the wall and began to see what Usqha meant. 'You there,' I ordered a warrior. 'Get some men and have them break this wall down.'

The man shouted down the tunnel, and soon men were hammering at the wall with their maces and clubs. The wall gave way, and began to crumble. Underneath the rubble, there were indications of fresh work and recent plastering. The hammering had broken through into another room—and there, placed reverently in a cove halfway up the wall, snuggled Thupa 'Inka Yupanki's *mummy*. It was unmistakable—a royal mummy, with fine robes and the royal tassel still on his head.

'Right, Usqha!' I said. My mind's on the next job. 'Clear the room. Get the men back to the complex entrance. If they find anything of value, they can have it—but no squabbling, or there will be trouble.'

'I can stay and help, if you want.' He meant well, but I sensed the reluctance—and who could blame him. Eternal damnation—that's what awaited me.

'It's all right, Usqha. Thanks, but I was given this assignment, not you. It's my destiny.' I tried to smile, but my heart wasn't in it. 'You just take the men and wait outside. Before you go, if you like—light me a fire. Get some wood and light it there in the middle of the room. That shouldn't put your spirit into jeopardy—but then I'd like you to leave. I won't be long.'

Usqha sent some men for kindling, some wood, and then sent them to the complex entrance. He lit the fire himself—and stood back. The fire took hold, and the smoke slowly filled the room. Coughing, Usqha half waved with his hand and left. I gazed after him while the smoke got into my eyes. Tears began to roll down my face, and I tried not to retch. I waved some of the smoke away with my hands and searched out Thupa 'Inka Yupanki's *mummy*. I lifted it, all the time praying silently to *Tiqsi Wiraqocha* to spare my spirit.

The dead of our people, especially the royal dead, remained powerful after death, like hot peppers. Food and attention was offered by supplicants of the cabal. The dead required food, clothing, and care. To enter the ancestral realm, a corpse had to be intact or it would be condemned to eternal damnation. The corpse was laid out, and allowed to dry naturally, and then the *mallqui* were ritually received by the living, and ceremonially reunited with other deceased kindred in communal repositories, mausoleums of the dead. They were entombed in the *llacta* mortuary complex, such as this *huaca* sepultura, high above Qusqu, guarded by the now dead sanctified attendants.

I placed Thupa 'Inka Yupanki's *mummy* gently and reverently on the roaring pyre, and stood back, head bent. I prayed for *my* spirit, choking with the fumes, and for forgiveness for this sacrilegious act. Deep down, I knew I was doing the right thing for my Lord 'Ataw Wallpa, for if the *cabal's* immortal remains were captured, then the *cabal* could be held hostage and forced into submission. But if the immortal remains were destroyed—so was the royal *panaqa*.

Tears streaming down my face from the smoke, I watched Thupa 'Inka Yupanki's *mummy* splutter in protest and then burst into flames. The flames seemed to roar up into the room's ceiling, but then subsided and sizzled with the remnants of what remained. Then it was gone, and I wiped away the sniffle and my tears.

My thoughts were sad and I said aloud in anguish, 'I hope I'm never ordered to commit such a sacrilegious act...ever again, because I have a feeling I will be forced to decline.' As I walked down the passage to join my warriors, I now felt an outcast within myself—I felt my soul was dammed by my foul desecration.

Kuraka "*Anka*" = Captain "eagle"

Kuraka = Captain

Second in command *Kamayuq* "*Usqha*" = "fast"

Kamayuq = Senior NCO

Runa = the "Inca" referred to themselves as "Runa" =
        people

Inti = Sun God, the major deity of the empire

Apu-punchau = another name for Inti the Sun God

Mama-Quilla = Inti's sister and consort was the Moon

Tiqsi Wiraqocha = originator, creator-god

Wiraqocha = god

Pacha Mama = mother earth

Pachakuti = Earthshaker (earthquakes)

Mayu = the 'celestial river' i.e. the Milky Way

Inka = King Emperor

Koy-Ya = principal wife of the Emperor

Panaqa = royal cabal

vara = ceremonial staff imbued with *huaca* and an
        emblem of authority wielded by nobles or
        people of inherited rank

aqha beer = prepared from the yellow *jora* maize/corn
                   liquor
ch'arki = jerky—preserved meats
huacas = sacred sites
ayllu = village, moiety
huaca ayllu = sacred village
llacta mortuary complex i.e. a *huaca sepultura,* where
          mallqui reposed in aboveground mausoleums.
llacta = town
mallqui = human mummy
mallquipavillac = sanctified priest attendants who
                      oversaw mourning rites and gave
                      consultations and replies on
                      behalf of the dead. Offerings of food,
                      drink, coca, and property were given
Saksaq Waman = Sacsayhuamán, meaning satisfied
                  falcon
Qusqu = Cuzco; Qusqu split into status upper *hanan*
          and lower *hurin* residential and social areas

*Smallpox was the disease that killed one third of the Inca before Pizarro arrived, and was directly responsible for the Civil War. Smallpox came up the Amazon and crossed the Andes with the Chiriguano, who had earlier contracted it from the coastal Charrua Indians. They in turn got it from European landing at the River Plate in 1516, when an expedition led by Juan Díaz de Solís, chief navigator of Spain, traversed the estuary as part of its effort to find a route to the Pacific, infecting the tribes as he went.

Oriental Enigma

'*What the hell happened?*' Serge wheezed.

Coughing, spluttering, trying not to breathe, he picked himself up from the rubble. From his leg pouch, he quickly extracted an air mask and clamped it to his face, breathing deeply.

'*Sophie*! Are you all right?' He went over to where she lay, dizzily shaking her head.

'I'm okay,' she managed, choking on the dust, sitting up, brushing rubble and dust out of her dark hair.

'I think we've fallen through the floor, into some kind of basement,' he answered his own question. 'Use your air mask,' he told her, waiting whilst she covered her nose and mouth.

Through her mask she asked with difficulty, 'Can you get some light going?'

Serge pulled out a glow-strip from his upper arm pocket, and flicked on the bright light, standing it in the dust on the floor.

Sophie took in a sharp breath of canned air. 'What brilliant walls,' she said, pointing over his large shoulder at the life forms beginning to be visible through the settling dust.

Serge's green eyes stared at the walls, at the vivid colours of the illuminated pictures. The glow-strip lighted various animals, barely recognisable from this mysterious long deceased civilisation. He pulled out another glow-strip and flicked it alight, holding it aloft, lighting up his own blond hair, giving brilliance to the other side of the room.

'It seems were in a large circular chamber,' he said unnecessarily. Then he took out his recorder and repeated the description for the record. 'The ceiling is slightly domed, and seems to be made of some huge tusk-like crystals stacked into a vertex.' He continued his descriptions, talking only into the recorder.

Like a cat, Sophie eased her lithe frame towards what looked like a circular doorway, three more doorways being situated at the other corners of the compass. Across the room through her mask she shouted, '*Come and take a look at this. There's some statues of the missing inhabitants over here.*'

Serge stopped recording and moved his massive frame towards her, craning his head to look at the hole in the dome ten meters above, through which they'd fallen. Then he looked more closely, trying to see through the dust, covering the floor. His gaze fell on a richly coloured glass-like marble inlay, containing some of the most intricate geometric designs he had ever witnessed.

The room around him had delicately sculpted tables—encrusted with layers of grime—standing in a circle. There were a large number of chairs, in the same delicate design, scattered all around, some lying on their sides, as if knocked over in haste by their long-departed occupants. Other unrecognisable items, some small, others quite large, lay strewn over the beautiful floor, all of it heavily covered with ancient dust.

Serge checked the scanner strapped to his left forearm. The air was barely breathable and heavily impregnated with the mustiness of ages; making it imperative that both planetary exo-archaeologists continue to use their air masks to supplement their breathing.

He reached Sophie's side and gave a little gasp. She was transfixed. The statue she gaped at had clearly defined human features. Even the costume on the statue seemed familiar, having a distinctive oriental style, albeit an ancient one.

'But how can this be?' Serge blurted out. 'Our scanner dates this site at some twenty-five thousand years in the past.' Before they fell through the hole, they had taken dating measurements at various points throughout the site.

'Serge! You realise what this means,' she gasped, astonishment on her face. 'This site is *dynamite*; once this gets out, it's going to attract some intense scrutiny by the big-wigs back on Earth,' she pointed at the statue.

'You have *that* right!' Serge agreed. 'We'd better be careful not to disturb anything.'

Sophie, ever the consummate professional, didn't need reminding how to do her job. She stood mesmerised, closely scrutinising the immobile figure.

'*This can't be*? Humans *here*, a hundred and fifty light years from the Solar System, at a time when we were still living in caves back on Earth?' A stubbornness crept into Sophie's voice. She just couldn't believe what she was seeing.

She wanted this contradiction to resolve itself, but had no idea how to achieve this; at least not immediately. Gingerly, she slid the circular portal doors open. The portal led into a corridor with a rounded ceiling. She went through, and Serge followed.

On either side of the long corridor, there were a number of other circular doorways. The first on the left seemed to have some sort of writing on either side. She gently rubbed the panels, clearing it of the ancient dirt.

On the left panel there was: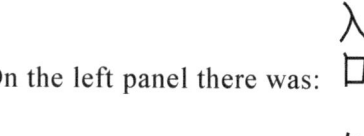

on the right: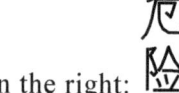

'Even these writings seem oriental ideograms.'

'Looks like Chinese,' Serge offered. 'If it's Chinese, it shouldn't *be* here. It's got no *business* being here.'

'I agree. So are we going to get on, or pretend it's not here. And we'd better go carefully. This is the archaeological find of the millennium.' She looked cautiously at the writing. 'Can you scan these ideograms; maybe get an idea of what they mean?'

'Sure!' He ran the scanner over the ideograms. 'The one on the left..... is coming up as...."rù kou," meaning "Entrance," and the one on the right......is...."wei xian," meaning "Danger".'

'So it's definitely Chinese?'

'That's what the scanner says.'

'This is spooky. If it says "Danger"—dare we go in?' She wanted his support.

'It *has* been twenty-five thousand years since anyone's gone through this door. That's right, isn't it? We're going to *have to* double-check the dates. I hope the *danger's* full of cobwebs. Do you want me to go first?'

She ignored the last remark and pushed the doors aside. The doors gave way smoothly, retracting into the walls.

'After all these years? The doors slide so *easily*!'

Serge held the glow-strip aloft.

Over her shoulder Sophie said, 'There's some stairs leading downwards.'

Both peered down the illuminated dusty passageway.

'The stairs seem disturbingly normal,' he commented.

She offered, 'As if they were made for human feet?'

Cautiously, they made their way to the next level. At the bottom, they were confronted by another doorway. Sophie managed to slide the grubby doors aside, this time with a little more difficulty. Serge pulled out another glow-strip from his upper arm pocket, lit it and placed it on the floor.

The room was enormous. A huge circular opening, to what seemed like a tunnel at the far end, immediately caught their attention. Its massive structure seemed to fill the room, although the tunnel seemed only two meters long. On either side, there were banks of inert electronic machinery, clearly relating to the immense portal.

'What do you think?' She looked into his face.

'There's a blank wall behind the tunnel. Hmm! Is that blank wall movable?'

'It doesn't look like another doorway,' she ventured.

'*Hang on*! Now don't go jumping down my throat. If…and I mean only *if*, it were possible to activate all this equipment, my guess would be, it's a jumpgate to other worlds. A sort of doorway through the Galaxy.'

'*What?* I don't think so. Wait! I've just had…an idea.' She stood thinking for a moment.

'Well? You gonna share it with me?'

'I warn you; it's bizarre.'

'What? More bizarre than my suggestion?'

'Well okay, here goes. I think it's what you said *and* a time portal.' She stood looking at his mask, his wide green eyes visible.

'Are you *serious*? That's only ever been a *theoretical* notion.'

'But it's the only thing that fits this layout, *this* situation—that oriental scribble. I've been giving this some thought. It would explain how humans come to *be* here. I mean not *all* of it, not the details.....The more I think of it, the more I'm convinced we're looking at a jumpgate *and* time machine—of some sorts.'

'There a large stack over there—possibly rotating—in the corner—look, on the right hand side, against the wall.' She sauntered over, and Serge followed.

'Look! It's got a lot of small square silicon wafers stacked in it. Operating instructions?'

'Shouldn't think so. They must have known how to operate it. Careful! After all this time—they'll fall to pieces.'

Picking one out, shaking the dust off, she said, 'No! They look quite sturdy.'

She pulled out her minivac, and sucked dust from a slot below the stack. Removed her air mask and blew down the hole, coughed, replaced her mask. Inserted the silicon wafer. Nothing happened.

'Serge? You're the electronics wizard. See if you can make this thing work. I think it's the reader for these wafers.'

He bent, looked underneath, unhooked an access panel. Placing the light beside him, he began to examine the circuitry with a small probe.

'The circuitry looks fine. You know; this stuff is at our current level of accomplishment. But twenty-five thousand years old...what the hell's going on?' Then he exclaimed, '*There's no juice!* That's the problem. If I isolate this circuit and use our mobile power pack, it might work.'

Fifteen minutes of fiddling, and the console flickered into life. Sophie slid the silicon wafer back into the slot. A small flat screen lit up, set into the wall above the slot. She wiped more dust away to reveal the screen properly. The images on the screen showed a number of oriental looking technicians busily adjusting the huge circular time portal." Sophie stood amazed, then pulled the wafer out. She began going through the dust-covered wafers one at a time.

Serge saw there was no stopping her, and he wandered around the room inspecting various electronic consoles, trying to make sense of them. After half an hour, Sophie gave a gasp, loud enough for Serge to hear despite his mask. He hurried over.

'I think I've come across a series of wafers depicting their history. They're right on the other side of the stack, near the end. The first of this series has the evolution of the original inhabitants of this planet. They're dinosauroids by the way. Three-quarters of the way through, there's a story regarding the Orientals. Watch!' She slid another wafer into the slot.

An oriental face was speaking slowly and precisely. Clearly, he seemed somewhat uncomfortable and conscious of the recording device.

'Can you programme the scanner to translate what he's saying?'

'I'll give it a go,' Serge replied. '.....there! That ought to do it.'

'Go back to the beginning of this fellow's speech.'

She removed the wafer and inserted it again. The screen showed the oriental sitting, beginning to talk. The scanner picked up the words and gave them the translation into their earphones.

"The following record is the story of our arrival on this planet. It is an instructional record for our young ones. They must be made aware of their history. It begins a little way back when our ancestors were building the *A Fang* palace."

It all came through their translator into their earphones—they were looking at a film with a voice-over. They viewed a sequence of introductory shots, with the old oriental seated, telling the following story:

"The scene shows Li Si, the Grand Councillor, hurrying to the newly completed throne room, summoned to an audience by Qin Shi Huangdi, the First Emperor of a united Zhonghua. Qin Shi Huangdi arrived from his capital at Xian Yang, unannounced, in a full-blown rage. He demanded an explanation for the delay in the building of his new palace. The new palace named *A Fang,* on the south bank of the Wei river, was well overdue, and Huangdi wanted someone's head for the delay. Eager to set up his court in *A Fang*, away from the choking crowds of the current capital—someone was resisting his will.

Li Si approached the throne on his knees, in the customary fashion of obeisance; then lay spread-eagled waiting for the First Emperor to speak.

'Fetch the architect,' the Emperor boomed. 'Well? What are you waiting for?'

'Sire, there is news of your son, Prince Fu Su.'

'Speak!'

'He arrived at Xian Yang in a great caravan with General Meng Tian a short time after you left.'

'Meng Tian? Then who's guarding our northern frontier if Meng's here? Those barbarian Xiongnu will have stormed our northern encampments by now. *Why has he left his post?*' shouted the emperor.

Li Si wisely lay supine, silent. The imperial architect arrived at a run. Quickly, he assumed the position of obeisance before the Emperor.

'*Why is my palace not finished?*' the Emperor yelled at the architect.

'Your heavenly radiance,' the architect began, 'we keep losing our workers to your army.'

'Go on,' Huangdi commanded.

'We started with 500,000 labourers, now we're down to 300,000. A hundred and fifty thousand were taken from us, conscripted into the army to fight in the north, then 50,000 taken to work on your tomb at Mount Li. If the labourers keep being removed from us, oh chosen of heaven, we will have great trouble finishing.'

Huangdi seemed to calm down, becoming thoughtful, alternately rubbing his black goatee beard, and then stroking his long drooping moustache. Huangdi subscribed to the Legalist doctrine of being a tough master, and apportioning blame to the *correct* person was part of the Law.

'If what you say is true, then I will have your labourers returned. This palace *must* be finished by the end of this year. Do you understand?'

'Yes, your magnificence.'

'You may go. *Li Si!* Get my carriage ready. We ride back to the capital. Maybe my son has found some Immortals?'

The thousand strong procession with two-wheeled carriages bearing the Emperor, his Grand Councillor Li Si, and the rest of the courtiers, raced the twenty kilometres back to the imperial capital. Huangdi's carriage, pulled by six black horses was setting the pace. Huangdi's favourite number was six and his preferred colour—black.

The Captain of the cortege urged the retinue to go faster as the procession approached the imperial city through the Shang Lin hunting park. They reached the bridge fording the Wei River, heading for the city gates.

The bridge, a marvel of construction, comprised sixty-eight spans of nine meters each, giving an overall measurement of more than six hundred meters. All the beams were made of wood, carrying a deck width of twelve meters. Piers close to the bank were made of stone. The carriages rumbled across at high speed.

The monumental beige coloured walls encircling the city, gave the impression of mighty power. Billowing black silk banners proclaiming the Qin dynasty, hung at intervals on the high walls. The procession sped through the tall gateway guarded by a grey slate covered barbican. Down the main thoroughfare, past bustling markets, hurtling by towering multi-storeyed pavilions. Speeding to the core of the city where the many Grand Palaces stood, themselves surrounded by tall walls.

The carriage hastened through the ornate Meridian Gate guardhouse, entering the lavish imperial park, decorated with glittering lotus lakes, winding streams, and luxuriant trees. The long drive to the Changle Palace was intended to impress, to calm foreign emissaries and visiting functionaries. Water was Huangdi's «element» liberally situated as ponds and lakes in the well-groomed park.

Nearing the extravagant palace, they passed a large group of General Meng's soldiers, taking their rest near the armoury that separated the Weiyang Palace, from the

Changle Palace. The Emperor's carriage went up the paved driveway, through the Gate of Supreme Harmony, into the large courtyard, directly to the long white marble palace steps.

A waiting litter swiftly removed Huangdi up the steps of the three-tiered terrace, each tier surrounded by a white marble balustrade. Past tall bronze elephants guarding the palace entrance on either side, into the Tai He Dian, the towering coffered long ceilinged Hall of Supreme Harmony, forested with thick lofty lacquered columns, carved with gilded dragon motifs. The hall, the main throne room, was peppered with standing charcoal room heaters. The elite corps of imperial litter bearers lowered the litter to the lacquered floor, a firm hand pulled the gold embroidered yellow silk curtain aside.

Huangdi, dressed all in black, his robes tinged with yellow and embroidered gold, deftly alighted, propelling his own ample frame up the golden steps of the raised platform. Head held high, the Lord of Ten Thousand Years, glided past the tall intricately cast bronze dragon urns containing incense, oblivious of the smoke from the urns, he moved towards his throne. In the nearby galleries, bells of gold and jade, heralded his ascent. The majestic seat cushion covered with imperial yellow silk, sat on a golden dais, flanked by a pair of imposing cloisonné cranes and a pair of cloisonné tortoises symbolising long life. The throne faced the direction of the benevolent spirits, southwards. The litter bearers lifted the empty litter, retreating to a distant corner near the traditional circular Chinese windows.

Emperor Qin Shi Huangdi, Son of Heaven, settled on the elaborately carved gold encrusted throne and shouted, '*Where's Meng*? Bring him here at once!'

No sooner had the words left his lips, General Meng Tian came towards the throne preceded by Crown Prince Fu Su, followed by the young Prince Hu Hai, and behind him, the chief of the army, General Bo Qi. The elderly chief eunuch, Zhao Gao, brought up the rear. All the courtiers wore black dress, at Huangdi's behest. Everyone approached the dais on their knees and on reaching the lower steps, lay prostrate before Huangdi.

'*What are you doing here*?' Huangdi bellowed at Meng. 'Who's guarding the frontier?'

Crown Prince Fu Su interceded quickly, rising to one knee, 'General Liu Bang, Father! *Father*, we have brought someone to see you. Someone from another planet.'

'Fu Su! Are you responsible for bringing Meng back here?' Huangdi demanded of his son.

'*Father!* We have encountered an alien not of this world. He wants an audience with you.'

'What is this nonsense; what are you blabbering.'

'May I approach?'

'Yes, my son. Come forward.'

Fu Su got up and approached Huangdi. He whispered in his father's ear for some minutes, whilst everyone remained in their prone postures.

Finally, Huangdi commanded, 'Get up—all of you. Zhao, you stay as you are.' He wanted the eunuch on his face. 'Well don't just stand there. Go get this alien. Bring him before me,' he commanded his son.

Huangdi looked at the prone figure of his chief eunuch whilst waiting for the stranger to be brought before him. *I'm going to have to watch Zhao. His gossiping is beginning to cause much trouble. I'm certain he was involved in that last assassination attempt.*

A black robed figure approached the throne. The figure made no attempt at obeisance, walking erect towards Huangdi.

'Have you taught him no respect,' Huangdi demanded of Li Si.

'*Your illustrious majesty,*' Li Si said in alarm.

A metallic voice boomed from the robed figure, 'Your magnificence, I come from the planet Rraladan, a hundred and fifty light years from this planet.'

The metallic quality of the voice was so alien, it momentarily stilled the Emperor's speech. Although he grasped the gist of what this alien was saying, terms such as 'light years' had no meaning for Huangdi. What he understood was, this black robed figure had come from far away.

The metallic voice continued, 'I bring a proposal from *my* emperor to you, one which will be of great profit and benefit to you.'

'Remove your robe; let us see to whom we're talking.' Huangdi's hawk eyes were alert; he stroked his black goatee as he studied the robed figure.

'I hope you will not be startled, your imperial majesty.'

The black robe fell from the tall figure. The alien stood in a red waistcoat and black trousers. Huangdi's mouth opened wide in astonishment; he prepared to call for the palace guard.

'Fear not your magnificence; I pose no threat to you. I am named Barran and come in peace.'

A complete silence descended on everyone in the throne room. Those not in the know, stared in horror; others shocked—shrank backwards. General Bo Qi almost drew his sword, a sacrilege in the presence of the emperor. General Meng stayed Bo's hand. Others looked on in fascination at the green scales, and yellow eyes, on the face of this alien manifestation.

'You're *not* human! What are you? A dragon?' Huangdi demanded.

The tall figure looked around the room. 'I am from another star. Not of this world. I come to trade. We need something; we're willing to give you something valuable in return.'

'How is it you speak our tongue?' Huangdi wanted to know.

'I have a mechanical translator,' Barran tapped a pouch hanging from a belt on his right side.

'So! What do you wish from us?' Huangdi's large face became inquisitive.

'We would like to buy some of your population.'

'Hmm!' The emperor stroked his goatee. 'How many, and for what purpose?' Negotiations, advantage, profit; Huangdi understood the language well.

'Fifty thousand. We need your people to act as labourers and servants.'

'Understood. You want to buy some serfs. What do you offer in return?'

'I offer you twenty-four wagons loaded with gold. Furthermore, I will show you how you can safeguard your northern frontier. Oh chosen of heaven, most important of all, I will show you how you may defeat your enemies in the afterlife.'

'Can you make me immortal? I seek the Immortals here on earth, but they evade me. Maybe you can tell me the exact location of the three isles where the Immortals live?'

'Your regal illustriousness, that may be included in our *second* trade negotiations, but I would wish to talk this over with *my* emperor. It is for him to decide whether he is prepared to include the elixir of life in our trade.'

The look of longing on Huangdi's face suggested he would deal with Yen Wang Yeh, Lord Yama of the Underworld, himself, if only he could get his hands on the long sought elixir of life.

Twenty-four wagons is six times four, thought Huangdi. *Six is my favourite number.* 'All right! I agree to your terms; but on condition, the *next* trade includes the elixir of life. Agreed?'

'If it is your will.'

'It is! Now, how do you propose to defend us from the barbarian Xiongnu?'

The alien spoke loudly so Bo Qi, Meng Tian and Fu Su could hear, 'In the great northern loop of the Huang He, there is an arid semi-desert area known as the Ordos. As yet, you have no defensive wall across it...'

Astonished, Bo interrupted, unable to contain himself, 'It is over 1,288 kilometres long...'

'I'm aware of its length General Bo,' Barran said sharply. 'Nevertheless, I propose you build a great wall across it from Gansu province in the west, to the Liaodong peninsula in the east. This is where your defences are the weakest. The wall must be higher and thicker than the walls of the past. If you planned for the future, you'd really need to build up *all* of the wall from east to west, all along your northern frontier. That would solve for ever, the problem of your northern barbarian invasions.'

Meng jumped in, 'The idea had crossed *my* mind, but the enormous scale of the project... I assumed the emperor would never sanction it.'

The alien looked at Huangdi. Huangdi had a scowl on his face from the interruptions—but nodded in agreement.

'Sire! It might be the only answer to prevent us being overrun,' Meng continued.

'*I've already agreed*,' Huangdi boomed back at Meng. 'Li Si! Assemble fifty thousand of the labourers working on the *An Fang* Palace, outside the city walls, tomorrow. Tell them to bring their families.' Huangdi returned to the alien. 'Now! How do you intend to allow me to defeat my enemies in my afterlife?'

'By proposing you construct an imperial guard made of terracotta. You must place them in a vault near Mount Li, so they are close to you, facing the lower Huang He valley; that is where your greatest threat comes from.'

'Are you saying these guards will come *alive* if I need them?' Huangdi took the outrageous proposal as if it were the most natural suggestion.

'It will be so, your imperial majesty,' replied Barran.

For the first time in its long history, it was now five years since Huangdi had succeeded in finally unifying all of Zhonghua, bringing all the various warring kingdoms under the suzerainty of one emperor. This momentous achievement had induced a vast sense of omnipotence in

Zheng, the former King of Qin. After his defeat of the various scattered kingdoms, Zheng had chosen the title Qin Shi Huangdi, meaning «Qin First Sovereign Emperor». Was he not divinely chosen by Heaven as the founder of an empire destined to last «ten thousand generations»? Bringing clay figures to life was merely one more minor miracle in a long miraculous career.

'Scribe! Come and write my decrees. First decree: *In the fifth year of the reign of Qin Shi Huangdi, General Meng is to go north and build a giant wall across the Ordos.*

'Second decree: *General Bo is to oversee the potter's guild in constructing a copy of my 8,000 strong imperial bodyguard. They are to be made life-size of clay; officers, chariots, cavalry, cross-bowmen, and infantry: all made as realistic as artistically possible. They are to be grouped in battle order, ready to fight, and placed in a subterranean vault near my tomb at Mount Li.* That is all. When shall I see the gold?' Huangdi returned to the alien.

'Sire. We are ready to produce the wagons by tomorrow.'

'You may all go; you are all dismissed,' Huangdi commanded.

The audience over; everyone backed out of the throne room. The alien was taken back to the Weiyang Palace by Prince Fu Su and General Meng Tian. General Bo Qi hurried out of the city to Mount Li, at Lintong, to implement the terracotta decree.

The next morning, a great hubbub could be heard outside the city walls as the labourers arrived in a forced march from the *A Fang* building site. A large force of soldiers surrounded the labourers, since Meng feared there may be reluctance for such an enormous body of slaves to be herded anywhere.

The labourers were encouraged to take their families with them, were promised good housing, good living conditions when they arrived at their new destination. They were also each given some gold coins. The coins were a minor miracle for the labourers. It was more money than they had ever seen in their lives before. The coins and the promises came from the alien; the backup coercion came from Meng. Carrot and stick had been a well-tried form of persuasion. It had seldom failed.

Ten kilometres south of the capital, in a secluded gorge, the gold was loaded onto the wagons by soldiers. Bar after bar of the yellow metal was brought through the circular time portal by muscular bipedal aliens with green scales and yellow eyes, dressed in strange clothes. Barran, Prince Fu Su and General Meng stood monitoring the transaction, counting the bars, watching until the last of the twenty-four wagons had been filled. The creaking wagons were sent on their way to the city, and soon the first of the labourers began to appear at the head of the gorge from the direction of the city.

A number of senior officials had been delegated by Huangdi to lead and control the labourers. The soldiers herded the column on either side, prodding them towards the time portal. The portal was only visible as a shimmering four-meter circle of light seemingly emerging from a rock face. What onlookers saw were aliens with green scales bringing gold bars out of that same rock face.

The column of labourers halted before the time portal; Barran conferred with the senior officials, then led the column into the seemingly solid rock. Hour after hour, the 50,000 labourers from *A Fang*, marched through the grey granite time portal. With their families, the whole column totalled well over 100,000 people.

At the other end of the time portal, the slaves came out into a lush green landscape, trees, flowers, and clean rich air. What really took the people's breath away were the two suns in the sky. True to their word, the aliens provided well-appointed clean accommodation for people more accustomed to mud huts and dingy squalor.

When it dawned on the former labourers they were to live more in the style of what they would have regarded as their own middle classes, they rejoiced, fully co-operating with the aliens.

The aliens ordered the small group of accompanying mandarins to teach the population to read and write. It was a prerequisite to their introduction to the intricacies of dinosauroid society. The humans took over sewage, waste disposal, transportation, and all the other mundane jobs. The aliens were relatively benign; somewhat self-absorbed, concentrating on their science, leaving the humans to their own pursuits when not on duty.

For reasons buried in their prehistory and history, all the dinosauroid's science was focused on time travel. Their religion was enmeshed in the «contracting-expanding universe» theory, and the dinosauroids were obsessed with going back in time to observe the "the point of first expansion," to pay homage to the event. It was for this reason they had needed to procure some extra helpers to carry out the mundane tasks within their society, releasing themselves for an increased effort to perfect their time travelling science.

The video film finished with the old oriental face coming back onto the screen, continuing his commentary. "Throughout the next thousand years, our people became the equals of their former masters, by dint of sheer hard work and due Zhonghuo diligence. Our two races shared the riches of the bountiful planet of Rraladan."

Abruptly, there was a short blank patch on the screen, followed by a different oriental face, much younger; harried and agitated.

"It is a tragic day for us all. Varral, the larger sun has spawned a gigantic sunspot. The enormous sun flare is gushing out a plasma filled solar wind, more accurately, a *solar hurricane*. When the radial outflow of the charged particles hit Zurral, the minor sun, a concatenating effect will double the outflow of charged particles flowing towards Rraladan. It is expected to overwhelm our «radiation belt»." The speaker paused to wipe the sweat from his face.

"The prediction is, flora and fauna on Rraladan will be bombarded with immense amounts of cosmic radiation. The effects will be lethal on those exposed, no amount of effort can save the population. The only escape is through time. The dinosauroids refuse to leave their planet and we humans have decided to share their fate. We have been linked with our former masters for over a thousand years now; bound closely in culture and affection. They have sustained us for many generations and in return, we can do no less than share their fate. It has been decided!

"Within a week, we expect most of the population to have died of radiation sickness. A few may survive below the planet's surface, but they will all be sterile. If anybody finds this recording, may they look kindly upon our decision in the light of this tragedy."

The screen went blank. Serge looked at Sophie, peering inside her atmosphere mask, and saw tears rolling down her cheeks. He put an arm around her shoulders and squeezed gently.

Zhonghua=China
Xiongnu=Huns
Huang He=Yellow River

The Philosopher's Brain

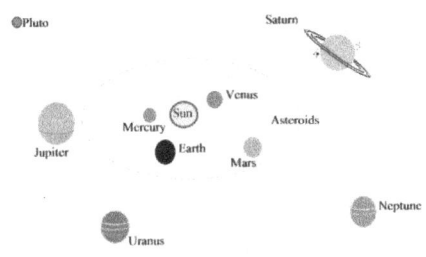

Itaupi was out on a furious jaunt along the Orion 'spur', on the inner edge of the Perseus Main Arm of the Milky Way, aiming his vessel at top warp speed for a system with nine planets.

He had set out from Palari in a raging temper having just slammed the proverbial door on his loquacious partner, Tewpi. *How dare she speak to him like that?* Fumed Itaupi not for the first time.

So he had ejected their egg prematurely, so what*? It's not as if it was to be the last egg. Anyway, it was* his *egg, his body. What right did she have demanding to be consulted?* The thoughts reverberated through his raging mind as his communicator antennas flashed his fury. *She may have supplied the nucleus but* he'd *supplied the major part, the cell.*

Even in such a foul temper he had remembered to stop off at the **BODYSHOP** to add to his depleted cryo-cupboard with a variety of computer controlled shell life-forms. Who knew; he might have to stop off at a planet somewhere and mix with the natives.

He had raced across from the other side of the galaxy at faster than light, in a furious attempt to work off some of his anger, dangerously but deliberately manufacturing near misses with comets, meteorites and other debris. He was angry at having become angry. His "emotional" research was rubbing off on him. He only became contemplative again as he neared the immense spherical cloud containing billions of rocky and icy bodies that surrounded this Solar System. He would leave the navigation through the debris field of the numerous bodies to his computer. He used his training methods to calm himself. It took them a while to get through this Oort cloud and the ship finally came out near a meteor belt on the edge of the Solar System proper.

Back on Palari, he made a fair living as a Consultant, a "thought" Consultant. On his *Intermesh* Holo-Grid site he had the logo, "Got a Balance Problem? Bring it to Itaupi!" Numerous people hit his Holo-Grid site every day. People always had problems and always would have problems, so for a budding intuitive empath such as himself, there was always going to be work. He was the only one of his species who could understand emotions.

Leaving Kuiper's meteor belt, he entered the system of the nine planets, being careful to cloak his small ship to prevent any prying eyes scrutinising his arrival. It was his first visit to this area of the galaxy, so he was being extra careful. If there were any life-forms in this system, he had to quickly discover the level of their civilisation. Were they friendly or hostile? Most importantly, could they do him any harm?

Some years ago he'd barged incautiously into another system, and the natives had trapped him with tractor-beams as neatly as a Parrion swooping on a small Laptoon. It took him six months to extricate himself from their clutches. Worse; it nearly bankrupted him. He wouldn't admit it, even to himself, but that little junket nearly cost him his life. It was a seminal lesson for him to be a lot more careful in future.

From the safety of the small frozen outermost planet, he looked into this new Solar system.

'*Computer!* Do a Spectral Analysis on everything coming out of this system.'

'As you command!'

He needed to establish if there were any Electromagnetic Spectrum emissions from any of the planets and if so, were they benign.

'Only natural background planetary emissions detected,' the computer reported.

So, no sign of any sentient output. Either nobody's home or they haven't reached the stage where they could put out electromagnetic waves yet. It began to look somewhat promising. Still cautious, Itaupi pointed his ship in an elliptic towards the sun and leisurely entered the nine planets system proper.

He approached a large bluish gaseous planet with high-level clouds that reflected sunlight above the atmosphere on the starboard bow of the ship. It had a large moon circling it, and a very small moon in an erratic orbit. There were no life signs there.

Further on in the same direction there was another large yellow-orangey planet with a belt of colourful rings. Neither on the planet with the rings, nor on its eight moons did his computer detect life.

On the other side of the Sun, on the larboard bow, there was a large greenish methane gas planet, a little smaller than the bluish one, with a clear cold atmosphere and five detectable moons. The dark shadings at the right edge of the sphere corresponded to the day-night boundary on the planet. No life signs. Itaupi was beginning to suspect that this particular Solar system might not yet have evolved any life forms.

Fine, on the larboard bow he was going to pass the largest planet in the system, a huge brownish gaseous giant with a striation of colourful bands. There were twelve moons circling this monster. From his past encounters these gaseous giants were unlikely to have contained any life.

Closer in, he encountered a thick belt of asteroids. Looking further in to the left of the sun he could discern two inner planets, juxtaposed to the right, there were two more. These four planets were inside the massive ring of asteroids. He pressed a couple of touch-sensitive panels with his right raptorial foreleg, and adjusted his course heading for the inner planets.

A little further in, he came across a few meteoroids. He then passed a sandy yellow-red planet with a very thin atmosphere; no signs of life. The whole reddish planet resembled a cold, high-altitude desert. He decided to take a closer look at the blue planet in between the red and a bright beige planet with a thick soupy atmosphere. The beige planet was far too hot and made up of swirling clouds of sulphur oxide and sulphuric acid. There was little point of looking for life there.

He was closing in on the blue planet in the middle of his holographic star-finder. There were streaks of seemingly white hydrous clouds surrounding it. *Now* that *looks more promising,* he deliberated. His earlier garrulous disposition had subsided, to be replaced by a cautious inquisitiveness. He kept a wary eye out for the slightest electromagnetic emissions, but didn't detect any. He parked his cloaked ship in orbit around the blue planet and began to survey his find.

Within a short time he realised the place was teeming with all sorts of life-forms: in the air, on land, under the water. There were large quantities of quadrupeds spread out over four of what looked like five continents. Itaupi took a particular interest in what he deemed to be the dominant life-form, a seemingly intelligent bipedal creature. The biped was only missing from one land mass, situated at one of the poles of the planet—a cold barren place entirely inhospitable to the bipeds form of life. Otherwise, the biped was everywhere.

Itaupi used the high resolution astroscope, and found clothed inhabitants surrounded by quadrupeds with humps, living in black tents in the middle of deserts. That was in one of the hottest parts of the planet. He found them in icy wastes, where the inhabitants hunted at the edges of the frozen ocean in their skin covered boats. Itaupi marvelled at the adaptability of this bipedal species.

Life! Its adaptability, its gritty mercenary determination to survive was a constant miracle to any rational traveller. Itaupi had seen planets where the low gravity bred tall lanky life-forms. Other planets where the high gravity bred short stubby multi-legged ground-hugging creatures. He'd seen atrophied life-forms in a micro gravity where they were slowly evolving into ethereal creatures, leaving their corporeal shells for life amongst the stars.

Yet the profusion of life in the vastness of the galaxy, a galaxy where the average distance between the stars was only five light years, never ceased to excite him. He was addicted to his exo-psychological research and spent every spare workaholic moment claiming many laurels on Palari for his efforts.

He worked overtime to find unusual specimens, to integrate them into his 'Emotional Potential' model and to receive their "thoughts." His craving for travel in his research knew no bounds. Yet again, here he was readying to make new contact, catalogue a new species; obtain new "thoughts." His juices were coursing through his body, his compound eyes were focused, invigorating his synapses; he tingled with the thrill of it all.

Itaupi entered the atmosphere, skimming silently over the largest continent, moving quickly from east to west. He brought the ship to a hovering halt near the western end of the landmass, over a southerly jutting mountainous peninsular of an inland sea. It seemed that the small westerly inland sea was pressing northwards in on the peninsula with a thousand arms. A grumble from his main stomach reminded him that he should take a little sustenance.

At the eastern end of the inland sea, there were thousands of small islands, and a small isthmus leading into another inland sea. Itaupi loved tracing the outlines of new geography with his sharp compound eyes. He was the first of his species to feast their eyes on this strange new planet; he gorged himself on its strange new geography.

From the console in front of him, he pulled a flexi-tube with his left raptorial foreleg and inserted the tube, grazing his right mandible, into this aperture, sucking in greedily the green glutinous mass into his foregut.

'Computer! Activate the cryo-cupboard and convert one of our shell life-forms into a simulacrum of those bipeds below.'

'As you command!' responded his computer.

'Now let's see,' he mused aloud to himself. 'Activate the alpha sensors.'

'As you command,' repeated the computer.

'Let's have a look at what these bipeds have for brains...hmm! *Enhance!*'

On the screen in front of him was a sample neural matrix of the combined brain patterns of around a hundred of the bipeds. His computer had copied the matrices without so much as a by-your-leave from the hapless owners, and integrated them into its bio-processors.

As he looked at the preliminary data collection displayed on the console, he gave a gasp...*that can't be right?* He pulled himself together and decided to let the computer finish.

It analysed the language patterns, the capabilities and weaknesses of the cross-section. It made a stab at extrapolating the potential and possibilities of the life-forms. The shipboard computer went far beyond anything a mere surgical theatre could perform in dissecting the bipeds. At its conclusion, the computer knew far more about the bipeds than the bipeds knew about themselves.

'Are you sure the emotional parameters are correctly set in the model?'

'Yes!' the computer replied.

'But that's the highest Emotional Factor we've ever recorded for any species,' Itaupi blurted out with excitement.

'I confirm that,' responded the machine.

'Now look, there! That's also interesting,' mused Itaupi. 'Computer! Do you concur that their Thought-Rapaciousness Potential Factor exceeds that of the Ga'aneri and stands at 0.4341 sotri.'

'I concur,' responded the computer.

'This is a brilliant find.' Itaupi said aloud, having long ago learned to openly talk to himself. It was the penalty he paid for travelling alone. 'Make a sweep and locate the brightest of the bipeds in the area,' he commanded.

'As you command,' said the compliant computer.

After a few minutes Itaupi began to get restive. 'Well? Have you found anything?' he demanded.

'There is a landmass to the south-east of the peninsula that exhibits a plus seven on the alpha sensor. It comes from a coastal city situated near the mouth of a river, a city with four harbours. The locals call it Miletus. I took that from one of the inhabitants.'

'Well, what are you waiting for? Get us close to it. Hmm...a plus seven—that's better than I'd hoped for.'

The cloaked vessel approached Miletus, the Greek city of the Ionian confederacy in Asia Minor, gently landing well into the interior as dawn began to replace the night. Itaupi put the ship down in a gully, first checking there were no roads or paths nearby, which might indicate that it was frequented by the natives. He was some twenty kilometres from the walls of the city.

'Have you finished the shell life-form?'

'I've transferred the shell from the cryo-cupboard. It is ready, waiting for you in the thawing cupboard.'

'Good! I'll get into the transfer-repository and you can initiate somatic transfer.' Itaupi got out of the pilot's seat and went to the back of the ship. He opened a door and climbed into a cupboard. 'Oh! Take it easy this time—give me time to adjust; I might be a bit unsteady with only two legs.'

A little time went by, punctuated by a few flashing lights on the console. Noise began to emanate from the thawing cupboard. The door was thrown open, and out he stepped.

Itaupi turned, stumbling a bit before he steadied himself.

He ordered, 'Computer! Turn the glass panel into a mirror.'

The Greek language sat somewhat uncomfortably in his dry throat. He walked to the mirror and looked at himself; then shuddered. His elegant colourful insectoid body with its protective rigid exoskeleton had been replaced by a ghastly Avatar, with a fragile soft skinned life-form. In the mirror, he observed a one point eight meters nude male human specimen. It had a typical muscular Mediterranean appearance, a medium long beard as facial hair. Growing from the cranium was dark long hair. The whole body was covered in a sallow skin, and instead of compound eyes, it had only two dark eyes placed horizontally.

'Hmmm...,' he scowled.

He began to doubt the wisdom of this trip. *I'm a martyr to my research,* he thought.

The worst part of it was, that he felt somewhat vulnerable as he moved his limbs, testing their flexibility, or lack of it.

'What do you think?' he asked the computer. 'Do you think I'll pass?'

'You've always managed it before,' the computer answered noncommittally.

'You're right! I always get nervous at the beginning of a first encounter: what of clothing? From what I could see, the natives wear a robe wrapped around them.'

'I'm replicating a conventional form of local Ionian attire. The life-form you seek is similarly dressed.'

'Good! It should be around mid-morning by now. The broach....? Ah! There it is. Won't do to forget the com-badge.

Computer! Listen carefully. I'll give the usual click series if I get into trouble. Lock on to the com-badge and get me out of there fast. Understood?'

'As you command!' responded his computer.

'In that case—I think I'm ready. Got the ring—and the abstracter.' Itaupi paused and brushed his hair backwards, looking at the ring.

The ring was his only means of defence and he compulsively checked the charge level. The abstracter had a holo-camouflage unit built into it so that the casual observer took it for a stone, a lump of ordinary rock.

'Now tell me—who is the target?'

'I gather his name is Thales....'

'That's the plus seven?'

'Yes! I've located him on the Acropolis of Miletus. He has a few friends with him, and they seem to be deep into some tortuous mental perambulations. Your abstracter should point him out. Look for them near the temple of the virgin goddess Artemis. Shall I teleport you to the Acropolis?'

'That's probably a good idea. I'm not sure how steady I'm going to be on these two legs.'

'As you command.'

The computer scanned the destination area and rematerialized Itaupi away from prying eyes, behind a small grey minor temple on the edge of the Acropolis. Itaupi took a few paces in the fresh air, and immediately felt dizzy. He leaned against the light grey ashlar stone. Trying to pull himself together, he made an effort, walked round the corner, found the nearest low wall, and sat.

People went past him and stared. A beggar ten meters away spotted him for an easy mark and approached him on crutches, hobbling on one leg.

He drew near, averted his eyes and held out his left hand, hoping for a few coins. 'Spare a couple of *mina* for an old soldier.'

Still Itaupi sat quietly trying to sort out his co-ordination. *Had the computer made a mistake with the shell life-form, maybe somehow wired it up wrongly?* Then his head cleared and the dizzy spell passed. A raunchy smell of urine hit his nostrils. It came from the beggar.

Itaupi looked at the beggar, 'Do you know the whereabouts of Thales?'

'Oh...! *That explains it.*' A scowl appeared on his weather beaten face. 'You're with *that* crowd!' He spat the words out with contempt. The beggar pointed a finger in the direction of the large grey-stone temple across the clearing. He then swung around, making a show of turning his back on Itaupi, and hobbled off.

Itaupi looked in the direction the beggar had indicated, and saw a small group of men gathered in heated discussion. To his right, he could see the blue sea below in the distance. The Acropolis was a natural fortified stronghold sitting on an eminence, rising precipitously from the surrounding region on the northerly spur of the vast harbour. It was the high point of the city that spanned out in a crescent around the bay, from the base of the inland facing hill.

Itaupi stood up and stretched himself. He checked his abstracter in the pouch round his waist, and proceeded to cross the agora heading towards the group of men. Now his mind had cleared; he felt fine, vigorous. As he advanced across the red clay agora, all barring one were oblivious of his approach.

The debate was getting louder; voices were being raised in protest at something being said by one of the group.

The man being orally abused by the others detached himself from the group, and headed towards Itaupi.

'Friend!' said the stranger to Itaupi, opening his hands as he neared.

'Hallo yourself!' Itaupi responded.

'You're not from Miletus.' It was a statement rather than a question.

'That's very perceptive of you,' replied Itaupi.

'From your robe I would venture to suggest you are a free man, a man of some substance.'

That startled Itaupi. He wasn't expecting such direct astuteness from these primitive bipeds.

'I'm from across the waters,' he said gingerly.

'*Water!*' exclaimed the stranger. He swiftly brought a vessel out from behind his back and threw the contents over Itaupi. 'There! Marvel at the primal substance. It will dry in a few minutes and you will be one with the universe.'

Not for the first time in his travels did he curse the need to get so close to his subjects with his abstracter. The abstracter had to be at least a meter from the subject's brain to be effective. Otherwise the synaptic emissions would dissipate before the matrices were firmly secured by the meshlock. *Why couldn't they build an alpha sensor tight enough to do the job from a distance? I can get a rough matrix but not a tight matrix from orbit,* he complained in his mind to nobody in general.

The stranger saw the shock on Itaupi's face at having water thrown over him by a complete stranger. 'Ahh..."water," the primary substance,' he repeated. 'This bodes well to our meeting. Are you from Hellas?' asked the stranger, ignoring Itaupi's shock.

Itaupi's head was loaded with information from the earlier neural matrices of the combined brain patterns of around a hundred of the bipeds. From that, he knew the stranger meant the peninsula across the inland sea.

'Can we sit whilst we talk,' Itaupi ventured still feeling damp. The hot morning sun was fast drying him. He headed in the direction of a stone bench beneath the shade of a cooling olive tree, by the low wall surrounding the Temple. This was well away from the group of men, now staring daggers at his companion. The stranger followed.

'Why are they so angry? Have you been throwing water at them too?' Itaupi asked, trying to change the subject.

'I told them that all religion is just superstitious nonsense. That it exists to support the lazy priests, and that if they wanted to obtain true knowledge, all they had to do was study the physical world around them—such as water.'

Itaupi narrowed his eyes and looked closely at this man. *He couldn't be a shell life form—another alien like himself? No...! That would be too much of a coincidence. Anyway, that last bit about "water" was totally lopsided. Still—this must be the plus seven.*

They sat, and Thales scratched himself, then yawned as he settled on his buttocks. There was no doubt; it could only be Thales, the plus seven.

'I'm sorry; am I keeping you awake?' Itaupi said quietly. To confirm the stranger's identity Itaupi reached into his pouch for the abstracter.

'You didn't answer *my* question. Are you from Hellas?' Thales persisted.

'No! From Olbia.' Itaupi thought that would be the end of that. It was far away enough for this Thales not to have visited it, maybe just heard of it.

'What! Past the Propontis, all the way up the Euxine Sea?' Thales exclaimed in astonishment. He thought for a few seconds, and then said, 'So what brings you to the mother city?'

By this time Itaupi had the abstracter in his hand and was adjusting some of the controls, pointing it at Thales.

'What is that rock you have?' queried Thales, as he saw Itaupi fiddling with it.

'A Scythian *shaman* gave me this stone as a mark of friendship. I sometimes rub it for good luck.'

'Mmm! Maybe he thought that "rocks" were the prime substance—he's wrong of course.'

'Of course!' agreed Itaupi, trying to humour Thales.

Itaupi pressed the "collector" on the abstracter and immediately saw a momentary glazed expression on Thales' face. In a flash it was over. He had what he came for. Thales' thought essence was now stored in the abstracter. *And what is this nonsense concerning "water,"* he thought irritably. In a moment of capriciousness, he reversed the polarity on the abstracter, and added to Thales' thought potential by doubling his synaptic connections. *That'll put an end to that load of absurdity.* Then an uneasy afterthought struck him; *I hope there's no knock-on effect from my benevolence.*

'What happened?' Thales was saying, shaking his head.

'It's the sun—and the arguments,' Itaupi tried to convince him.

Thales raised his left eye, as if he had only just noticed this foreigner in front of him for the first time.

Itaupi got up saying, 'Excuse me! I must find the public toilet. Don't go away—I'll be back shortly.'

He headed back to the spot where he had first rematerialized. As he rounded the corner of the small grey temple, he glanced around to make sure he was alone, then gave the clicking signal to his on-board computer. Immediately he was transported back to his veiled ship.

He ran to the thawing cupboard, hurriedly opened the door, and climbed in. Within a few minutes he was his old self again. The adjacent cupboard door opened; out stepped Itaupi preening his antennae compulsively in an attempt to somehow rid his memory of being in such a disgusting soft body. All his instincts told him that the life-form was the wrong way round; that the hard skeleton ought to be on the outside, not the inside.

'I'd mark that up as another success,' he said to no one in particular.

He went back to the cupboard and retrieved the abstracter.

'Computer! Put the shell life-form back into the cryo-cupboard.'

He inserted the abstracter into a slot in the console. 'Transfer the contents to your data banks,' he decreed.

'As you command!'

'Now where....? Did you manage to locate any others whilst I was away?'

'Another plus seven in an easterly direction,' the computer informed him.

'Well? What are you waiting for? Set a course in that direction.'

'As you command!'

Itaupi settled at the work table in the middle of the vessel to admire his new acquisition. Thales' complete neural matrix was displayed as a three dimensional holo projection sitting in the middle of the table. It was superimposed on a complex grid of reference points that were intended to classify the Emotion Potential with respect to other species.

'This looks very promising....' aloud he said to himself.

'We have arrived!' the computer announced.

'What? So soon?'

'It was only a short distance across the plateau we were on.'

'All right! Let's have a look.'

On a wall screen to his right he had a vista of the terrain below.

'Very mountainous this planet of theirs,' complained Itaupi. 'Well! Where's this other plus seven?' he inquired somewhat grumpily.

'He is located on the banks of a river below. The river runs into a large inland sea. His name is Zarathustra and he seems to be seeking some form of enlightenment. That's all that seems to be in his conscious neural circuits.'

'I assume you've prepared another disgusting shell life-form for me to use?'

'I am just downloading the sample information matrix into it right now,' the computer informed him.

'Well, here goes nothing!' Itaupi went to the thawing cupboard and climbed inside.

Within a short time, he was again standing looking at himself in the mirror.

'The sooner we finish, the happier I'm going to be.' He put on the trousers and shirt; then the boots and sheepskin jacket. 'These clothes are a lot different than last time.'

'He is a Mede and Thales was an Ionian. The data bank has it that different cultures dress differently on this planet.'

'Have you located a spot for me to put down?' Itaupi wanted to know, as he checked his com-badge, his ring and abstracter.

'Three hundred meters back from the river bank in some tall grass. There is nobody in the vicinity.'

'Why is he all alone? This species is supposed to be social, mixing in groups like the last one. Are you certain he's a plus seven?'

'That is what the alpha sensor indicates. I have double checked.' There was a sense of outrage from the computer, on being questioned on its competence.

'You stay up here, hover five hundred meters above us; keep an eye out for any danger. Well then, put me down.'

It was late in the afternoon when Itaupi rematerialized in the tall grass. The first thing he noticed was the aroma of carbohydrates tickling his nostrils. *Must be oil somewhere near the surface,* he concluded. He heard the water, but could not see it. Looking around, he concluded the oil smell was coming from somewhere behind him.

He made a bee-line for the sound of the water. Within ten minutes of walking, stumbling through the tall grass, the sound of the river was becoming a roar. The tall grass had dampened the noise at a distance, but now he could hear nothing but the roar of the water rushing on an urgent journey impelled by gravity.

As he reached the water, he saw a blazing fire a little to the left of him, up-river. A human was sitting staring into the fire, pocking it with a stick, totally oblivious of his surroundings. The fellow was dressed only in a loin cloth held together by a belt. Cautiously, Itaupi approached the absorbed squatting figure, trying to look nonchalant, as if he were out for a simple stroll.

The figure didn't move a muscle, continuing to stare into the fire. This was going to be awkward. *To disturb or not to disturb; that was the question? Was the man aware of him, and playing some subtle game, or was he so unaware of his surroundings that a wild animal could creep up and devour him?*

Itaupi decided to risk all, boldly marching up to the blaze.

'Hallo friend!' he said loudly extending his open palms.

No answer. He tried again, 'Are you *ateshperest* and is this of *atesh-gah*?'

The man turned his head, his eyes wide in amazement. 'Are you Vohu-mano, the spirit of wisdom?' he asked in a hoarse voice.

Itaupi had got the man's attention by the simple ploy of getting onto the same wave-length as his subject. An old effective trick he had used many times in the past.

'I am the sacred mortar; I bring you the sacred cup and the words of Ahuru. I am Atar, the supreme light,' and Itaupi twirled his ring, which promptly surrounded him with the holo image of fire.

Zarathustra screamed and bowed his head to the ground in front of Itaupi.

Barely above a whisper Zarathustra mumbled, 'Wise Lord, I am your servant. What do you require of me?'

'That you get up off the floor and allow me to join you round the fire. That for a moment, you treat me as an equal.'

Itaupi used many tricks to acquire his material, but deep down; his rational make-up abhorred adulators, preferring to talk to his subjects on an equal footing. They may be primitive, but their Emotional Potential was the reason he was visiting them at all, collecting their brain patterns. The least he could do was respect their potential.

'But Lord...! How am I, a mere mortal, to treat my God as an equal?' Zarathustra kept his head firmly glued to the ground.

'I command you to lift your head,' Itaupi said firmly.

Zarathustra lifted his head, but averted his eyes.

'Look at me!'

Zarathustra forced himself to look at Itaupi. The halo of fire had gone, to be replaced by the visage of a shepherd, or at least to Zarathustra, he looked like an ordinary shepherd.

'Come, sit with me round the fire,' Itaupi commanded.

Reluctantly, Zarathustra sat back on his haunches, then swivelled around to face the fire. Itaupi joined him, sitting next to the distressed Zarathustra. The man looked thirty, was muscular and had the dark countenance of all Medes. He had obeyed Itaupi, but was still feeling visibly uncomfortable in his presence.

'Have you nothing to offer me?' Itaupi inquired, raising his eyebrows.

'I'm sorry Lord.' Zarathustra reached behind him, away from Itaupi, and produced a water skin. 'This is your drink Lord, made of the sacred *haoma* plant.'

Itaupi removed the stopper and put the neck to his lips. His data base told him that this *haoma* was a herb that the locals pressed through a strainer producing a liquor—this was then fermented. When drunk, it was supposed to heighten spirituality: in fact, it was a mild hallucinatory drug that distorted reality. It ought to have no effect on him. He took a long quaff at the draught.

At that moment, for some aberrational reason, a large eagle swooped at Zarathustra, missing him by a meter. It flew away in the direction of a small hill not far away and landed, staring at the figures around the fire.

Zarathustra had dived sideways onto his stomach to avoid the swoop. 'Damn pest!' was all he said.

'A friend of yours?' Itaupi inquired.

'He's been having a go at me for weeks. Suddenly dived on me one day for no reason.'

'They are all Ahuru's creatures. Maybe he wants to play with you?'

Zarathustra looked on in admiration. *Maybe I should try to make friends with the eagle.* This was going to be a definitive moment in his life; he could feel it. He gazed greedily at everything around him, trying to persuade his mind's eye to engrave it in his long term memory.

He had spent seven long years at the bottom of a cave atop a mountain, remaining silent, staring only at the images of Ahura Mazda, Vohu-mano, always trying to ward off Angra Mainyu, the cold spirit of the North, who came to tempt him.

For a moment, Zarathustra felt a little dizzy; shaking his head, he looked back at Itaupi-Atar and saw the Lord pointing a rock at him.

'Am I to take the rock, Lord?' he asked.

'No! I am weighing your soul against this rock and am pleased with my findings,' Itaupi lied. 'It is now time for me to depart.'

'Must you go so soon, Lord?' Zarathustra asked, alarmed at the short time he had spent with his God.

'Go now my son and spread my message,' and with that he gave the clicking signal.

He dematerialised before Zarathustra's startled eyes. *What more fitting departure could he have made as a God*, he asked himself, chuckling silently.

Back on his vessel, hovering five hundred meters above ground, he added Zarathustra's brain patterns into the three dimensional holo projection on his work table. Something that was being hinted at before, now came closer into focus.

Most species that he had studied to date, had little or no Emotion Potential. His species for instance had no emotions to speak of. Were emotions a blessing or a hindrance? His research was to determine if there was a benefit to a species having emotions—if so—could his species be bio-formed, changed to so that emotions would grow over time.

However, the current indications, with the two plus sevens' integrated into the computer model, suggested that this particular species had an extremely rich emotional life. Incorporating and extrapolating the data would produce a stochastic view that would finally end the speculation. Was having an emotion good or bad? If he could discover the reason species had emotions; maybe—just maybe, he could circumvent the lack of emotions in his own species.

'Computer! I've decided to go amongst them for a little while. Find me a large populous area; somewhere I can roam around unnoticed.'

'As you command!'

Itaupi wanted to gather a large database of actual brain patterns, thousands, possibly millions. This would give his statistical analysis something concrete to work on. Any anomalies would be firmly grounded. The larger the sample, the greater the accuracy of his stochastic analysis.

'We have arrived!' his computer announced.

'And exactly *where* have we arrived?'

'We are at the southern tip of a large sub-continent. It is heavily populated from this tip to the large range of mountains up in the North. I have assumed that you wish to gather large numbers of brain patterns for the model. Is that correct?'

'That is correct.'

'Then may I suggest that you beam down during their day, collect the matrices and beam back for the night. If you work your way up the central spine of the sub-continent, I predict that it will only take around fifteen of their planet's seasonal rotation to reach the mountains.'

'Are you trying to take over this research?' Itaupi demanded.

'I'm sorry. I was only being efficient. Did I offend you?' There was a mix of contriteness and sarcasm in its tone.

'You didn't offend me. But let me organise *my* schedule. After all, *I'm* the one who's going to be down there collecting the data.'

'As you command!'

Itaupi was of a species that had managed to extend their life span to around a thousand Earth years; so fifteen years to Itaupi, was the equivalent of around one month and three and a half weeks to a human. Even had it been fifteen Palari years, Itaupi would not have hesitated, considering the importance he placed on this research.

Anyway, it would serve her right if he never came home at all. He was referring to Tewpi of course, his loquacious partner. He hadn't forgotten her—or her piercing remarks. Although it seemed their sting had lessened with distance and time.

After fifteen gruelling years of trampling the roads, of feigning interest in these creatures' miserable lives, Itaupi finally reached the huge range of mountains in the north of the sub-continent. He had managed to acquire some hundred thousand brain patterns averaging around twenty per day over the seven hundred and eighty weeks.

He had input the brain patterns into his statistical model and the stochastics had firmed up the benefits of having an Emotional Potential. The reason as to why there might be a benefit, had not yet emerged. Naturally, there had to be a reason. Nothing seemed to resolve itself; no neat explanation he could then manipulate or unravel for his own specie's advantage.

'I need to get more plus sevens, or even higher,' he declared aloud.

'I have been working on that,' replied his computer.

'And...!' Itaupi tapped the table impatiently with his foreleg.

'I think I have located a plus eight.'

'You're exasperating sometimes—are you going to tell me where?'

'Over these mountains, to the north-east.'

'What are you waiting for...? Take us there.'

'As you command.'

Itaupi turned his attention back to the model, rubbing together his two communication antenna.

Within a short time his computer announced, 'We are here.'

'The cryo-cupboard! Have you thawed one out?'

'It is waiting for you.'

'Have you got this plus eight's name yet?'

'Li Er. He lives in a small state called Song.'

Itaupi climbed into the transfer-repository and the computer initiated somatic transfer. He climbed out of the thawing cupboard and again looked at himself in the mirror. A middle aged face with half-closed eyes looked back at him. A wispy beard and moustache made of dark hair sat on a round face. Long dark hair flowed from the cranium. Itaupi scowled and looked for his clothes. They sat on a couch behind him.

He covered his lower body with a long white silk apron and put buskins on his legs and knees. A black silk divided skirt was wrapped over the apron. Double-soled fur lined shoes went on his feet. He wrapped himself in a casual long silk black loose *shenyi* robe, a sort of overcoat, and tied it at the waist with a long belt. Finally, he donned his *guan*, his cap.

'This is unnecessarily cumbersome,' he complained. 'Are you sure I need all this?'

'It is the standard formal clothes worn in Song state,' his computer responded. 'It will be the style of clothing worn by Li Er.'

'Where is this Song state?'

'A little way westward from a large ocean, next to Lu and Chu states. It is a minor state with its capital at Shangqiu. That is where you will find Li Er.'

'Are you ready to set me down?' Itaupi was irritated by the layers of clothing he had to wear.

'Li Er is reading in the garden of his father's house. I think materialisation at the external entrance door to the garden would be appropriate.'

'Is the area empty?'

'It is.'

'Initiate.'

'As you command.'

Itaupi reappeared at the door to the garden. He rang the bronze bell loudly and waited.

It was some time before a grate in the door opened and a young face asked him what he wanted.

'I have come to talk to Li Er. Is he available?'

'What business do you have with him?' The fellow was being cautious.

Itaupi was certain he was talking to Li Er, aged around twenty, but he wanted to be sure. *Why was he being so circumspect?*

'I'm not prepared to shout my business through the grating,' replied Itaupi.

Li Er looked Itaupi up and down, noting his costly apparel. He must have decided to take a chance, because the grating closed and the door bolts were pulled back; the door opened.

'Well? What business do you have with Li Er?' asked Li Er.

Itaupi put his foot inside the door, leaned forward and whispered, 'I seek knowledge of the Celestial Master of the First Origin.'

Li Er's face lit up with suspicion. 'Who sent you?'

'Lao Tien Yeh—Father-Heaven!'

'Recite the Supreme Triad!' Li Er demanded.

Clearly he was testing Itaupi. This was where his prior preparation would be put under scrutiny.

Itaupi obliged. 'The Heavenly Master of the First Origin. The August Personage of Jade. The Heavenly Master of the Dawn of Jade of the Golden Door.'

Li Er opened the door wide, 'I bid welcome to you as a fellow traveller along the Dao.'

Itaupi entered the garden and walked by Li Er's side. 'What are you reading?'

'The *Chunqui.* Have you read it?'

'I am familiar with the history of the *Spring and Autumn Annals* period. I would have thought that the chivalry it extols would be something beneath you. Why waste time on such pompous distortions?' Itaupi was teasing the young man.

'Know your enemy! To scorn chivalry you must first be able to recognise it,' Li Er responded earnestly.

Itaupi put his hands in his robe pocket and brought out the abstracter. '*You* are Li Er then?'

'I am. I am also prudent with strangers. Until I know what they want, I prefer to keep my counsel.' Li Er noticed Itaupi's abstracter that had been reconfigured to look like a lump of Jadeite. 'That is a beautiful piece of jade you hold there.'

'A gift from a grateful Zhou Prince for services rendered. He told me that it was said to be a part of the treasure of The August Personage of Jade.'

Li Er looked at the lump of Jadeite more closely. 'A Zhou Prince you say?'

'You might do worse than go there. I have seen their archive and it contains some of the most ancient manuscripts anywhere.'

A glazed look crossed Li Er's features as Itaupi pointed the abstracter at him.

'What did you just do?'

'I beg your pardon?' None of his subjects had ever been aware of him using the abstracter before. It nonplussed Itaupi for a moment.

'You did something that made me feel dizzy. What did you do—and how did you do it?'

Li Er seemed *certain* that Itaupi was the cause of his dizziness. *Could a plus eight be aware of my activities?* Itaupi decided to bluff it out.

'I was informed by the Zhou Prince that this Jade possessed powerful magic. Maybe you felt its power?'

'Hm! I suppose that could be it. Of all the earthly elements, jade is linked to the most primordial forces of nature. I have identified myself with its underlying primitive vitality in an effort to understand and harness those forces. May I hold your jade for a moment?'

'I was told by the same Prince not to let anyone else handle this, for fear of losing its power. I'm sorry; I'm going to have to refuse—you understand.'

Li Er looked disappointed. 'Of course.'

'I came to look you up—to introduce myself. Now I must take leave to go to another. I shall return this way; maybe I could call on you again?'

'I shall look forward to it.'

Li Er led the way back to the exit door, opened it, and let Itaupi out. The future Lao Zi would remember the meeting with Itaupi when he wrote the *Daodeijing*

After the door was closed, Itaupi took a few steps to his right and bumped into a blue-jacketed militiaman who had stepped out from a nook and barred his way. 'I'm sorry he mumbled.'

The man raised his hand and around ten others surrounded Itaupi. 'Why are you visiting this blasphemer? What is your business with him? *Speak man!*' his colleagues pressed in, closing the circle.

'I'm a respected merchant; why do you trouble me?' Itaupi stared the man down.

'This house is off limits,' he asserted. 'He has insulted the Gods with his inventions, and we have many complaints about him,' the head militiaman insisted.

Itaupi gave the clicking signal and his computer whisked him off to his ship, leaving a bewildered group of militiamen staring at an empty space.

He changed back to his normal self and then input Li Er's brain pattern into his statistical model. The plus eight brought a certain clarity to that which had been hinted at. Not entirely—but enough for Itaupi to want to get back to his larger computer facility back on Palari.

The thought of getting back to Tewpi made him feel a little frisky.

'Set a course back to Palari.'

'As you command.'

❋   ❋   ❋   ❋

Back on Palari, he made up with Tewpi, who managed to persuade him to settle down into a cycle of domesticity. In time they produced nine offspring, which made it virtually impossible to continue his jaunts throughout the galaxy.

Then a prestigious position was offered to him with the Palari Scientific Academy and Tewpi had insisted he take it. He worked hard and prospered, but his own research, as opposed to his official research, had been put on a back burner, and was almost forgotten.

One day in a pique of frustration he called the files back into the three dimensional holo projection, and gazed as the brain pattern matrices settled into the statistical model. Without saying anything to anyone, he raided the **BODYSHOP**, stocking up with shell life-forms and pointed his Spacecruiser back in the direction of the system with nine planets. Fifty-five earth years had gone by since Itaupi had returned from the blue planet. It was the feeling of excitement that he had missed which prompted his momentous decision to continue his research. He arrived back into orbit around the blue planet.

'Computer! I want you to find me a plus nine.'

'I will commence the search immediately.'

'Why don't we start the search over the place where we found Li Er previously.' Itaupi expected, not unreasonably, that the plus nine might have genetic companions that would turn up in that region.

'The signal is veering to the sub-continent where you spent a long time gathering you large sample of data,' his computer informed him.

'Really! Oh, well! Lay in a course to follow the signal.'

'As you command.'

Itaupi went back to his table, staring at the holo model, as if he could somehow penetrate the mock-up with his mind, and suck out the secrets he knew, deep in his many guts, it must hold.

'We are hovering near a place the natives call Kasi. From my data banks it is a sacred place for these people. Not far from Kasi, a man sits under what they call a Peepal tree, and is deeply depressed.'

'Good! Good! Place a shell life-form in the thawing cupboard—and don't forget the clothes.'

'I have already done that in anticipation.'

'Splendid! Well, find me a spot where I can put down.' Itaupi went to the back of the ship and climbed into the transfer-repository for somatic transfer. He climbed out of the thawing cupboard a dark-skinned simulacrum of the populace below.

'I recommend a small group of tall bushes near a group of trees a kilometre away from Siddhartha. That is the name of your target plus nine. He is a Prince of the clan Gautama of a small Kingdom centred on Kapilavistu, up against the large range of mountains to the North. He seems to be very frustrated and depressed about something.'

'Fine! These white wraparound robes remind me of that Thales fellow. All right! Put me down.'

Itaupi rematerialized amongst some tinder-dry bushes, which immediately caught fire. What should have been a surreptitious arrival turned into the spectacle of a man beating at his clothes and running from a fire. Luckily there were few prying eyes directed at the little grove.

Itaupi was more bemused by the incident than angry. Quick wits and swift action had meant that he was just a little singed, nothing more. The grove was burning furiously but was isolated and the fire wasn't able to spread.

He left the fire behind whilst a small number of people had gathered to make sure the fire didn't get out of hand. They saw Itaupi saunter off, but thought nothing of it. The harder the times, the less likely that someone would interfere in other's business. People tended to keep their counsel, and not look for more trouble to add onto their already overburdened shoulders.

Itaupi walked up a path in the direction from where the plus nine signal had come. After a kilometre, he noticed on his left, an awkward looking tree on a spot a good distance from the banks of a river, silhouetted against a range of low hills. Below a tree sat a man, naked from the waist up, with his two hands folded in his lap. By this time it was noon, and his human stomach began to make noises.

Leaving the path, Itaupi scrambled over a ditch by the side of a field. He walked on the edge of the field towards the seated figure. It was then that he noticed two other seated figures that had been obscured by the trunk of the large straggly fig tree.

He slowed his walk as he approached the seated figures. The two that had been obscured sat two meters away from the one with his hands folded on his lap.

'Greetings!' hailed Itaupi, opening his palms to them.

'I've been expecting you,' said the seated figure unfolding his hands.

'Have you?' Itaupi had difficulty in hiding his surprise.

'Yes! I felt you in my mind a little while ago, trying to determine who I was.'

This was *not* how the conversation was scripted by Itaupi. The seated figure was telling him that he had felt the alpha sensor probing his mind for information. For the first time on this planet, Itaupi was losing the initiative and was feeling flustered.

He pulled himself together, and sat in front of Siddhartha. 'Are you aware of who I am?' he asked.

'You originate from out there.' Siddhartha pointed up into the sky. 'Even now your questor hangs up there waiting for you.'

'Are you sure? How do you know that?'

'I am sure. I see it in my mind's eye.' It was said with undoubted ease and such self-assurance.

Itaupi beheld a pauper before him, but the Prince was coming through loud and clear. He glanced sideways at the other two nearby figures, and was surprised to see one of Li Er's race amongst them.

'He brings knowledge of the Dao from his people. They are far away to the north-east, across the mountains. I have renamed the Dao—Nirvana, so my people may know of it.'

'I'm astounded that you've heard of the Dao.'

'I am deeply distressed by the human misery that surrounds me, and the sorrow of the endless succession of births and deaths in this turbulent stream of existence. The way of the Dao is the law of Karma, the law of retribution for the sins and evils that is the curse of all men. If it could be alleviated by people living a life of perfect justice and virtue, it would lead to Nirvana—the ultimate liberation of the soul, which would then enter into a state of unity between itself and the universe along the Dao. I have left my wife and son and a life of luxury, to escape from the material burdens of existence—to walk the Dao and liberate the effect of my Karma.'

'How do you propose to achieve *this Nirvana*?' Itaupi asked facetiously.

'I have realised that asceticism, like overindulgence, is futile. Through a middle way of meditation, I have found what I have named "the Four Noble Truths." It can be ended by following "the Noble Eightfold Path" through which a person eventually arrives at Nirvana, the extinction of all craving for things of the senses, the *moksha*-release from the cycle of rebirth.'

'I wish you well. But tell me, how did *he* get here?' Itaupi pointed at Li Er's countryman. 'He didn't cross the mountains, surely?'

'No! That way is much too difficult. He came by way of Gandhara, Bactria, Sogdiana and the desert to the north. He describes a journey in an arc with many hazards. Talk to him; let him explain.'

'Do you know why I'm here?' Itaupi wanted to know how far Siddhartha's insight went.

'You wish to learn from me.'

In a way that was right. Taking his plus nine brain pattern, and using it, had to be considered a form of learning.

Itaupi took the abstracter from his pouch and showed it to Siddhartha. 'What do you make of this?'

'It is many things to many people. It looks like an ordinary lump of rock, but in reality it is a powerful rock of knowledge.' Itaupi tried not to let amazement show on his face.

The lump of rock in his hand wasn't dismissed as it should have been, as simply a piece of rock. In his own limited technical vocabulary Siddhartha had been accurate as to what the abstracter was used for.

'May I use this powerful rock of knowledge on you.'

'I fear little of this world. You may proceed.'

Itaupi pointed the abstracter at Siddhartha and was shocked by *not* seeing a glazed look on his face.

'You have what you came for. I would now ask you to leave so that we may meditate in peace. The strangeness of your mind disturbs me.'

That shocked Itaupi even more. He was being dismissed. It could not have been worse if Siddhartha had got up and kicked him in the groin. He was tempted to reverse the polarity on the abstracter and do what he had done to Thales, but on this particular plus nine; he feared the consequences. So with a look of bemused disgust, Itaupi turned and headed back the way he came, towards the field and path. He felt Siddhartha's mind nudging him on his way. Out of sight in the ditch by the path, he gave the clicking signal.

Back on his ship he opened up on the computer. 'The next time you drop me in an arid zone, you could make damned sure you don't fry me.'

He was letting off steam for having been dismissed by one of the primitive natives of this perplexing planet. *Dismissed indeed!*

'I am most apologetic,' responded the computer.

'I was almost burned to death by your clumsiness.'

'It won't happen again.'

'It had better not. Anymore slip-ups and I'll disconnect you.'

That was an empty threat. Nothing could function without the computer. He would be stranded. Instead of further blustering, he went and changed back to his old self, and then ingested some nourishment.

'I have located another plus nine in the land where you met Li Er. Do you wish to go there?' the computer asked him.

He'd just had the shock of his life with this Siddhartha and wanted to reassess the native potential threat to himself.

'No! Set a course back to Palari.'

'As you command.'

He went back to the table in the middle of the ship, and pulled up the three dimensional holo projection that held the complete neural matrices he had captured so far. He fed Siddhartha's brain pattern into the model and let it settle into the complex grid of reference points.

After all these years, the prior hint took a more concrete shape, and the classification of the Emotion Potential with respect to other species began to filter out as a genetic trait impelled by the social environment of this species. *I might have guessed! What was so exceptional in their social evolutionary makeup that might have made them special?* His mind kept nagging at the problem.

Fifteen earth years more were to pass before Itaupi managed to restock his cryo-cupboard with fresh shell life-forms and head back to his research.

'We are at the spot you requested,' his computer told him.

'What? Oh, yes! Well, who is this plus nine?'

'Someone called Kong Qiu from the *shi* class, educated and pretentious.'

'Did I ask you for a value judgement?'

'No! My apologies.' The computer did not sound apologetic.

There's something going on with the computer. I'm going to have to have it checked when I get back home. It seems to be developing a personality of its own. He went to the back of the ship and switched bodies. The clothes were identical to the ones he'd worn for Li Er.

Suitably dressed he asked, 'What is this Kong Qiu doing at present?'

'He is teaching some pupils. He's in a small room of a large house in the centre of Linzi, the capital of Qi state.'

'See if you can find me an empty room in the same house that I can transport to.'

'As you command.'

Itaupi rematerialized in what turned out to be an empty scribe's room, indicated by all the parchments lying on a worktable. The room was on the first floor. Now he had to find where Kong was.

He quietly left the room and made his way along the corridor. He tried a door, opened it and popped his head round the corner. He was looking into a long room with women in various stages of undress. A shriek—was followed by a thrown jar. He quickly closed the door. From the room he could hear shouting and screams of abuse, no doubt aimed at him.

He then heard footsteps approaching. Two guards with pikes turned the corner, rushing towards the room. Itaupi clicked furiously and was snatched back to the ship.

'Find out *exactly* where this Kong is teaching,' he shouted at the computer, 'then put me down in an empty room *close by.*'

'As you command.'

Again Itaupi rematerialized in a room. He looked around and found himself in some kind of reception room. Single chairs with small tables were lined up in rows. *I wonder what this is used for,* he scratched his head. *It's not a reception room; I was mistaken.*

He went to the door and cautiously opened it. A bit of a commotion was coming from upstairs, but there was nobody in the corridor. Kong's room ought to be the next one on the left.

He knocked on the door and heard a voice say, 'Come in!'

Itaupi cautiously opened the door and beheld a man in his middle thirties, trying to teach his pupils the finer points of propriety, "*li.*" Charcoal scribbles specified the proprieties on one wall of the room.

'Yes! What can I do for you?' Kong asked.

'I have just come from Lu. I am told that you would appreciate news of the uprising there.'

'Yes, I certainly would.'

'The news of the uprising in your home state of Lu is good. The government forces are beginning to make headway against the rebels and the uprising is being suppressed. The bad news is, that the rebels have done a great deal of damage and many have lost their lives. Qufu, the capital was almost destroyed when the rebels set fire to it.' Itaupi had prepared well for this meeting.

The last bit of information regarding Qufu, had hit Kong quiet hard and lines of anger danced on his face.

'I was born there as was my wife and our children,' Kong lamented.

'I'm sorry,' Itaupi sympathised.

'At least, order is being re-established.' A look of determination replaced the anger. Then he added as an afterthought, 'I must see if I can get in touch with my father.' He was talking more to himself than to others.

'It is right that you think of your family,' Itaupi agreed.

Kong turned back to his pupils, attentively listening to the interchange. Then he continued with the lesson, 'It is the moral order and observance of the family, their ancestors, and the social relationships of authority, obedience, and mutual respect that are at the heart of propriety.

'The proper emphasis on tradition and ethics underpin the moral virtue of all right thinking men. The benevolent sovereign deserves the obedience and respect of his subjects that lie at the heart of law and order. When that balance is disturbed, then rebellion and anarchy ensues.

'Witness what is happening to my homeland to the south. The sovereign was too harsh, or too absorbed in his pleasures, neglecting his people, who then rose to demand that he deal with their grievances. He was passive to them and they took up arms.

'All of it was totally unnecessary—had the sovereign been thinking of propriety. I have told you many times; the origin of harmony is in the union of yin and yang, of the passive and active principles achieving balance. Please make a point of remembering that. Well, we will end the lesson there. Bright and early tomorrow!'

Kong returned his attention to Itaupi. 'I teach them the *Wujing*, with some of my interpretations thrown in,' Kong explained.

'Ah, yes! The *Yijing*, the *Shuching*, the *Shijing*, the *Liji*, and the *Chunqui*,' recited Itaupi.

Always get on the same wavelength as your subject, Itaupi reminded himself.

'I see you're familiar with the Five Classics!'

'It is an ignorant person who is not.'

Itaupi was fumbling in his pocket and clumsily managed to drop the abstracter on the floor.

'That is a beautiful piece of jade you have there,' Kong exclaimed.

'A present from my wife,' Itaupi lied hurriedly.

He picked it up and aimed it at Kong. The eyes glazed for a second.

Kong resumed, 'Your wife has an eye for value *and* beauty.'

Itaupi was startled that Kong had not felt anything or been aware of what had just transpired. *So not all plus nines are the same?* Itaupi thought. He'd been expecting another indignant outburst couched in oblique language. None came.

He put the abstracter back into his pocket and bade farewell to Kong. 'I hope everything turns out all right for you,' Itaupi said as opened the door.

'My fear is for my parents. Anyway, thank you for bringing me the news. It was most thoughtful of you. Goodbye.'

Itaupi went out into the corridor, looked around to see if he was alone, then gave the clicking signal.

Back on the ship, Itaupi hurried to discard the humanoid body, trying to rid himself of the vulnerability the soft exterior skin always made him feel.

'I'm not sure I want to accept your apology regarding the value judgement you gave Kong Qiu when I left the ship,' he told the computer playfully.

'I only called him pompous,' squirmed the computer.

'I'm afraid you were right—the man was pompous. That's why I can't accept your apology.'

'Very well! I have located a plus eight waiting for your attention, if you wish it,' the computer changed the subject.

'We might as well. Where is he?'

'In a city next to the one where you met Thales. A place called Ephesus. It's in the next large bay north of Miletus.'

'Oh, well! Set a course for this plus eight.'

'As you command.'

Itaupi was getting a bit fed up that his research hadn't thrown up the conclusive factor why there might be a benefit to having emotions. Why did such strong and rich emotions separate these humanoids from all the other species he had studied? Had he been able to concentrate all of his time on his research he might have found a solution by now. Damn Tewpi! She had ensnared him at a crucial point in his research. It was so frustrating. Mind you, he had to admit; it took two to tangle.

'How long has it been since Thales?'

'Eighty-five of their earth years.'

'Well, let's get to it. Get the shell life-form ready; clothes. And this time find the right spot and make sure it's safe.'

'The name of the plus eight is Heraclitus, of royal blood, who has turned his life to philosophy. He is currently haranguing a crowd on the steps of a temple.'

'Hmmm...,' he scowled. He glared at himself in the cupboard door mirror. 'Ring, com-badge, abstracter. Okay, let's go.'

The computer set him down behind a far pillar to the left, in the temple of Artemis, on the Acropolis of Ephesus. Itaupi looked around and was surprised at the elaborate interior. A profusion of splendid grey marble Ionic columns stood in six long rows holding up the roof of the nave, three rows on either side of the aisle. Each column was painted and gilded at the top.

He moved quietly out into the open aisle and gazed at an altar that was dominated by a huge marble statue of a Goddess, armed with a golden bow and arrows. She was decked out in ivory and gilded gold. On either side of her stood splendid wild bears rampant. At her feet were a number of marble sculptures of other wild beasts.

From the direction of the entrance to the temple, he heard much shouting. It sounded like a large crowd baying for blood. He had to go out there to look for his plus eight and somewhat cautiously he headed for the area. He approached the immense bronze doors, and cautiously peered round them. Some six meters away on the top step of the temple entrance, stood a young man in his mid-twenties, declaiming to an assembled crowd. The crowd was smaller than the noise they made in trying to shout the young man down.

'Change is the only reality', he was shouting at them.

'So change into a monkey,' shouted a heckler. That was followed by loud laughter.

'Only the orderliness of the succession of things remains the same,' he yelled back at them.

When the crowd didn't understand one of the young man's phrases, it was met with silence.

'The universe is in ceaseless flux: the world is eternal fire,' he bellowed at them.

'Your robe's on fire,' shouted a wit.

'Fire is the primary substance, not water, as that eccentric neighbour of our insisted. That so called seeker after half-truths, Thales.'

'I object to that,' shouted an elderly man at the front of the crowd.

'Ah! Hecateus. No offence meant to your city!' responded the young man kindly.

'Get on with it,' someone yelled.

The crowd had come for some fun and was getting impatient. The young man looked over the shoulders of the crowd, pointed and proclaimed, 'What say the Persians?'

A squad of soldiers had been milling around at the back of the crowd, waiting for an excuse to break the gathering up.

'Here we are on the steps of one of the great wonders of the world, yet we can't defend ourselves against a bunch of Persians...'

The crowd were aghast. A complete silence descended on the mob. Stirring up the populace against Darius and the Persians was a capital offence. The young man was deliberately seeking a confrontation, and was hoping to use the assembly as his weapon.

The soldiers present were all Ionian Greeks, but the King of Ephesus was a suzerain of Darius and had to tread a delicate road of appeasement. The leading officer had drawn his sword and was pushing his way through the crowd to get at Heraclitus.

Suddenly, the ground began to shake; small chips of marble began to fall from the temple facade. The crowd shrieked in terror and began to run away from the temple onto open ground.

The tremor subsided as quickly as it had begun, but everyone was aware that there may be more to come. Earthquakes always had slight warning tremors to start with, before the big one.

Itaupi rushed forward from behind the door, grabbed the young man's arm and pulled him round the temple corner, away from the bewildered soldiers, who were now panic stricken by the earth tremor. He pushed and pulled the reluctant Heraclitus out towards the agora, to open space.

'Who are you?' Heraclitus wanted to know. 'What do you want from me?' The young man was trying to break Itaupi's iron grip on his arm.

'I'm trying to save your life,' Itaupi answered impatiently.

Heraclitus broke free and stopped in the middle of the agora. 'The tremors have stopped, or hadn't you noticed?' he said sternly.

'The tremors may have stopped, but the soldiers are still on your tail; look!' Itaupi pointed at the squad that had regained their composure and now came looking for the rabble-rouser.

Itaupi led the young man at a trot to the side path leading from the Acropolis, heading towards the city proper. The soldiers had not spotted them yet, and there was no pursuit. Nevertheless, Itaupi rushed Heraclitus along as if they were being pursued. This time the young man didn't protest and matched Itaupi's pace.

They sped along the winding path and soon arrived at the base of the Acropolis hill.

'I know of a tavern not far from here where we can imbibe a little wine,' offered Heraclitus.

'Good! Lead on.'

They went along a narrow lane, between some low roofed houses, and came to a small open plaza. Directly in front, stood a dingy tavern with an empty table out front.

'Spiro!' Heraclitus called. 'Bring us some of your best slop. We'll take it out in the open.'

Heraclitus sat at the table and invited Itaupi to sit. 'I suppose I ought to thank you for pulling me out of there,' he offered a little abashed. 'Why did you rescue me?' Heraclitus looked penetratingly at Itaupi.

'I had set my heart on doing a good deed today. It seems the Gods elected you for my attentions.' Itaupi tried to laugh the gratitude off. 'But let me ask you, what's all this about "fire"?'

'The world is in a constant state of flux. You'll have to take my word for that. The history of the world is periodic. That is to say; it comes in cycles. When the balance is disturbed for one reason or another, fire takes the upper hand, and the world is destroyed. Then after a while, a new world arises again, and the cycle repeats. Fire lives on after the death of earth, air lives on after the death of fire, and water lives on after the death of air. You see! It's all cyclical.'

I've never heard so much rubbish, except from that Thales fellow, thought Itaupi. 'I see,' he said aloud.

'Look! I'll draw it on the ground for you.' Heraclitus picked up a small stick lying near the wall and began to draw on the ground. 'The transformation of fire occurs like this....'

Itaupi looked at the drawing and scratched his head. *It's completely meaningless, yet this lunatic thinks it's the answer to everything.* 'I see,' he repeated.

'Fire is the primordial substance from which all else is created. Surly you can see that.'

'But Thales thought it was water, now you think it's fire. Where do you get this stuff from?'

'One cannot step in the same river twice,' said Heraclitus smugly.

'You mean time moves on,' queried Itaupi.

'Precisely! Nothing in the world ever stays the same, hence my dictum, "All is flux, nothing stays still."'

'But from where do you get the idea that "fire" is the basic primordial substance?'

'Isn't it obvious? Fire is the great destroyer, and conversely, it *must* be the great creator—fire is much stronger than water, so water cannot be the primordial substance. Can it?'

'But water can easily put fire out,' objected Itaupi, half getting sucked into the senseless argument.

'Only if the fire is small,' responded Heraclitus.

There is no arguing with this fellow, Itaupi concluded. He took the abstracter from his pouch and pointed it at Heraclitus. The young man's eyes glazed over for a second.

Heraclitus continued, unaware of the theft of his brain pattern, 'Those people in Miletus are confused. They're out of date; mark my words.' He sat back and took a deep draught of wine from his beaker, licked his lips and closed his eyes.

Itaupi shrugged his shoulders and said, 'I'm sure you're right. Well, it was interesting meeting you, but now I must leave you.'

'Really! Must you go? We were just getting to the nitty-gritty. I was so enjoying our little chat.'

'No! Really, I must go; I have to meet someone.'

'Well, you know where to find me. On the steps of the temple.'

'I would advise you not to go there for a little while. Let things die down a bit.'

'Oh! I can deal with my brother—he's the king of this place you know. I'll talk to him tonight and things will be back to normal tomorrow.'

Itaupi got up and walked down a narrow lane. He took one final look back at Heraclitus and shook his head in amusement. Heraclitus was sitting back with his head against the wall, no doubt conjuring up some further nonsense for the next day to entertain the crowd with.

The lane was quiet and well shaded in the afternoon heat. Itaupi gave the clicking signal. Back on his ship he began to berate the computer even before he changed back into his own body.

'Why didn't you pull me out of there before the earth tremor started? Don't you know how dangerous these geological shifts can be?

'I was aware that the tremor would be slight and that you were in no danger, otherwise I would have retrieved you immediately,' the computer answered noncommittally.

'It didn't seem like that to me at the time.' Itaupi knew the computer was right, but the experience had given him a fright, and he wanted to take it out on someone.

'Was the trip useful?' asked the computer.

What's this? Itaupi was shocked. *The damned computer has changed the subject on me. That's it! It's definitely due for an overhaul when I get back to Palari.* Itaupi ranted at the computer inside his head as he headed for the thawing cupboard.

Once inside his own body, he input Heraclitus' brain pattern into the holo-model on the table.

That's better! Now the reason is becoming clear.

Emotions clearly enriched the imagination, which in turn drove intelligence. The greater the Emotional Potential the greater the potential of the intelligence. One fed on the other. Anxiety, anger, and depression were counterbalanced by peace, calmness, and exaltation. But those were the extremes. The subtlety and richness of the area in between black and white, all that bountiful grey, the appreciation of beauty, of music, of art. That was where the emotions expressed and expanded themselves, in the aesthetic, enhancing the intelligence as a by-product.

Emotionality led to cognitive appraisal of the stimulus, sometimes many differing interpretations as to its cause, until a conclusive reason was finally settled on. Other species cognitively appraised their stimulus, but an intuitive leap could often by-pass a lengthy set of logical progressions, a distinct advantage when time was at a premium. It was patently clear to Itaupi that there was a huge advantage to a species having developed mature emotions, and somehow he would have to find a way of engineering emotions into his own species.

'Set a course back to Palari,' he ordered the computer.

'As you command,' replied the errant computer.

ateshperest — fire-worshipper
atesh-gah — a place of fire
Atar — fire

Kong Qiu = Kong Fu Zi = Confucius
Wujing — *Five Classics*, originated before the time of Kong Fu Zi, and consisted of:
i) the *Yijing* (*Book of Changes*),
ii) the *Shuching* (*Book of History*),
iii) the *Shijing* (*Book of Poetry*),
iv) the *Liji* (*Book of Rites*), and
v) the *Chunqui* (*Spring and Autumn Annals*).

Sasha Garrydeb

The Chameleon Fell Onto St Albans

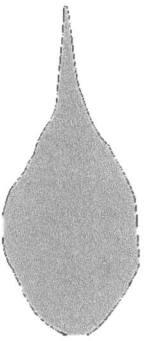

The first of the strange rains fell on the valley of the River Ver, more precisely, on the city of St. Albans, late in the year 2025. People reported the drops as red in colour—that was contradicted by others who insisted they were orange. Others were just as adamant that the drops were a light yellow—but they all agreed they later changed to a green, then to a blue, then indigo, and finally violet.

The rain lasted a short time—not longer than fifteen minutes—but it changed the face of St. Albans. A fungus like growth sprouted wherever the raindrops hit the ground. The odd quality of this fungal growth was, it continually changed colour as people watched—flushing like an excited chameleon.

From the air, St Albans looked like a circular kaleidoscopic spread, a neat two kilometres rainbow ring with its focal point on the Broad Way in the city centre, spreading to the edges of Prae and Batch Woods. It attracted lunatic treasure hunters, who insisted there *had* to be a crock of gold at the end of the rainbow. They dug holes whenever they could get past the resilient leathery fungus, and wherever they could, in Clarence Park, in fields, and even in the open space of the old Roman ruins of Verulamium at the bottom of the hill, to the utter outrage of the local archaeologists, who treated the fungus merely as a passing phenomenon in the two millennial view they'd caged for themselves.

Experts from the Ministry of Defence came and took samples to Porton Down for analysis. The local lady Bishop prayed for protection from the colourful display, surrounded by her frightened congregation. The local *Herts Advertiser*, tongue in cheek, asked if this was the second colourful coming, always willing to deflate the Bishop's pompous opportunism. End-of-world placards propagated on the streets, mostly outsiders bringing news no one wanted to hear, invading this ancient archaeological city. Posters appeared outside the arch of the Waxhouse Gate, "**Down with Normans—Bring back Offa's Church**." Others announced Boudicca's second destruction of St. Albans imminent.

The peculiar rain prompted a number of strange sightings—weirdoes burrowing out in swarms from the woodwork. Some reported seeing the ghost of John Ball prowling near the Clock Tower. Ulsinus was said to have been seen at night in the marketplace. Others even reported sighting Alban on the east bank of the Ver, roaming the vicinity of the Cathedral, site of his martyrdom. An old drunk swore he'd heard the curfew bell. It got so bad, one old lady insisted she had seen the ghost of Tasciovanus, Prince of the Catuvellauni, chasing Alban with a Celtic long sword.

In a short space, more crank calls were received by the local police than in all the last twenty five years of the new millennium. There were even a bunch of women from the Temperance League camped down Abbey Mill Lane, beside the river Ver, keeping vigil outside the octagonal timber-framed inn, the *Ye Olde Fighting Cocks*, claiming to be the oldest inhabited pub in England, and so the starting point of all evil drink in England.

The fungus, if that's what it was, stayed a week, and then vanished, as if it had never been. One moment the city was the centre of world attention, the next, it returned to being the sleepy residential suburb for commuters on the outskirts of North London.

National newspapers reported similar rains had fallen on Sellafield and York, but St. Albans was the first to receive the benefaction. Although more experts arrived and performed various medical tests immediately after the visitation, nothing more transpired for a lengthy interval—until—twelve years after the event, children conceived during that memorable week, found their hair shimmered thorough the colours of the rainbow upon reaching puberty. Both boys and girls were affected—forty-seven in St. Albans alone. The national papers, prompted by the local *Herts Advertiser,* dubbed them "the rainbow children," always obligingly eager to put a catchphrase label on any event.

News broadcasters told a different story...... *"reports are coming in of a group of vigilantes attacking two "rainbow children," brothers of a family on a York housing estate, amid a clamour for action from a number of quarters regarding the alien invasion"*...Government responded by sending in the army. Around two hundred thousand people were quarantined, with army units surrounding York, Sellafield, and St. Albans.

The world watched—and reported—on the extreme measures enacted by a democratic government on its own population. The strange rain had endowed only the three locations in England—nowhere else on the planet had the visitation. Only the British Government had any reason to act. From inside the quarantined area—silence. Spin Doctors for the Coalition Prime Minister insisted the situation was calm, and the people were being *assessed.* When asked by an Italian journalist from *Corriera della Sera*, what that meant, the Spin Doctors replied....*"we are making an official scientific determination if any threat exists to the rest of the population from the recent unfolding events"*...

On the outskirts of the isolated areas, sat an enormous gaggle of journalists feeding a worldwide twenty-five hour a day industry. The Americans were the worst—sending reports back that were pure invention—being true to their motto—"if you can't establish the facts, create them." According some of the more sensational pieces, the "rainbow children" had mutated into super beings and were holding the rest of those secluded, captive. Captain America at its best. Another report, even more bizarre, had the "rainbow children" hungry for human flesh, and eating their way through their captives. That was the Hollywood input.

Following such stories, the Spin Doctors were at pains to point out all was well, that all the isolated were being given a thorough genetic profiling to determine if any others were infected. In St. Albans, huge military helicopters were seen going in and out for days running—all leaving heavily laden, heading South. A French reporter from *Libération* was able to disclose those helicopters were off-loading detainees on the half cleared island of the Isle of Wight, off the south coast of England. It later transpired, England had asked the Scottish Government if it could use one of its vacant islands, but it was told it wasn't a dumping ground for the "rainbow children."

Large military convoys began moving significant parts of the population of York down to the Isle of Wight, where workmen in contamination suits, to accommodate 100,000 people, were readying an enormous barrack camp. In the meantime, the news media had renamed the "rainbow children"—"chameleon brats."

The UN wanted to know from the English Government, what they intended to do to the detainees. The Coalition Government told them, they were being well treated, and that it was none of their concern. This was an internal matter. Thus England stuck two fingers to the UN—and got away with it. A precedent set for the early 21st Century.

After months of keeping the story alive, fatigue set in, with both journalists and audience alike. Slowly the news changed to an Earthquake in Turkey, and a horrendous Tsunami that devastated the Solomon Islands. Every Thursday, relatives of the disappeared took to parading round Parliament Square bearing placards with photos, asking, "Where is *so and so*, what have you done with him?" On the whole, they were ignored.

York and St. Albans returned to the business of existing, surviving, and turning a profit. The empty houses were refilled and the "chameleon brats" forgotten—well almost. An occasional tenacious journalist tried to scuba past the military *cordon sanitaire* thrown around the Isle of

Wight—and promptly—disappeared. That sent a message to the other scoop chasers, and the media caught amnesia on the subject.

In St. Albans, down Fishpool Street, a little old lady gently hummed a tune from a long forgotten musical, and ambled to her kitchen sink to fill a watering can. She had a number of plants in the house, sitting on the windowsills—but she cooed to her favourite, encouraging it to grow.

She now went and stood by the plant and said, 'You know, you're the most beautiful of them all—and we must keep you from prying eyes.'

The plant, a fungus like growth, shimmered happily like a chameleon, through all the colours of the rainbow, responding positively to her cooing, as if......

Other novels by Sasha Garrydeb

Worlds Beyond Ours

Sasha Garrydeb

In the fourth millennium humans finally invent the warp-drive and set out to explore the Galaxy. The first mission is sent to our nearest star, Alpha Centauri, and the starship returns to a stormy acclaim by earth's population. It then comes as a shock to our planet when aliens visit earth and announce that the Galactic Federation intends to lift its quarantine around the Solar System. Since humans now have warp drive capability, would they like to join the Galactic Federation?

This story brings humanity for the first time into contact with a variety of alien life-forms when Earth's Embassies are sent to other worlds: elfin-like creatures, dinosauroids, insectoids, and many more. As the humans fan out from their home world, they encounter a number of adventures which shape humanity's future for generations to come. Wonders like floating cities in the sky, terraforming other planets and genetic advertising.

The story at the end comes full circle when it culminates in another first contact, but this time from our neighbouring galaxy for this Galactic Federation.

The Wizard of Kalar

Sasha Garrydeb

On the distant planet of Kálar the two hundred year old life cycle of the Schánda once again menace the idyllic lives of the Bólani, a small tribal village of forest dwellers living in their hollowed Lándo trees.

The schánda stand half a cubit high, have a two hundred year life-cycle and normally live up on the northern edges of the tundra of the planet of Kálar. They are an insect, something like a cross between a spider and a scorpion. The adult form has no poisonous stinger and isn't carnivorous. Then the mating urge mutates the schánda into a massive swarm of ferocious carnivores. It doubles in size, grows the stinger and large claws in its fourth and final moult, then begins its long march from its home-ground in the North of Kálar, south to its mating grounds on the shores of the Golden Sea.

In its path live the small peaceful Bólani tribe who make their homes in living Lándo trees in the forest. Around the same time as the schánda begin their journey, the Bólani's collective unconscious, an imbedded memory of these carnivorous insects, triggers nightmares. They dream of an unstoppable carnivorous procession intent on eating their way to their mating grounds, heading their way.

The Bólani must gather their possessions and flee ahead of the encroaching swarm. They escape south to the shores of the Golden Sea just ahead of the voracious insects. Their long march to the shores of the Golden Sea takes them through a series of adventures with small blood sucking insects, vicious storms, predatory birds, unfriendly villages, lakes of volcanic lava, and desert worms. Only the skill of their apprentice wizard, Morác, saves them from disaster—transforming his powers in the process. Even when they reach the Golden Sea their problems are not at an end. Imprisoned by a coastal tribe and then buffeted by storms on their flimsy rafts the dynamics of the tribe are changed forever before they finally manage to return to their small forest village back up in the far North.

This is an eco-fantasy tale stretching the imagination beyond the solar system.

Murder in Hattusas

Sasha Garrydeb

Murder in Hattusas is the 1st Volume of the Hittite Trilogy.

At the close of the Old Kingdom in 1420 BC, the realm of the ancient Hittite Empire is in chaos. Muwatallis, the king has been assassinated in the capital, Hattusas, by the feared Kaska Assassin's Guild. Muwas, the dead king's brother blames the two sons of the previous king, Huzziyas, and he insists he be the one to succeed his brother. The two sons of Huzziyas, Kantuzzili and Himuili, insist the next king be Tudhaliyas, son of Himuili, since rewarding Muwatallis' previous assassination of Huzziyas, is unthinkable. Neither side is prepared to give way, and the scene is set for civil war. Tagrama, the High Priest of the temple of the Storm God Taru, tries to broker a peace, but is up against outright stubbornness.

Muwas then hires Harep, of the same Assassin's Guild, to kill Tudhaliyas. Only Mokhat, the former spiritual adviser to the Assassin's Guild, knows what Harep looks like, and he is determined to stop all the damnable assassinations. He's had enough of the Guild's murdering ways.

Muwas calls upon his Mittani allies, the Mittani King Saustatar, who sends his son Artatama with an army to Muwas' aid. The Kizzuwatna King Shunashura changes allegiance and abandons the Mittani in favour of Kantuzzili's faction, sending an army to help Tudhaliyas.

The Pharaoh Amenhotep II threatens to invade Mittani unless they pull their army out of Hatti. Saustatar refuses.

When Tudhaliyas meets Nikal, he falls for this daughter of the Kizzuwatna king. They announce their engagement. Harep, the hired assassin, makes a number of attempts on Tudhaliyas' life, but is foiled. The major Battle of the Wide Plateau settles the civil war but in the mean time, Harap manages to kidnap Nikal.

The protagonist, Mokhat, is in search of himself after his sordid ministrations to a bunch of murderers. It is a bronze-age thriller, which includes a romp through the Hittite landscape, a civil war, and chariots in battle. This is a tale of love and adventure set in the most fascinating recently discovered culture of the ancient world. Volume 2 is due for publication in February 2011.

A must for all fans of the Hittite civilisation.

Madduwatta's Rebellion

Sasha Garrydeb

This is the second volume of the Hittite Trilogy.

It has been three years since the Battle of the Plateau put Tudhaliyas on the throne in the Hittite Empire, yet instead of feeling secure, he feels menaced. His chief spy, Satipilli, has vanished, and trouble is brewing in the west, possibly from Ahhiyawa. The Mittani are threatening Isuwa on the eastern border, seeking revenge for their humiliation in the civil war. All this requires reliable intelligence reports. Tudhaliyas is forced to turn to the unknown faces of Mokhat and Palaiyas and asks them to go to the west, to Millawanda, and discover what has happened to Satipilli, the chief spy of the Hittites.

On their journey, they are followed and someone keeps trying to kill them; with each failure, their attempts become more desperate. The assassins follow Mokhat and Palaiyas but are finally dissuaded; then they suddenly reappear in Khemet (Egypt). Somebody doesn't want them to complete their mission.

At the close of the Old Kingdom in 1417 BC, Madduwatta, the Governor of Lukka, a nominal vassal of Tudhaliyas, has plans of his own. How is he implicated in all this? He has his eyes on Arzawa. He badly needs friends, and will ally himself with anyone prepared to help him achieve his goal. But who has stirred him up? Who has gone to all these lengths to create a rebellion for the Hittites?

Meanwhile, Ahhiyawa is in the grip of a Civil War, with two brothers fighting it out for the throne in Millawanda. The outcome of the conflict will impact on their neighbours, Arzawa, the Hittites, and the Governor of Lukka.

Palaiyas, a Prince of Tiryns, decides to go home to make peace with his father, the king. While in Tiryns, he's abducted by his uncle, Elektryon, the king of Mycenae, and brought to account for his desertion; then forced to complete his tour of duty on Keftiu (Crete). Mokhat follows him and rescues him. After Khemet (Egypt), Ugarit, and Lukka, they finally discover the truth. Mokhat falls in love in this romp through the ancient Med, all in a search for Satipilli.

Mittani Kidnapping

Sasha Garrydeb

This is the third volume of the Hittite Trilogy.

Ammuna, a disaffected senior Hittite General has had enough of the Hittite King's interference in his career and has sold himself to the Mittani Crown Prince Artatama for golden shekels. Worse, he's kidnapped King Tudhaliyas' 6 year old daughter, Princess Asmunikal, for those golden shekels.

It is now six years since the Battle of the Wide Plateau put Tudhaliyas on the throne (Vol 1—*Murder in Hattusas*), in the realm of the ancient Hittite Empire, and three years since Madduwatta's Rebellion was dismantled by Tudhaliyas, (Vol 2—*Madduwatta's Rebellion*), both times with Mokhat's help.

In this third volume of the Hittite trilogy, the reader is invited to participate in a seventeen-day pursuit from Hattusas to Nineveh, in a romp through the landscape of ancient Mesopotamia, when Mokhat's *special forces* chase rogue General Ammuna and his gang of mercenaries into the heart of Assyria, trying to rescue the kidnapped daughter of grief stricken King Tudhaliyas and his consort, Queen Nikal.

Tudhaliyas invades Mittani to force Artatama to release his daughter. The Kizzuwatna army is on the march, in support of the Hittite King, as is the Pharaoh, both allied to Hattusas by binding treaties. Cities allied to the Mittani come under attack one by one. There are catastrophic consequences for Artatama's father, King Saustatar of Mittani when a Hittite army appears on his doorstep. Has Artatama overstretched himself? Has his ambition become his downfall? Will the *special forces* rescue the princess? These are the questions this third volume proposes to answer.

Galactic Sniffers

Sasha Garrydeb

This is the first volume of the Praut Agency SF series.

Humans were spreading, as they once did on earth, into every niche that would sustain them. There were human colonists on the rim of the Milky Way looking longingly across the empty chasm of intergalactic space at our neighbouring galaxies, hoping a way would be found to bridge the chasm. The way to the next galaxy was through a stabilised wormhole. Yet this last piece of the technological puzzle was being sabotaged.

Out there, an entity was undermining humanity's one way of reaching the other galaxies. The scientists were on the verge of succeeding in stabilising the wormhole yet all the information on wormholes was under threat. Any enterprise trying to stabilise wormholes was being attacked. The culprits had to be found. Humanities interstellar dream demanded it.

The Praut Investigation Agency is hired to uncover the guilty party. This begins a chain of events leading to murder, war, and mayhem. The reader is taken across the galaxy, following Praut's ingenious sniffers, to various planets in pursuit of the culprits.

On one occasion, they follow a sniffer to a bizarre hippy planet, yet on another planet, they are rescued by Sámi reindeer herders from a crash landing in the tundra.

Praut and his people are forced to suffer hardships, trek through snow, fight their way through numerous adventures. All in a search of the mysterious guilty perpetrator who is out to destroy the technology with which humankind hopes to reach out into the universe.

The final outcome shocks Praut and his companions, and threatens the very existence of humanity for some time to come.

Sasha Garrydeb